Rave reviews for *New York Times*
bestselling author

SUSAN MALLERY

Hot on Her Heels

"[T]his glimpse into glitzy Texas high society
and the dark underbelly of business
is a thoroughly enjoyable read."
—*Publishers Weekly*

Straight from the Hip

"One of the Top 10 Romance Novels of 2009!"
—*Booklist*

Lip Service

"Mallery breathes real life into these former
lovers hoping for a second chance."
—*RT Book Reviews*

Under Her Skin

"Bestseller Mallery's Lone Star Sisters series
opener draws in readers with intriguing
characters and a precisely assembled plot."
—*Publishers Weekly*

Sweet Spot

"I strongly recommend *Sweet Spot*, especially to
readers who like their family melodramas spiked
with lots of laughter and hot romance."
—*The Romance Reader*

Sweet Talk

"*Sweet Talk* is one sweet read! Susan Mallery
delivers a deliciously satisfying first book in her
new wonderfully written Bakery Sisters trilogy."
—*The Romance Readers Connection* (4½ stars)

SUSAN MALLERY

SOMEONE LIKE YOU

HQN™

Recycling programs
for this product may
not exist in your area.

ISBN-13: 978-0-373-77465-4

SOMEONE LIKE YOU

To Jenel, for making this the best
it could be.

SOMEONE LIKE YOU

CHAPTER ONE

"I LOOK LIKE A FREAK," Shelley said as she plopped down in the chair and covered her face with her hands. "I'll have to move under the cover of darkness so I don't frighten small children."

Jill Strathern sat down next to her assistant and patted her back. "You're not a freak."

"You're right." Shelley raised her head and sniffed. "Being a freak would be an improvement." She gave a strangled sob.

"This is all fixable," Jill reminded her. "You're not scarred for life."

"My psyche is."

"I think you'll recover."

In fact, Jill was sure of it. Shelley had left work the previous evening excited about her appointment at a new and trendy salon. She'd gone in expecting some subtle highlights and a few layers. She'd left with a botched body perm, orange brassy color and a cut that could only be described as…unfortunate.

"You know what? I have a great idea." Jill stood and walked around her desk where she flipped through her electronic Rolodex. "I know exactly who can fix this for you."

Shelley looked up. "Who?"

"Anton."

Shelley sucked in a breath and for the first time that morning, hope filled her swollen eyes. "Anton? You *know* him?"

Anton, like Madonna, was famous enough not to need a last name. Two-tone highlights and a styling cost as much as a small imported car, but the rich and famous swore by his magic fingers.

"I'm his lawyer," Jill said with a grin. "Now let me call him and explain we have a hair emergency. I'm sure he can take care of everything."

Fifteen minutes later, Shelley had an appointment for early that afternoon. Jill promised to let her make up the time by coming in early for the next couple of days.

"You're the best," Shelley said as she walked to the door and stepped out into the hallway. "If you ever need me to do anything, let me know. I'm serious. A kidney. Have your baby, whatever."

"Maybe you could look over the brief I left on your desk," Jill told her with a laugh. "It's due first thing in the morning."

"Absolutely. Right this second. Thanks."

Jill chuckled as she turned back to her computer. If only all of life's problems could be solved so easily.

Two hours later, she looked up from her research. Coffee, she decided. A nice, little jump start to keep her brain going. She stood and headed for the centrally located lunchroom where jumbo carafes full of liquid energy waited.

On her way back, she detoured around to the other

side of the offices where her husband, also a third-year associate, had his office. They'd been working so many hours the past few weeks, they'd barely seen each other. Her calendar was free. If Lyle's was, too, maybe they could grab lunch together.

His assistant was gone and his door closed. Jill knocked lightly once, then pushed inside. She moved quietly, not wanting to interrupt if he was on the phone.

He was busy, all right, but not with a call. Jill stopped in the center of the room. Breath left her body as the mug of coffee fell to the carpeted floor. She didn't remember letting go, but she felt the hot liquid splash onto her legs.

Her husband of three years, the man she lived with, worked with and cooked for, stood beside his credenza. His jacket was over his chair, his pants around his ankles and he was busily banging his assistant. So busy, in fact, he hadn't noticed Jill's entrance.

"Oh, yeah, baby," Lyle breathed. "Just like that."

But the woman saw Jill. Her face paled and she shoved Lyle away.

Later Jill would remember the silence and how time seemed to slow. Later she would recall the way papers had fluttered to the floor as his assistant scrambled off the credenza and jerked up her panty hose. Later she would want to kill Lyle. But right now she could only stare in disbelief.

This wasn't happening, she told herself. He was her husband. He was supposed to love her.

"Next time you should knock," he said as he bent over and grabbed his pants.

She had, she thought, too stunned to feel much of anything. Then she turned on her heel and ran from the room.

FORTY-NINE HOURS and eighteen minutes later, Jill decided that being buried alive was too good for Lyle. Still, she was due some serious revenge. Unfortunately, as she had no idea on how to *get* the revenge she so desperately needed, she contented herself with imagining him lying on the edge of a desert highway, gasping for breath as she zoomed by at a comfortable ninety miles an hour. She liked the vision of her soon-to-be ex-husband as roadkill.

"Lying weasel rat-fink dog," she muttered as she slowed at the bottom of the freeway off-ramp and turned west.

The lying weasel rat-fink dog was currently back in San Francisco, moving into what should have been *her* junior partner office with a window. No doubt he would celebrate what should have been her promotion by taking out his assistant, then seducing her with wine from the collection *she'd* put together, and carrying her off to what had been *their* bed.

Yes, it was true. Jill's day had gone from bad to worse. It wasn't enough to catch her husband in the act; later that afternoon she'd been fired.

"I hope Lyle gets a sexually transmitted disease and Big Willie falls off," she said aloud, before correcting herself. "Not exactly 'Big' Willie. In fact, nothing to be proud of. I had to fake most of those orgasms, you rat bastard lying weasel dog."

Worse, she'd cooked for him. Jill could accept a bad sex life, but to think she'd ducked out of important meetings so that Lyle could come home to meals she'd prepared really made her teeth ache.

She wanted to roll down the windows and scream into the sea-soaked air that she hated her husband and couldn't wait until their divorce was final. She wished she'd never met him, had never fallen for him and had never married him. But there was no point in frightening the seagulls on the sidewalk and the two old guys playing checkers in the park.

The only bright spot in an otherwise completely black situation was that Shelley's hair had turned out movie-star gorgeous. Something to hang on to, Jill thought as she pulled to a stop at a red light and looked around for the first time since leaving San Francisco. Really looked.

Jeez, she was back in the one place she never wanted to be. Obviously her string of bad luck had continued, she thought, as she realized she was the only person on the planet who really *could* go home again.

Los Lobos, California—a small, touristy coastal town where folks vacationed every year. You could get homemade ice cream at the local Treats 'n Eats, homemade pie at Polly's Pie Parlor, and the best fajitas in the state at Bill's Mexican Grill. Residents never locked their doors, except during tourist season. The pier was a national treasure and the Halloween Pumpkin festival on the beach was one of the biggest events of the year. For some it was paradise; for Jill, it was like being sentenced to serve time in hell. It was also something else Lyle was going to have to answer for.

At least the family home had been turned over to the Conservancy Society, so she was saved the humiliation of having to live in her old bedroom. The house where she'd grown up was in the process of being restored to its original Victorian prissiness, and so she was temporarily moving in with her aunt Beverly.

The thought of the older woman's gentle smile and potpourri-filled house pushed Jill's foot down on the accelerator. She drove through the center of town—such as it was—and came out on the south side. After making a series of turns, she pulled up in front of a two-story house built in the 1940s. The wide porch had an overhang supported by stone-covered pillars. Several worn pieces of rattan furniture filled the space and offered a place to sit and watch the world go by. Jill found herself in more of a "curl up and lick her wounds" kind of mind-set, but that would pass, and when it did she would appreciate the old rocking chair by the swing.

She parked in front of the house and climbed out. Aunt Bev must have been watching from the big bay window because she stepped out of the house and started down the stairs.

Beverly Antoinette Cooper, known as Bev to her friends, had been born into money. Not gobs and gobs but enough that she'd never had to hold a job, even though she'd spent a couple of years as a schoolteacher when she'd first graduated from college. Petite, with fiery red hair and a big smile, she'd been the younger of the two children in her family. She'd moved to Los Lobos when her sister had married Jill's father and had decided to stay.

Jill had never been more grateful for the family connection. Her aunt wasn't one to judge or criticize. Mostly she offered hugs, affection and occasionally odd advice. Bev considered herself gifted—psychically—although the jury was still out on that one. Feeling better than she had since walking in on Lyle and his assistant going at it on his credenza, Jill walked around to the sidewalk, where she stopped and smiled.

"I'm here."

Her aunt grinned. "Nice wheels."

Jill glanced at the gleaming black BMW 545. "It's transportation," she said with a shrug.

"Uh-huh. Lyle's?"

"California *is* a community-property state," Jill said primly. "As he acquired the asset after our marriage, it's as much my car as his."

"You took it because you knew it would piss him off."

"Pretty much."

"That's my girl." Her aunt glanced at Jill's shirt and raised her eyebrows. "Takeout?"

Jill looked at the stain on the front of the hundred-percent Egyptian cotton custom-made shirt she'd shrugged on over her jeans. The sleeves hung well past her fingers and she could have fit inside the garment two and a half times, but this was Lyle's *special* shirt that he'd ordered from Hong Kong at the tidy price of five hundred dollars. He'd owned four. The other three were tucked inside her suitcase.

"Burrito," she said as she rubbed at the brownish-red smudge just under her right breast. "Maybe some hot sauce. I stopped at Taco Bell on the way down."

"Tell me you ate in the car," Bev said impishly. "Lyle always did have a thing against eating in the car."

"Every bite," Jill told her.

"Good."

Bev held out her arms. Jill hesitated only a second, then flung herself into the smaller woman's warm embrace. She'd been holding it together for two days, only allowing herself to deal with the logistics of packing up her world. All her emotions had been stuffed down until it was safe to let them go. That moment turned out to be right now.

Her face heated, her chest tightened and a shudder raced through her.

"I saw him doing it with her," she whispered, her voice thick with pain and the tears she tried to hold back. "At the *office*. It was so disgusting. He didn't even take his clothes off—his pants were hanging around his ankles and he looked ridiculous. Why wouldn't she make him get naked?"

"Some women don't have any self-respect."

Jill nodded. "At least I always made him get naked."

"I know you did."

"But that wasn't what hurt the most," she continued,

her eyes burning. "He stole my promotion. I'd been working so damn hard and I brought in all that business and he got my promotion and I got fired."

The tears broke free. She tried to hold them in, but it was too late. They scorched her skin and dripped onto her aunt's shoulder.

"And what I really d-don't understand is why I'm more mad than hurt," she said, her voice cracking. "Why do I care more about my job than my marriage?"

Jill asked the question rhetorically. She had a feeling they both already knew the answer.

"Want to scratch his car?" her aunt asked.

Jill straightened and wiped her face with the back of her hand. "Maybe later."

"I made cookies. Let's go have some."

"I'd like that."

Bev took her hand and led her toward the house. "I've been doing some research. I think I might be able to put a curse on Lyle. Would that help?"

With each step, Jill felt her pain easing just a little. Maybe Los Lobos wasn't her idea of a good time, but her aunt's house had always been a haven.

"A curse would be good. Could we give him boils with pus?"

"We could sure try."

TWO HOURS LATER Jill and her aunt had split nearly a dozen double-chocolate-chip cookies and had knocked back several brandies.

"I don't want to do anything malicious," Jill said, pretty darned proud she could say malicious, what with the way the liquor had heated her blood and turned her brain to foggy mush. "So instead of outright scratching the Beamer, maybe I'll just park it by the high-school baseball diamond. All those foul balls could make a real impact on it." She giggled. "Get it? Impact? The two meanings of the word?"

Her aunt sighed. "You're drunk."

"You betcha. And I feel pretty good, if I do say so myself. I didn't think I would. I thought I'd be depressed for days. I mean practicing law here." She grimaced and felt her good mood slipping away. "Okay—that goes on the do-not-think-about list. Not my new practice here, although I use the term loosely. At least that's just until I get a *real* job. Not Lyle. The divorce is good, though. I really want that. I want our marriage to never have been." She reached for another cookie. "Could we vaporize him? Would that technically be murder?" She sighed. "Never mind. I know it would be. I don't want to be disbarred. That would be too depressing for words."

Cookie crumbs fell on her shirt right next to the damp spot where she'd sloshed her brandy. She brushed at the crumbs only to smear chocolate on the shirt.

"I need to go clean up," she said, and put down the half-eaten cookie. "I didn't shower before I left San Francisco this morning."

As she spoke, she reached behind her head to grab her mass of curly, frizzy hair. While she'd showered the previous morning, she hadn't bothered with her usual blow-dry, flatiron, forty-seven-hair-care-product regimen required to tame her impossible hair. As a result, she was left with a mass resembling Frankenstein's bride after the woman stuck her finger in an electrical socket. On the attractive scale, she knew she approached absolute zero.

Jill pushed herself to her feet. Between not sleeping much in the past two days and the brandy, the roses on the wallpaper in the kitchen began to swirl.

"That can't be good," she murmured.

"You'll feel better after a shower," her aunt said. "You remember where everything is, don't you?"

"Uh-huh. Top of the stairs." Although right now the thought of climbing stairs made her dizzy.

A timer dinged at the same instant that someone knocked on the front door. Her aunt rose from the round table by the window and motioned for Jill to head for the front of the house.

"See who it is. I don't trust you to remove hot cookie sheets in your present condition."

"Sounds like a plan."

Jill walked down the hall, only plowing into the wall once. She got a vision of herself as a bumper car, which made her giggle. She was still caught up in the humor when she pulled open the front door.

There were only a handful of things that could have made her present situation worse: The death or injury of someone she loved, the belief that she would never escape from Los Lobos to work in a big-city law practice again, and seeing Mackenzie Kendrick while she looked like cat gack.

So it was a one-out-of-three chance, she thought, as

she stared at the man standing on her aunt's doorstep. Couldn't she have just been struck by lightning?

Apparently not, she thought as she looked into dark blue eyes and studied the familiar, painfully handsome and strong features that made up his face. He looked older, but who didn't? He could still make her toes curl and her heart convulse like the bouncing ball on a karaoke monitor. Or maybe that was the brandy acting out.

Last she'd *heard,* Mac Kendrick had moved to Los Angeles where he'd been zipping up the ranks of the Los Angeles Police Department. Last she'd *seen* of Mac, she'd been eighteen and he'd been home on leave from the army. She'd shown up in his bedroom, dropped her dress to the floor, offering her very naked self to him, and he'd promptly thrown up.

Memories like that put the end of her marriage in perspective.

"Mac," she said, going for pleasant and cheerful and hoping she didn't end up sounding manic.

He frowned. The movement made his brows surge together and his eyes get all crinkly. Jill had to work hard not to sigh at how delicious he looked. She remembered the stains on the huge shirt she wore just as his expression cleared.

"Jill?"

She offered a little waggle of her fingers. "Uh-huh. Hi. I'm uh…" *Visiting* wasn't the truth and she knew she was too drunk to lie. Maybe better to avoid the issue of why she was in town. "So what are you doing here?"

"I live here."

She blinked. "In town? Here? In Los Lobos?"

"I'm the new sheriff."

"Why?"

He smiled. The curve of his mouth made her stomach somersault.

"I like it here," he said.

"I guess everyone gets an opinion."

He stared at her for a long time, then touched the edge of his upper lip. "You have some crumbs...."

"What? Oh. The cookies." She swiped with her hand, then reached for the edge of the shirt and wiped it across her mouth. A quick glance told her there had been chocolate in those crumbs. Great.

"Mac? Is that you?" Bev joined them. "I'm sure you want to confirm everything. Come on in. Jill, step back and let Mac inside."

Jill did as ordered. Somewhere between the first and third brandy, she'd kicked off her shoes, which meant she was barefoot on the gleaming hardwood floor. The sensation reminded her too much of the last time she'd seen Mac and she hurried to lead the way into the living room where at least there was carpeting against her toes.

She heard the thud of his footsteps as he followed, along with her aunt's pleasant conversation as she chatted about the warm afternoon and how pretty the sunrise had been. Bev was big on watching the sunrise. Something about the first light of morning cleansing her psychic energy.

Jill crossed to the rocking chair and sank down. The

chair swayed forward and back, causing the corners of the room to fold in just enough to make her want to giggle. Maybe this was good, she thought, as she curled up on the thick cushion. She'd always wondered what would happen if she ever saw Mac again. After that disastrous last meeting, she'd been afraid of what she would say or he would say. Or how he would look at her. But being drunk seemed to take the edge off. If he pitied her, well, wasn't that just how her life was going?

"So, you're the sheriff," she said when he'd settled on the long sofa opposite the window and Bev had disappeared for refreshments. Jill had a feeling Mac wasn't going to be offered brandy.

"Just. I started work two weeks ago."

"Why?"

"That's the date we agreed on."

She reached up to tuck a strand of hair behind her ear and froze when her fingers encountered the Brillo mop. Oh…my…God. She'd *completely* forgotten about her appearance. Now what?

She winced silently and realized there was nothing she could do but tough it out and hope he hadn't noticed.

"I meant, why did you take the job of sheriff?"

His dark blue eyes settled on her face. Even as she felt her insides begin to melt, she reminded herself that he was probably trying to figure out why she had chocolate stains on her cheeks. She rubbed her skin and let the alcohol make her not really care.

"I wanted a change," he said. "Plus it's a great place for Emily to spend the summer."

Emily? What were the odds of that name belonging to his aging but adored Saint Bernard? Zero, she decided, as her string of bad luck continued.

"Your wife?" she said with a smile and what she hoped was an expression of polite interest.

"His daughter."

Bev spoke as she walked into the living room. She set down the tray of cookies along with three glasses of milk.

"Mac's little girl is eight."

Jill tried to get her mind around the concept. Over the years she'd imagined him with an assortment of women who were nothing like her, but she'd never thought of him as a father.

"I have her for the summer," he said, and took a cookie from the plate. "Bev has agreed to help out with day care."

Jill turned her attention to her aunt, at the same time swinging her head. Instantly the entire room tilted on end before settling back to a normal axis. Two thoughts filled her brain—the first, that Mac wasn't married. At least, not to his daughter's mother. The second thought was more troubling.

"You don't like children," she reminded her aunt. "That's why you gave up teaching."

Bev handed her a glass of milk. "I don't like them in groups," she corrected. "Maybe I read *Lord of the Flies* too many times—I've always felt children could turn rabid at any moment. But individually they're fine." She smiled at Mac. "I'm sure Emily's an angel."

Mac looked startled by Bev's theory on children and

their potential. "What?" He shook his head. "No, she's just a regular kid."

There was something in his voice, Jill thought, as she grabbed a cookie and took a bite. Something... wistful. Or was that her liquor-laced brain doing the talking?

She sipped her milk, swallowed and nearly gagged. "I can't," she said, thrusting the glass at her aunt. "After the brandy, my stomach won't like this at all."

"Of course it will. Just pretend you're having a Brandy Alexander. In two courses."

"Oh. Okay."

Mac looked at her. "You've been drinking?"

Faint disapproval sharpened his gaze and tightened his mouth. A quick glance at the clock told her it was a little past three in the afternoon.

"It's after five in New York and I've had a bad day."

Make that a bad week, possibly a bad life.

"Don't worry. Jill's not a wild woman," Bev said with a comforting smile. "She's just a little out of sorts. When does Emily arrive?"

"Around five. I'll bring her by in the morning. I didn't want to work on her first day, but I have to appear in court."

"Don't think a thing about it," Bev told him. "I'm excited at the thought of the two of us spending the summer together. We'll have fun."

Jill thought about warning Mac about her aunt's "gift" and how she sometimes passed from normal to just plain odd. But what was the point in worrying him? Besides, Bev had a way of making a person feel special and loved and maybe that was something every eight-year-old little girl needed.

Mac rose and murmured something about heading home. Jill wanted to rouse herself enough to ask where exactly that was. His house. Not that she planned any more midnight intrusions. One humiliating moment like that was enough for anyone's life. Nope, she would avoid Mac as much as she could while trapped in the hell that was Los Lobos. She would practice whatever form of law they expected here, handling their petty problems while sending out her buffed-up résumé to large law firms all over the state.

And in her free time, she would plot revenge. Mean, hard-hearted, satisfying revenge that would reduce her rat-bastard ex-husband to a quivering mass. She smiled at the thought and felt something cold and wet drip onto her leg.

"Oh dear."

Her aunt sounded concerned, which made Jill want to ask her what was wrong, but she couldn't seem to open her eyes or speak. Something was taken from her hand.

"How much brandy did she have?" a man asked.

Mac, Jill thought hazily. Yummy, sexy Mac. She'd had a crush on him since she was thirteen years old. But he'd never noticed her. Not really. He'd been nice and friendly, but in a distant, big-brother kind of way.

It was because she hadn't gotten breasts. Not real ones like her best friend Gracie. Nope, Jill had what Gracie's mom had referred to as "discreet curves." Jill didn't want discreet. She wanted blatant, sexy, in-your-face boobs.

She felt herself slipping down in the chair, then suddenly she was high up in the air. It was like floating or flying or both.

"On the sofa?"

"Yes. I'll get a blanket. I'm sure she just needs to rest."

"Or drink less," a man said with a chuckle. "She's going to feel like crap in a few hours."

That won't be anything new, Jill thought as she burrowed into the pillow that found its way under her head. She'd been feeling like crap for two days. Only this was better. It was warm and cozy and she felt safe again. She let herself drift off and vowed that when she woke up, everything would be different.

MAC GAVE UP the pretense of not watching the clock somewhere around four forty-five. He had the thought that the waiting would be a whole lot easier with a beer in his hand, but he wasn't going there. Not with Emily on the line. Not with it all being his fault.

He wanted to blame someone else, to point the finger and say he wasn't responsible, but he couldn't. Not when he'd taken every step himself. He couldn't even blame Carly. His ex-wife had been more understanding and forgiving than he deserved.

Because she was organized and didn't see the value in making him sweat, she arrived five minutes early. He watched the Volvo pull up into his driveway and was outside before either of the occupants had a chance to open their doors.

"Hey, kiddo," he said as Emily stepped out.

His daughter was slight and blond, with big blue eyes and a smile that could light up the heavens. Only she wasn't smiling now. Instead her mouth quivered at the corners and she wouldn't look him in the eye. She clutched Elvis, her tattered, stuffed rhino, to her chest and stared at the ground.

He hadn't seen her in nearly two months and it was all he could do not to grab her and hug her forever. He wanted to tell her he loved her, that she'd grown and gotten more beautiful, that he'd thought about her every day. Instead he tucked his hands into his jeans pockets and wished he could go back in time and make things different.

"Hello, Mac."

He turned his attention to Carly. Petite, well dressed, with her gold-blond hair cut to her jawline, she walked around the car and moved toward him.

"You look good," he said, bending down to kiss her cheek.

She squeezed his upper arm. "You, too. Cute little town. So this is where you grew up?"

"This is it."

"How does it feel to be back?"

He'd spent the past two weeks torn between hope and impending disaster. Too much was on the line.

"Good," he said with a casual confidence he didn't feel. "Let's get the luggage and go inside." He turned to Emily. "Your bedroom is upstairs, kiddo. Want to go check it out?"

She glanced at her mom as if asking for permission. When Carly nodded, Emily darted inside.

"She hates me," he said flatly.

"She loves you, but she's scared. She hasn't seen you in weeks, Mac. You didn't show up the two weekends like you promised. You broke her heart."

He nodded and swallowed the rising guilt. "I know. I'm sorry."

He crossed to the trunk and waited for her to unlock it.

"Apologies don't work on an eight-year-old," Carly told him. "You disappeared from her life without a word and now you're going to have to prove yourself to her."

He already knew that. The question was how? How did a father go about regaining the trust of his daughter? Was it possible? Had he crossed the line and was it already too late?

He wanted to ask Carly her opinion, but he figured he'd already used up all his currency with her.

"You didn't have to do this," he said as he lifted out two suitcases.

Carly grabbed a cooler. "I know. Part of me wanted to turn my back on you, but you've always loved her more than anything." She closed the trunk and stared at him. "I want to believe you, Mac. I want you to have this chance. But make no mistake. If you screw up even one time, I'll haul your ass back into court and make sure you never see your daughter again."

CHAPTER TWO

JILL WOKE in darkness to the sound of the grandfather clock in the hall. She counted ten chimes, then shoved back the blanket and gingerly pushed into a sitting position.

Her memory blurred as she tried to figure out where she was and why she'd fallen asleep on a sofa. Bits and pieces returned as she recalled arriving at Aunt Bev's place and the liberal consumption of brandy.

The quiet of the house told her that her aunt had already headed upstairs. Not a surprise—those who liked to be awake and perky for the sunrise usually had to go to bed fairly early. Jill was more of a sunset kind of gal, although she'd missed it today, what with sleeping off her stupor.

"There'll be another sunset tomorrow," she reminded herself as she stood and tensed in anticipation of a blinding headache or double vision. Neither occurred. Actually, she felt pretty good.

"That's a plus."

She made her way to the guest room and smiled when she saw the folded-back covers and fluffed pillows. Her aunt had even left a tray with water, a glass and a package of Alka-Seltzer.

"An amazing woman."

Jill ignored the bed and walked to her suitcase. After collecting toiletries, she hit the bathroom and turned on the shower.

Twenty minutes, one shampoo and an application of sweet-pea-scented body lotion later, she felt practically normal. She debated between PJs and sweats before settling on the latter. With her hair still in a towel and a wide-tooth comb in her hand, she walked downstairs and out onto the back porch.

The wooden structure was nearly as wide as the front porch and just as furnished. There was an old swing, a rattan table and chair set along with a bench, a few bug-zapper lamps and a trellis covered with bougainvillea.

Jill ignored it all and sat on the rear steps leading down to the grass. The night was cool and pleasant. A clear sky twinkled with a thousand stars she couldn't see when she was in the city. She supposed there were those who thought small-town life was made perfect by things like stars and unlocked doors. They were, of course, hideously wrong.

She pulled off the towel and reached for the comb. Just then the back door of the house on the left opened and someone stepped out.

Jill froze, her arm raised, the comb barely touching her hair. Even in the dim light of the porch she recognized the tall, broad-shouldered man. Mac.

She figured the odds of him visiting a neighbor at this hour were slim, which meant he probably lived next door to her aunt. Wasn't that just how her life was going? No doubt he'd moved in with his wife and...

Hazy memories clicked into place. Something about a child. A daughter maybe? But no wife. Or at least not the kid's mother. Or had that been wishful thinking on her part? Horror swept through her as she thought she remembered passing out in his presence.

She shifted to stand and creep back inside, but a board creaked, Mac turned, then started toward her. Jill glanced down at the T-shirt she'd pulled on over sweatpants. Oh, yeah, a fabulous "aren't I sexy" look. She supposed her lack of bra could be considered provocative, if she had actual breasts larger than fried eggs.

"How are you feeling?" he asked as he approached.

His voice rumbled into the quiet of the night. The sound seemed to rub against her skin like velvet on silk. Her insides clenched and her mind emptied of all rational thought.

"Ah, better," she managed. "I needed that."

"The nap, the brandy or passing out?"

"Maybe all three."

He paused in front of her and leaned against the railing. One corner of his mouth curved up.

"Do you remember *anything* that happened this afternoon?"

She had a feeling that he wasn't talking about the drive from San Francisco. The question made her uneasy.

"Why? Did I do anything memorable before, um, passing out?" Had she thrown up, or worse? *Was* there worse than throwing up?

"Nope. You got very quiet, spilled your milk and passed out."

Inwardly she winced. "Sounds charming." She recalled waking up. "So how did I get to the sofa?"

Mac's half smile widened into a full grin. "You're welcome."

He'd carried her? She'd actually been in Mac's arms and she hadn't been conscious for the moment? Could her life *get* any more unfair?

"Ah, thanks. That was really nice of you."

What she wanted to know was had he enjoyed the experience? Had he thought of it as anything more than a chore? Had she even once crossed his mind in the past ten years?

He moved to the foot of the stairs and sat down. His thigh was amazingly close to her bare toes. If she moved her foot a scant inch, they would be touching. Jill jerked the comb through her still-wet hair and swallowed a sigh of frustration. One would think she would be more grown-up and mature by now, but one would be wrong.

"So you're back in town," she said when no wittier bit of conversation occurred to her.

He pointed to the house on the left. The one she'd seen him walk out of. "Right next door."

"With your daughter?" she asked, hoping her wisps of memory were accurate.

The humor fled his face, leaving behind only tightness and something that might have been pain.

"Emily."

"I'm sure she'll enjoy Los Lobos. It's a great place for kids. Especially in the summer." Jill hadn't started to chafe at the restrictions of small-town life until she'd entered college.

"I hope so. I haven't seen her in a while. After the divorce…" He shrugged, which didn't explain much.

"Was her mother difficult about things?" she asked.

"No. Carly was great. It was my fault. I wasn't around for a while. That hurt Emily. She's just a kid, I should have realized. I want joint custody, but I need to earn the privilege. That's what this summer is about."

His words left her with more questions than answers, but she decided not to push.

"I hope things work out," she said.

"Me, too. Em means the world to me." The smile returned. "Your aunt agreed to help me with day care. Should I be rethinking that?"

"Because of what I said about her not liking children?"

He nodded.

Jill shook her head. "She didn't like teaching very much, but she was always great when I was growing up." There was the whole psychic gift thing, but maybe it was better to let Mac find out about that on his own.

"Good to know," he said.

"Your daughter arrived earlier, right? Did everything go okay?"

He glanced toward the house. "It was fine. Carly drove her up from L.A. and stayed through bedtime. All I had to do was hang around in the background. The real test will be in the morning."

"You love her," Jill told him. "That counts for a lot."

"I hope so."

She was about to expand on the point when she remembered she had absolutely zero experience in the kid department. Not that she hadn't wanted them. But the lying weasel rat bastard had thought they should wait and, for reasons not clear to her, they had. Of course now she was glad—children would have complicated the divorce.

"So what are you doing back in town?" Mac asked. "Vacation? Last I heard you were practicing corporate law in San Francisco."

Jill felt her eyes widen. He *knew* about her life? Had he been asking? Had he thought about her? Was there—

She quickly slammed a mental door on those thoughts. No doubt Mac had simply picked up small-town gossip. Nothing worth getting excited about.

"I was, until recently," she said. "I worked for a corporate law firm in San Francisco. I was about to make junior partner." She resumed combing her damp hair.

"Past tense?"

"Yup. My soon-to-be ex-husband managed to get me fired. He also got my promotion, my window office and our condo." She tugged through a knotted strand. "Not that he'll get to keep the condo. It's community property. He cheated on me, too. I saw him, and let me tell you, there's a visual I want erased from my brain."

"That's a lot for one day. How'd he get you fired?"

"I'm still working on that one. I brought a lot of business into the firm. More than any other associate.

But when they fired me, I wasn't allowed to speak to any of the senior partners to find out what was going on. I sent a couple of e-mails and letters, so we'll see. In the meantime, I'm temporarily back in Los Lobos to take over the law practice of Dixon and Son."

"And you're not happy about it."

"Not even a little." She tried to tell herself at least she was still practicing law, but she didn't actually believe herself.

"I take it Mr. Dixon didn't have a son."

"Apparently not. Or he wasn't interested in taking over the family firm. So that's me." She set down the comb and forced herself to smile. "I'm a small-time litigator. In my free time I'll be planning revenge on Lyle."

"The ex?"

"Uh-huh."

"If the revenge involves breaking the law, I don't want to know."

"Fair enough. I probably won't do anything illegal, though. I don't want to be disbarred." Which cut into the possibilities. Not a problem, though. She could rise to the occasion by being more creative.

"Have the summer softball leagues started yet?" she asked.

Mac nodded. "Sure. Games every weekend."

"Good. I think I'll park the car by the practice fields. There should be plenty of fly balls zipping around."

He winced. "Is that 545 Lyle's car?"

"Technically it's community property. He bought it with joint assets."

"If I were you, I'd make a note of that to tell the judge."

"I will."

He chuckled.

Jill pulled her knees to her chest and sighed. This was nice—fun. If she'd been sixteen, talking to Mac in the dark would have been the answer to her prayers. At twenty-eight, it wasn't half-bad, either.

"Why here?" he asked. "You could have gotten a job anywhere."

"Thanks for the vote of confidence. This gig is temporary. Actually it was my father's idea."

Mac stared at her. "He suggested it?"

"Oh, yeah. When I told him what had happened, he told me about the vacant practice here. You'd think that moving clear to the other side of the country would make him less of a meddler in town affairs, but no. It's as if he's still around the corner instead of in Florida."

"He does keep a hand in," Mac said. "Judge Strathern told me about the vacancy in the sheriff's office."

Jill didn't know which surprised her more—that her father kept in contact with Mac or that Mac referred to him so formally. They'd known each other for years. Mac had practically grown up in her father's house. Of course Mac being the housekeeper's son probably put their relationship on a different level. Not that she'd cared about things like that. When she'd been a teenager all she'd cared about was how gorgeous Mac had been and how her heart had beat like hummingbird wings every time he smiled at her.

"So my dad's to blame for both of us being here," she said. "Although *you* like it."

"Maybe the town will grow on you."

"Like a wart? No thanks."

She fingered her hair and realized it had started to dry. In a matter of minutes it would be a wild and wooly mess. She reached up and began to weave it into a loose braid.

"I don't remember your hair being that curly," he said as he watched.

Jill thought about how she'd looked earlier that day—a stained, drunk, frizzy mess. "It has a mind of its own. I tame it with a combination of iron will and hair products. Blow dryer, flatiron and an assortment of bottles and jars. Give me electricity, my tools and an hour and you'll see sleek, perfect hair."

"Why go to all that trouble?"

Spoken like a true man. "To keep it controlled and borderline normal."

"Curly hair is sexy."

Four simple words that made her stomach clench and her mouth go dry. She wanted to shake her head and flaunt her curls. She wanted to dance on the lawn and announce to the heavens that Mac thought she had sexy hair.

"Especially when it's long, like yours."

The world just got better and better.

"Thanks."

Ooh, she sounded so cool and casual. Good thing he couldn't see the chorus line of hormones doing the happy dance.

Mac stood. "This has been nice, Jill, but I need to get back and check on Emily. I wouldn't want her to wake up and find the house empty."

"Good point."

She held in the regretful sigh and managed not to say how she wished they could talk about her sexy hair a little bit longer. Maybe next time.

She waved as Mac walked toward his house, then turned toward her own back door. Just as her fingers touched the door handle, she froze.

Maybe next time? Had she really thought that? No, no, no, no, no. There was no this time or next time or anytime. Mac was here—small-town sheriff makes good with kid. She was there—big-city corporate law shark. That was her—swimming for freedom. She did not want to get trapped here in Los Lobos. She wanted big bucks and bigger revenge on the rat fink lying weasel dog. Hunky guys next door were not part of her plan. And in case she was tempted, she needed to remember what had happened the last time she'd thrown herself at the guy in question.

He'd taken one look at her naked body and vomited. There was a lesson there—one she would do well to remember.

EMILY KENDRICK SQUEEZED her eyes as tightly closed as she could. She squeezed until her whole face hurt and she thought she might squish her eyeballs. She clenched her teeth, raised her shoulders and held her breath until the burning went away. Then she relaxed.

Okay. Better. She wasn't going to cry. Not here. She

wasn't sure why she thought she shouldn't give in to tears. It wasn't as if someone had told her not to cry. The message came from inside her—that scary dark place that got bigger when she thought about the summer with her dad and her mom going away and how nothing had been right for a long, long time.

She could hear noises from downstairs. Something clanged onto the stove. Before, she would have giggled at the thought of her dad cooking. He'd done it sometimes, on Sunday morning or when she'd been sick and he'd stayed home with her. Then he'd made fun stuff, like grilled-cheese sandwiches cut up into the shape of a boat, or caramel corn they'd baked in the oven. He'd always let her help. He'd—

The burning came back. Emily sucked in a breath and willed it away. She wouldn't think about before. About when things had been good and her dad had tossed her in the air and told her he loved her and her mom had laughed all the time. She wouldn't think about that, or how one day she and her mom had gone away and her dad had never, ever found them.

She walked to the bed she'd made so carefully and picked up Elvis. The worn rhino fit into her arms the way he always had and that made her feel better.

"Mommy left us," she murmured into the bare spot behind his ear—the place she always whispered her secrets. "She left last night after she tucked me in bed and I'm mad at her."

Emily didn't want to be mad at her mom, but mad was safe. She liked being mad right now because when she was mad she didn't care so much.

"We have to stay the whole summer and be with some lady because my dad has to work. He's the sheriff."

She didn't know what being the sheriff meant. He'd been a policeman before. She'd liked how he looked in his uniform—big and brave and she'd known he would always keep her safe. But then he'd let her go away and daddies weren't supposed to do that. They were supposed to be with their little girls always.

She didn't want to be here, Emily thought as she stared at the door to her room. She'd begged her mother to let her stay home. She'd promised to be good and clean her room and not watch too much TV, but it hadn't mattered. Her mother had brought her here and had left her.

Emily's stomach growled. She was hungry because she hadn't eaten much dinner the night before.

Slowly, carefully, she opened the door and stepped into the hallway. The house was old, but nice. Big, with a second floor and lots of big trees. Her mom had told her that the ocean was real close and that her dad would take her to play on the beach. Emily had liked that but hadn't said anything.

The stairs creaked as she walked downstairs. She could still hear her dad in the kitchen. She smelled bacon and maybe pancakes and her mouth began to water. Her grip on Elvis tightened until she was afraid she would pop him like a balloon. Finally she hovered at the entrance to the kitchen.

The room was big, with lots of windows. Her dad stood by the stove. He looked so tall and strong and just like she remembered him. For a second she almost ran over to be picked up and hugged. She wanted to feel his arms around her, holding her close. She wanted him to tell her that she was his best girl always.

Her throat got all tight and her stomach felt squishy instead of empty. And when he looked up and smiled at her, it was as if her feet had somehow glued themselves to the floor.

"Hey, kiddo, how'd you sleep?"

"Okay," she whispered.

She waited for the hug, or a wink or *something* to tell her that he still thought she was his best girl. She leaned forward to hear him tell her that he loved her and he was glad they were together. That he'd missed her and looked for her every day but he hadn't been able to find her.

But he didn't. Instead he pulled out a chair at the table in the center of the room.

"Have a seat. I made pancakes. You always liked them, right? Oh, and bacon."

Emily felt very cold on the inside, as if that dark, scary place inside of her had just frozen over. She didn't want pancakes, she wanted her *dad*.

He waited until she was seated, then pushed in the chair. Emily put Elvis on the table next to her place setting and waited while he slid three pancakes onto her plate. Bacon was next. She looked from the food to the glass of orange juice just to her right.

Funny how she didn't feel hungry at all. She didn't feel anything.

"Here's some strawberries," he said, putting a bowl of the cut-up fruit on her left.

Emily squared her shoulders and carefully pushed the plate away. "No, thank you," she said in a voice that was so small she wondered if she were starting to disappear.

"What? Aren't you hungry?"

She wanted to grab Elvis and hold him close, but then her dad might guess she was scared and sad. Instead, she squeezed her hands together so tight that her nails dug into her skin.

"The color's wrong," she said, trying to speak a little louder. "I'm wearing purple."

He looked at her T-shirt and shorts. "So?"

"If I'm wearing purple I can only eat purple."

His mouth got straight and his eyes narrowed. He didn't look happy anymore and she was afraid. But she didn't give in. She couldn't.

"Since when?" he asked. "How long have you been color-coordinating your food with your wardrobe?"

"A while now."

"I see."

It was barely after eight in the morning and Mac already felt tired. Damn it all to hell—he didn't want to let Emily win this battle. It would set a precedent, forcing him into a corner.

"Wait there," he told his daughter as he walked out of the kitchen and headed for the small den at the front of the house.

He'd set up an office in the narrow space, sliding a desk between built-in bookcases. Now he grabbed the phone and punched in Carly's number. Couldn't she have warned him what was going on with Emily?

They'd had the whole evening. Was it too damn hard to say "Gee, Mac, the kid only eats the color she's wearing."?

Still caught up in his temper, he barely noticed when a man answered the phone.

"Hello?"

"What?" Mac started to say he'd dialed the wrong number when he realized that maybe he hadn't. "Is Carly there?"

"Sure. I'll get her."

"It's Mac," he added, not sure why.

"Just a second."

There was the sound of the phone being set down, then a low rumble of voices too quiet for him to hear the words. Obviously Carly was seeing someone and the man in question had spent the night. Mac turned the idea over in his brain, then shook his head. He didn't care if she slept with the entire NFL as long as she didn't do it in front of his daughter.

"Mac? What's wrong?"

"Why didn't you tell me she won't eat a color she's not wearing?"

From a couple hundred miles away, he heard his ex-wife sigh. "Is she doing that? I'm so sorry. I'd hoped she'd let it go. We talked about it."

"You and she talked about it. You didn't say squat to me."

"I should have."

"How long has she been doing this?"

"About six weeks. I talked to the pediatrician. She thinks it's a way for Emily to have some control in her life, and maybe a way to get us to do what she wants. She didn't get a say in the divorce or having you gone. She's punishing us."

"Couldn't she just throw a tantrum and be done with it?"

"Tell me about it."

He sat on the corner of the desk. "So how does this work? She ate last night."

"Sure. She wore red. I brought spaghetti, a salad made of red-leaf lettuce and we had strawberry short-cake for dessert. What's she wearing this morning?"

"Purple. I made pancakes and bacon. So far she's ignoring it."

"Blueberries are good on purple days. Although… when I saw the doctor last week, she pointed out that if we were willing to hold out against her and not give her what she wanted, eventually hunger would force her to eat."

Starve his daughter? He couldn't imagine it. "Did it work?"

"I was too chicken to try."

"Great. So I get to be the bad guy?"

"It's only a suggestion. You have to do what you think is right."

His gut told him that the doctor was on to some-thing—Emily would eventually get hungry and eat what was served. But was that how he wanted to start their summer together? There was also the matter of the so-cial worker. He could only imagine *that* interview as Emily complained that her bully of a father hadn't fed her in two days.

"How the hell am I supposed to know what's right?" he asked, more to himself than Carly.

"You were always a good father, Mac."

"Absolutely. Right up until I disappeared from her life. Some kind of hero, huh?"

Carly was silent for a couple of seconds, then she said, "Emily doesn't know I'm seeing anyone. Brian and I have been dating about two months, but I haven't introduced them. I want to be sure it's going to last."

He didn't care about his ex-wife seeing a guy, but he hated the thought of his daughter having another father in her life.

"I won't tell her," he said.

"Thanks. I wish I could be more helpful on the food thing."

"I'll deal with it. I suppose in some courts, the judge would say I earned it."

"You need to give both of you some time," Carly told him. "That's what this summer is about."

"I know. I'll send you an e-mail in a couple of days and let you know how things are going."

"I appreciate that. Take care, Mac."

"You, too."

He hung up the phone and returned to the kitchen.

Emily sat where he'd left her. The only change was the stuffed rhino in her arms.

"Elvis have any advice for me?" he asked.

Wariness filled her wide blue eyes as she shook her head.

"Just like a rhino. I can't get him to shut up when I'm

driving. He's always telling me what lane to be in and where to turn. But now, when I need some instructions, he doesn't say a word."

Emily bit down on her lower lip. Mac hoped it was to keep from smiling.

He gave an exaggerated sigh. "Purple, huh?"

She nodded.

"Okay, kiddo. Let's hit the grocery store and get you some breakfast."

"Can I have Pop-Tarts?" she asked as she slid off the chair. "They're purple."

"Unless I can find some purple bacon, we may end up there." He made a mental note to get some kid vitamins. The multicolored kind. And wondered what on earth he was going to cook on the days she wore blue.

CHAPTER THREE

JILL CAREFULLY LOCKED the BMW before leaving it parked by the foul line of the practice fields. A quick glance at the sign-up board told her that there would be several teams practicing over the next few days. With a little luck, they could all have a close encounter with the 545.

Maybe she should look into a rental car while she was in town, she thought, as she shifted her briefcase to her left hand and began the three-block walk to her new office. If she left Lyle's car all over the place, how would she get around? Not that there were all that many places to go in Los Lobos.

The morning had dawned cool and clear, which was good. Fog was death on her hair. She'd blown it dry, used the flatiron *and* her forty-seven products to produce a sleek, smooth cascade of stick-straight hair before coiling the whole length into a neat knot at the base of her neck. In deference to working in the more casual setting of a small town, she'd put on a pantsuit instead of a skirted suit, but the label still read Armani even though she knew the elegance would be lost on her clients. No matter, it was really all for her. When she dressed better, she felt better about herself. And today she would need all the help she could get.

The law offices of Dixon and Son were on Maple Street—a road with plenty of trees but no maples. Trendy antique stores leaned up against old bookstores. There were coffeehouses, cafés and the chamber of commerce on the corner. It was quiet, picturesque and pretty much as it had always been for the past fifty years.

Jill tried to convince herself that it wouldn't be so bad—but she knew she was lying. She'd only been in Mr. Dixon's office a couple of times, but the details of his building were firmly etched in her brain. She didn't mind that the place was old, musty and in serious need of paint. What she most objected to was the fish.

Mr. Dixon had been an avid fisherman. He'd gone all over the world, fishing his heart out and bringing back trophies for his office. The fish he'd caught were often stuffed, or whatever it was one did with dead fish one did not eat, and mounted onto plaques. These plaques hung in his office. Everywhere.

They stared down at clients, frightened small children and collected dust. They also smelled.

"Please God, let them be gone," Jill whispered to herself as she opened the glass door that led into the foyer and reception area and stepped inside.

God was either busy or chose not to oblige. Jill stopped on the scratched hardwood floor and felt dozens of eyes focus on her. Small, dark, beady fish eyes.

A huge swordfish hung up by the beamed ceiling. Midsize fish about ten or twelve inches long mounted on dark wood plaques circled the room just above the bookcases. There were fish by the light switches, fish along the wall leading upstairs, even a fish mounted on the front of the reception desk.

The smell was exactly as Jill remembered it—an unpleasant combination of dust, pine cleaner and old fish. The lone piece of toast she'd had for breakfast flipped over in her stomach.

A chair squeak jerked her attention from the large multicolored, large-toothed creature on the front of the desk to the woman sitting behind it.

"You must be Tina," Jill said with a warmth she didn't feel. "How nice to meet you at last."

Tina—her assistant/secretary/receptionist—stood up with a reluctance that made Jill think she wasn't the only one not happy about the change in circumstances. Tina was in her midthirties, with short brown hair in a sensible cut. She looked efficient, if not particularly friendly.

"You're in early," Tina said with a tight smile. "I thought you might be, so I had Dave get the kids off to school. I don't usually get here until nine-thirty."

Jill glanced at the old grandfather clock in the corner. It was 8:25 a.m.

"This is about when I start my day," Jill said. In San Francisco, it had often started closer to five-thirty, but she wasn't on the partner track anymore.

"I have three kids," Tina said. "They might be out of school, but I still have to get them off to their activities. Little Jimmy's in the baseball camp down by the park and Natalie is…" She pressed her lips together.

"I don't think you're that interested in my children, are you?"

"I'm sure they keep you very busy," Jill told her, trying not to stare as she noticed the other woman was wearing a polo shirt and Dockers. In a law office?

Tina caught her gaze and tugged at the front of her shirt. "Mr. Dixon didn't care if I dressed casually. You didn't want me to wear a dress, did you?"

Her tone indicated that it didn't much matter what Jill wanted. "You're fine," she said, reminding herself that it wasn't important. Who was there to impress?

"Good. Then I'll just show you around. This is the reception area. You probably guessed that. Recently closed cases are in that cabinet back there." She motioned to a set of dark wood file drawers.

Not even locked, Jill thought in amazement.

"The older files are all stored upstairs. Your office is in here." Tina walked through the open door and Jill followed.

The fish motif was in full swing. Dozens and dozens of those from under the sea had been mounted on wooden plaques and hung on nearly every inch of available, paneled wall space. Fishing net draped across the front of the large wooden desk, where a couple of long-dead starfish hung on precariously.

Bookcases lined two walls, while two open doors led to what looked like a storage room and a bathroom.

"It's very…" Jill turned in a slow circle and searched for the right word. Or any word. "Clean."

"There's a service that comes in once a week," Tina told her. "The coffeemaker's in the storeroom. I guess I could make it if you want me to, but Mr. Dixon always made his own." Her dark brown eyes turned misty. "He was a wonderful man."

"I'm sure."

"The heart attack was very sudden."

"Was he at work?"

"No. Out fishing."

Of course, Jill thought, trying to avoid beady fish-eyed glares from the décor.

Tina took a step back toward the reception area. "The paralegal comes twice a week. She's home with twins, so sometimes she can't make it in, but she gets the work done. I'll let you know when I have to be gone. I try to bunch up things like games and doctors' visits, so I'm not always running back and forth."

Jill had a feeling that Tina would go out of her way to make herself scarce.

"Where are Mr. Dixon's open cases?"

Tina pointed to the desk. "There are a couple of wills, that sort of thing. Oh, and you have some appointments. Mr. Harrison later today and Pam Whitefield on Wednesday."

The latter name startled Jill. "Is this the same Pam who married Riley Whitefield?"

"That's her. She said she had some trouble with a real estate transaction." Tina shrugged.

"I'm surprised she's back in town." Pam had been a couple of years ahead of Jill in school and had always made it clear she was destined for a great future that didn't involve Los Lobos.

"She never left." Tina inched toward the door. "I'll be out front if you need me."

Jill glanced around the office. It was like standing in the middle of an aquarium for deceased fish.

"Mr. Dixon caught all of these himself?" she asked.

Tina nodded.

"Perhaps *Mrs.* Dixon would like them as a reminder of her late husband."

"I don't think so." Tina shifted back a bit more. "She told me she liked knowing they were here in the office. Sort of like a tribute."

"I see."

While Jill didn't want to get stuck with the aquatic menagerie, she couldn't blame the widow for not wanting them in her home.

"Thanks, Tina. What time is Mr. Harrison coming?"

"About eleven-thirty. I have to leave about noon to take Jimmy to the orthodontist."

Why was Jill not surprised? "Of course you do. Will you be back?"

Tina's shoulders slumped. "If it's important to you."

Jill looked at the fish, the paneling, the net and the long-past-dead starfish. "I'm sure we'll be fine without you."

IT TOOK JILL less than two hours to bring herself up-to-date on Mr. Dixon's open cases. She contacted the clients, offered her services and was prepared to give referrals if they preferred.

No one did. Every single one of them made an appointment to come see her, which would have been gratifying if anyone had showed the slightest interest in his or her legal issues. Mrs. Paulson summed it up perfectly.

"That old will," the elderly lady had said with a laugh. "I don't take it very seriously. I mean, I'll be dead. What do I care? But sure, honey, if it makes you happy, I'll keep my appointment."

Rather than tell the woman that very little about the situation made her happy, she put a check mark next to the time and date in the appointment book and told Mrs. Paulson she was looking forward to meeting her.

"Your daddy was a fine man," the older woman said. "A good judge. I'm sure you'll do us all proud, just like he did."

"Thank you," Jill said before she hung up. As her father had talked her into being here, he wasn't one of her top-ten favorites at the moment.

With all the appointments confirmed, Jill pulled a disk out of her briefcase and slid it into her computer. With a few keystrokes she was able to pull up her résumé and began to update the information.

Mr. Harrison arrived promptly at eleven-thirty. Tina didn't bother knocking—she simply pushed open the door and showed him in.

Jill stood to greet him. There hadn't been any hint as to his problem in the appointment book, but she figured she could handle it.

"I'm Jill Strathern," she said, walking around the desk and holding out her hand. "How nice to meet you."

"Likewise," the older man said.

Mr. Harrison was one of those thin elderly men who seemed to shrink with age. His hair was white and thick, as were his eyebrows. Wrinkles pulled at his features, but his blue eyes were clear and sharp and his handshake firm.

When he'd taken the leather chair in front of her desk and just to the right of the fishing net, Jill returned to her seat and smiled.

"I didn't find any notes in Mr. Dixon's file on your case. Had you been in to see him before?"

Mr. Harrison dismissed the other man with a flick of his wrist. "Dixon was an idiot. All he cared about was fishing."

"Really?" Jill murmured politely, as if she wasn't aware of dozens of beady eyes watching her. "So what seems to be the problem?"

"Those bastards stole some land from me. Their fence is about twenty or twenty-five feet on my side. I want it moved."

He spread out several large sheets of yellowed paper showing deeds and land tracts. Jill stood and leaned over the desk while Mr. Harrison traced the various property lines. She found her interest piqued.

"We'd need an official survey to determine the boundaries, but from what I can see here, you're right. Your neighbors *have* put a fence on what is clearly your property."

"Good. Now they can take it down."

Jill grabbed a legal pad and sat. "What kind of fence is it?" she asked as she began to make notes.

"Stone. About six feet wide."

Her head snapped up as she stared at him. "You're kidding."

"Nope. I'm not saying it's not a nice fence and all. It works, but it's in the wrong place."

A stone fence? She'd been picturing chain link or cedar. "Why didn't you stop them when they started to put up the fence? A project like that would have taken weeks."

"I wasn't around. Besides, it's not my responsibility to patrol my own borders. This isn't Iraq."

"Fair enough." But a stone fence. That had to cost a fortune. "Have you talked to your neighbors about this?"

His mouth tightened. "They're young and they listen to rock music. Cotton wool for brains. No point in talking to them. They probably take drugs."

She sent up a quiet prayer of thanks that Mr. Harrison didn't live next door to *her*. "When was the fence built?"

"Near as I can tell, 1898."

The pen slid from her fingers and landed on the hardwood floor. Her mind simply wouldn't wrap itself around the information.

"That's over a hundred years ago."

His gaze narrowed. "I can do math, little lady. Why does it matter when it was built? It's stealing, plain and simple. I want that fence moved."

Jill might not know a lot about real estate law, but some truths were universal—one of them being that a fence in place for a hundred years was unlikely to be moved anytime soon.

"Why are you dealing with this now?" she asked.

"I don't want to leave a big mess after I'm gone. And don't bother telling me no one will care. Dixon already tried that argument." He glared at the nearest fish.

Jill felt the first stirrings of a headache. "Let me do some research, Mr. Harrison. There might be a legal precedent for what you want to do." Although she had her doubts. "I'll get back to you next week."

"I appreciate that."

Mr. Harrison rose and shook her hand, then headed for the reception area. As he didn't close the door behind him, she heard him clearly when he spoke to Tina.

"What were you going on about?" Mr. Harrison asked the receptionist. "She doesn't seem like she has a stick up her ass to me."

MAC CROSSED THE STREET from the courthouse to the sheriff's office and pushed through the double glass doors. He nodded at the deputy on duty and did his best not to make eye contact as he walked toward his office in the back corner, but Wilma caught up with him in less than two seconds.

"You have messages," the gray-haired dispatcher said as she thrust several pink pieces of paper into his hands. "You can ignore the ones on the bottom, but the top three are important. How'd it go in court?"

"Good."

He'd managed to keep one bad guy behind bars for

a couple of years. That had to count. He glanced down at the notes as he kept walking.

"The mayor called?" he asked, knowing that couldn't be good.

"Uh-huh."

Wilma had to take two steps for every one of his. She barely came past his elbow and, according to legend, had been around since before the earth's crust cooled. She was a tough old bird and one of the first of his staff he'd known was a keeper.

"Mayor's calling on behalf of the pier centennial committee. They want a temporary alcohol permit to serve beer at the car wash."

Mac stopped in the middle of the room and glared at her. "What? Serve beer? High-school kids are going to be doing the work."

"The mayor said the beer was for the patrons."

He felt his blood pressure climbing. "He wants to serve beer to people who are going to get back in their cars and drive around town? Of all the stupid, ill-conceived, ridiculous, backward—"

"I said you wouldn't like it," Wilma told him. "But he didn't listen."

Mac had already had a few encounters with the mayor and he hadn't enjoyed a single one. "Does he ever?"

"No."

He swore. "Fine. I'll call him back and tell him there's no way he's getting the permit."

"He won't be happy."

"I don't care."

She grinned. "That's one of the things I like about

you." She poked at the messages in his hand. "You also have a call from someone named Hollis Bass. The boy sounded like nothing but useless trouble. He's not a relative, is he?"

Mac flipped through the notes until he found the one with Hollis's number. "No. Not a relative. A social worker." Just what he needed—one more thing. "What else?"

"Slick Sam is getting released on bond today and someone needs to go tell the judge's daughter not to get messed up with the likes of him." Wilma wrinkled her nose. "Slick Sam is proof our criminal law system is in serious need of an overhaul. Want me to give her a call for you?"

Mac glanced at the big clock on the wall. It was barely twelve. He'd promised Emily he'd be back for her by one. There was still time to drop by Jill's office and warn her about Slick Sam.

"I'll do it in person," he said. "Then I'll call the mayor and the social worker from home. Everything else can wait."

Wilma's hazel eyes widened slightly. "I figured you had to know Jill."

"We go way back."

"Her father may have retired to Florida, but he still stays informed."

Mac grinned. "I'm going to warn her about a potentially difficult client, not seduce her."

"It always starts with conversation. You be careful."

With Jill? He doubted it was necessary. She might

be gorgeous, sexy as hell and recently single, but she was also the daughter of the one man who'd practically been a father to him. No way he would betray that relationship by getting involved with Jill.

"You can stop worrying about me, Wilma. I have everything under control."

"That's what those lemmings always say right before they jump off the cliff."

"I HEARD ABOUT what happened with Lyle," Rudy Casaccio said in his low, smooth voice. "I can arrange to have him taken care of for you."

Jill winced, then switched the phone to her other ear. "I know you didn't mean that the way it sounded and if you did, I don't want to know."

"You've provided excellent service to our organization, Jill. We believe in rewarding that."

"You send a fruit basket at Christmas. That's more than enough. As for Lyle, I'm going to handle him myself."

"How?"

"I haven't exactly worked that out yet, but I'll come up with a plan." She glanced at the résumés spitting out of her printer. "Maybe I'll go with that old standard of living well as being the best revenge."

"Are you staying in Los Lobos?"

"No. I'll let you know as soon as I land with another firm."

"Good. In the meantime, we want you to continue to handle our business."

Real corporate law, she thought wistfully. Wouldn't

that be fun? "You need to stay where you are right now," she said regretfully. "I don't have the resources to handle your concerns."

"Are you sure?"

"Yes, but it was sweet of you to offer."

Rudy chuckled. "Not many people call me sweet."

She could imagine. Rudy was one tough businessman, but he'd always been good to her.

"Are you sure about Lyle?" he asked. "I never liked him."

"I'm beginning to think I shouldn't have, either. Thanks, but don't worry. I'll be fine."

"If you change your mind…"

"I won't. I'll call when I'm with a new firm."

"You do that, Jill."

Rudy said goodbye and hung up. Jill did the same. She allowed herself exactly two minutes of pouting over what Lyle had cost her, then went over to check the printer.

Her résumés looked great, and the content was even more impressive. Rudy was a man of his word, so she knew she could bring him over to whatever law firm hired her. The senior partners would appreciate the extra three million a year in billings.

A knock on her closed door made her turn. It couldn't be Tina—for one thing, the woman never knocked. For another, she'd disappeared shortly before noon.

"Come in," she called, then caught her breath when Mac strolled into her taxidermy aquarium.

"How's it going?" he asked.

"Great."

The single word was all she could manage. Man oh man did he clean up good, she thought as she took in the dark tan uniform that emphasized broad shoulders and narrow hips. She had the sudden urge to throw herself on her desk and pretend to be a music video slut.

"Nice," he said as he glanced around the office. "I don't think I've been in here before."

She wrinkled her nose. "It's hardly the sort of place you'd forget. Welcome to fish central. If you see one you like, let me know. I'm thinking of having a yard sale."

Not that she would, really. The fish belonged to Mrs. Dixon and, until Jill talked the widow into reclaiming her property, she was stuck.

Mac turned in a slow circle, then slowly shook his head. "Generous offer, but no thanks."

"Figures. I bet I couldn't even give them away. Are you here officially? Should I ask you to sit down?"

"Do I only get to sit under certain circumstances?"

She laughed. "Of course not." She circled around her desk and waved at the leather visitor chair. "Be careful not to get caught in the net there."

"Thanks."

He sat and looked at her. Jill felt his gaze settle on her face with a connection so intense it was nearly physical. She wanted to ask him if he saw anything he liked. She wanted to lean closer so he could replace his gaze with his fingers. She wanted to know if he thought she was beautiful and sexy and irresistible. She settled on checking to make sure her hair was in place.

"It's straight," he said, motioning to her head.

"Thanks to the miracles of modern hair-care products, yes."

"It looks nice, but I like it curly better."

A piece of information she would file away for later. "I'm going to guess that's not why you're here."

"Nope, I'm here to give a friendly warning. Slick Sam was arrested for passing bad checks. He got out earlier today and may come looking for representation. You probably want to tell him no."

Her back stiffened. "Why is that? Do you think I couldn't handle a criminal case? I assure you I'm more than capable of defending my clients against any number of charges. Furthermore, I don't appreciate you judging me. You don't know one thing about my legal experience. For all you know I could have—"

One eyebrow rose as he leaned back in his chair.

"What?" she demanded.

"Go on. You're doing all the talking."

"I…" She pressed her lips together. Okay, maybe she'd overreacted. She cleared her throat and straightened the papers on her desk.

"So why did you want to warn me about Slick Sam?"

Mac grinned. "I thought you'd never ask. The last lawyer he hired, also a woman and also very attractive, ended up letting him move in with her, where he made the moves on her teenage daughter, trashed her house, then took off with her cash, her credit cards and her car."

Mac thought she was attractive? How attractive? Could she ask?

Not in this life, she told herself, then laughed. "I appreciate the advice and I'll be sure to be out when he calls. But I have to tell you, I'm tempted by a client willing to steal my car."

CHAPTER FOUR

JILL ARRIVED home shortly after five. As she was used to working until at least eight or nine every night she wasn't cooking for Lyle, she wasn't sure what she was supposed to do with an entire evening. What did people who worked regular hours do with their lives? Was this why they had hobbies? Would *she* like a hobby?

"How was your day?" Bev asked as Jill walked through the front door. "Any dents on Lyle's car?"

"I didn't go by and check. I thought I'd do that in the morning."

She set her briefcase by the coatrack and wondered why she'd bothered to carry it home. There wasn't any work inside.

She leaned forward and kissed her aunt's cheek. "I have high hopes, though. A nice high fly to the side door would make my heart beat with joy."

Her aunt smiled. "I'm so happy for you, dear. How was work?"

Jill thought of Tina, the fish, and the hundred-year-old fence dispute. "You don't want to know."

"That bad?"

"Technically, there's very little I can complain about, so I won't."

"Dinner will be ready in half an hour. You have time to change."

Jill hugged the woman who had always been there for her. "I love you taking care of me, but I didn't come here to invade your life. I'm going to start looking for a place of my own tomorrow."

Bev shook her head so hard, her long red hair flew back and forth like a flag in the breeze. "Don't you dare. I know you're not moving back to Los Lobos permanently, but I want to be with you for the time you're here."

"Are you sure? I'm not crimping your social life?"

Bev rolled her eyes. "Oh, please. You know I don't date. I have to worry about the gift."

Ah, yes. The gift. Bev's psychic connection with the universe that allowed her to *see* the future. As her aunt had explained many times, the gift came with responsibilities—one of which was to stay pure…sexually.

"Don't you ever get tired of being alone?" Jill asked, because whether or not she believed in her aunt's gift, for the most part Bev lived as if *she* believed it. There had been very few men in her life and no long-term relationships.

Bev smiled. "I've been rewarded for my sacrifice. Over the years I've helped many people and that's a great feeling."

"Sex can be a great feeling, too." She thought about her own pathetic sex life with Lyle. "Or so I've heard."

"We make choices in our world. Staying pure for the gift was mine."

Jill raised her eyebrows. "You mean semi-pure," she teased.

"Well, there were one or two occasions when things got a little out of hand, but as they weren't my fault, they didn't count."

Jill grinned. "I like your rules. I always have."

"Good. Now go get changed before dinner. Oh, Gracie phoned about an hour ago. I gave her the number at the law office. Did she catch you before you left?"

"No," Jill said, disappointed to have missed the call. "I'll try her right now."

She hurried up the stairs and into the airy guest bedroom she'd claimed as her own. After peeling off her suit and pulling on shorts and a T-shirt, she flopped onto the bed and grabbed the phone.

Thirty seconds later she heard Gracie's answering machine and left a message. When she hung up, she closed her eyes for a second, wishing her friend had been home and they could have talked. She needed to connect. So much had changed in such a short period of time, it seemed as if her world had started spinning out of control. Gracie had a way of keeping things in perspective.

"Tomorrow," Jill whispered to herself and headed downstairs.

She found her aunt in the kitchen, fixing a salad. "Let me help," she said as she moved to the sink to wash her hands. "I smell lasagna, which means you worked hard this afternoon."

"Gracie not home?"

"No. We'll talk tomorrow. So what happened today with Emily? What's she like?"

"A sweet girl. A little unnerved by all the changes in her life."

Jill dried her hands on a dish towel, then crossed to the island and picked up a cucumber and a knife. "Mac's worried about them bonding."

Bev nodded. "She's been living with her mother for the past couple of months, so being with her father is strange." She sighed. "There's so much pain inside of her. I can feel it. She dresses monochromatically. Today was all purple. Shirt, shorts, socks, everything. And she'll only eat the color she wears."

Jill stared at her. "What?"

"I know. It's a silly way to express her pain, but she's eight. How many choices does she have? Mac wasn't happy when he explained the problem to me, but I didn't mind. It made making lunch much more interesting."

"What did you do?"

Bev's green eyes twinkled. "I cheated. I had some beef stew in the freezer, which I defrosted for lunch. While she was setting the table, I mixed a little of the liquid with beet juice and put it in a white bowl. Of course it looked completely purple. Then I asked Emily if the color was all right. She said it was. I served lunch in colored bowls so she couldn't tell it wasn't purple. We agreed that bread was neutral, so that was good. Oh, and we made sugar cookies with purple icing."

"Smooth move." Jill sliced the cucumber. "Aside from the color thing, what was she like?"

"Friendly. A little sad and confused, but good-hearted. Smart, too. We read some this afternoon and she's a couple of grades ahead."

Jill dumped the cucumber into the salad bowl. "You didn't do her cards or anything, did you?"

"Of course not. She's a child. Besides, I'd ask Mac first."

"Good idea." She could only imagine what he would say if his baby-sitter wanted his permission to read his daughter's future in tarot cards.

"You'll meet Emily tonight. Mac's dropping her off in a few minutes. He has a meeting with the social worker." She sighed. "I hope he can handle it."

"Mac? Why wouldn't he?"

"There's a lot of pain there," Bev said as she shook the bottle of dressing. "That man needs to be loved."

"Don't look at me. I'm not interested." Jill smiled. "Okay, so maybe I'm a little interested, but not in something serious. Could we substitute sex for love? Because then I'd sign right up."

The phone rang before Bev could answer. Her aunt glanced at Jill. "It's for you."

"You just do that to creep me out, don't you." She walked to the phone and picked it up. "Hello?"

"Jill? What the hell do you think you're playing at."

Lyle. She wrinkled her nose. "You never did see the value in common courtesy, did you, Lyle?" she asked, more resigned than annoyed. "That was always a mistake."

"Don't you talk to me about mistakes. You had no right to take the car."

"On the contrary, I had every right."

"You really pissed me off."

"Huh. Thanks for sharing. Do you want to talk about all the things *I* have a right to be angry about? Because that list is a whole lot longer than a car."

"You're playing a game, Jill, but you won't win. By the way, the new office is really great. I can see the bridge."

Bastard. He had her office and her junior partnership while all she had was a stupid car and a bunch of fish.

"Was there a point to this call?" she asked, holding on to her temper with both hands. "I've filed for divorce. You'll be served tomorrow. Except for the property settlement, this is long over."

"I want my car back."

"Sorry, no. You drove it for a year, now it's my turn. Community property, Lyle. You remember that, don't you?"

"I *will* get it back and when I do, there better not be a single scratch on it. If there is, I'll make you pay."

"I doubt that. I've always been the better lawyer. If you want to discuss anything else with me, do it in e-mail. I don't want to talk to you again." She hung up without saying goodbye.

Her insides shook a little, but other than that, she felt okay. Not great, but not crushed, either. Still, she wished he hadn't called.

"He wants his car back," she said as she turned back to face her aunt.

"I gathered that." Bev turned off the oven and pulled

out the bubbling lasagna. "He isn't going to play fair on the divorce. Have you protected yourself?"

"Yeah. I did all that before I left town. I transferred half of our savings into my own account, canceled all the credit cards in both our names, that sort of thing."

"Is he really being served with papers?"

"You bet. They're coming to his work. I almost wish I could be there to see the whole event."

Her aunt poured a glass of red wine and handed it to her.

Jill took it. "After what happened with the brandy yesterday I was going to lay off liquor for a while, but maybe not."

MAC ARRIVED with Emily exactly at six. Bev let them in, which gave Jill a chance to brace herself for yet another close encounter with the guy next door. He didn't disappoint when he entered the kitchen. Gone was the sexy uniform from earlier. Now he was dressed in a sports shirt and slacks. He looked like a powerful man ready to close the five-billion-dollar deal over drinks at an exclusive club.

Which only went to show how active her imagination had become where Mac was concerned. He was going to be nothing but trouble, she thought as she turned her attention to the little girl behind him.

Emily was small and slight, with big blue eyes and short blond hair the color of champagne. A beauty, which made Jill instantly dislike the girl's mother. No doubt another stunner. But then, when had Mac ever dated a female who wasn't gorgeous?

"Hi," Jill said as she smiled at Emily. "I'm Jill, Beverly's niece. Nice to meet you."

The girl smiled shyly back. "Hi. Bev told me you're a lawyer. That you make sure people are following the law."

"On my good days."

Mac touched Bev's arm. "Thanks for doing this for me. I'll keep the appointment as short as possible."

"Not to worry. Emily and I had a brilliant time together this afternoon. Tonight will only be more fun. Isn't that right?"

The eight-year-old nodded.

"Great." Mac glanced at his watch. "I'm running late. I'll be back as soon as I can."

Jill trailed after him as he walked to the door. "Are you eating dinner?"

"Maybe later."

Typical guy. "Good luck with the social worker. If you decide you need any legal advice, let me know."

He paused on the threshold. "You're a corporate lawyer. This isn't your area of expertise."

"True, but if I can't research it, I'll know someone with the answer."

"I'll keep that in mind."

MAC ENTERED the county services building at 6:28 p.m. and walked to the stairs.

The reception area on the second floor was typical government issue. Formica-covered countertop with a couple of desks behind. A shelving unit held dozens of different forms while posters reminded pregnant women they needed prenatal care and kids that it wasn't cool to smoke.

Most of the overhead lights were off, but he saw light spilling into the hallway and he stepped behind the counter to head that way. He stopped in front of a nameplate reading "Hollis Bass" and knocked on the partially open door.

"Come in," a man called.

Mac pushed open the door and entered.

Hollis Bass's office was as neat and prissy as the man himself. Two large plants sat on top of gray file cabinets in the corner. The paperwork in the open shelves had been neatly stacked and perfectly centered in each cubbyhole. The folders on the desk lined up with military precision and the pens and pencils rested in a perfectly straight row.

Hollis looked as if he'd never outgrown that adolescent awkwardness of too-long arms and legs. He was tall, thin and painfully tidy, wearing creased khakis and a long-sleeved button-down shirt fastened up to the collar. Small, round glasses made his brown eyes appear close-set.

Lord, he was a kid, Mac thought as he shook the man's hand. Maybe twenty-four, twenty-five. Great. Just what he needed. Some fresh-out-of-college, idealistic, save-the-world little prick determined to prove himself against a big, bad grown-up.

"Thank you for dropping by," Hollis said as he motioned to the folding chair in front of his desk. "I'm sure you're very busy."

"I didn't know the visit was optional."

"It's not." Hollis settled behind his desk and carefully folded his hands together on the blotter. "Mac... may I call you Mac? I prefer to be less formal on these visits."

"It's your party," Mac told him.

"Good. Mac, I want to give you a feel for how this process is going to go."

They had a process?

"The court mandates that you and I meet every other week for as long as you have Emily. I may also arrange more frequent meetings if I deem them necessary. While I will do my best to accommodate your schedule, these meetings are mandatory. If you skip even one, I will notify the judge, and your daughter will be returned to her mother within twenty-four hours."

"I'm aware of that."

"Just so we're all clear. Now, you are welcome to reschedule. I would imagine in your line of work, your time isn't always your own."

Mac had been in law enforcement for over a decade and he'd learned a lot about people. One thing that had been easy was spotting those who didn't approve of what he did for a living. Just his luck—Hollis was one of them.

"I appreciate your flexibility," he said, leaning back in his chair.

"It's part of my job." The corners of Hollis's thin mouth turned up, but not in a friendly way. "In addition to our meetings, I'll want to speak with Emily from time to time. I won't make appointments for that. I'll simply drop by."

Of course. All the better to see if Mac screwed up.

"She'll either be with me or her day-care provider. I've already given your office that information."

"I have it right here." Hollis opened a file. "Beverly Cooper, a local resident. Fifty-three, single. A bit eccentric, but considered to be a good person. No criminal record."

Mac's temper flared. The little twit had investigated Bev? He wanted to say something. He wanted to *do* something. But he sat quietly and reminded himself that he'd made the choices that had brought him to this place. He had no one to blame but himself.

"You're familiar with the terms of the custody agreement?" Hollis asked. "You must maintain legal employment, meet regularly with me, maintain a suitable house for your daughter and see that she is provided for. In addition you're not to commit any criminal acts or even be charged with any criminal acts."

"None of that is a problem."

"I'm glad we're clear." Hollis closed the folder and leaned forward. "Mac, I'll be blunt with you. I don't think men in law enforcement make good fathers."

This was one of the few times Mac hated being right. "What is that opinion based on?" he asked, even as he had to grind his teeth to keep from reacting.

"Personal observation. Men on the edge have trouble relating to their families, especially their daughters. Too much tension, too much violence, has a way of changing a person. Look at your own situation. Based on what I read about the testimony, it was your time in the gang unit that caused your divorce and your separation from Emily."

Mac hated that the kid had a point.

"So how are things going with her?" the social worker asked, his voice low and gentle.

Mac thought about Emily not speaking to him, about her monochromatic food issues and her emotional distance.

"Just peachy," he said easily. "Couldn't be better."

Hollis sighed. "Whatever you may think of me personally, I do want to help."

"I'll keep that in mind."

"All right. I'll see you in two weeks."

MAC SAT ON THE EDGE of his daughter's bed. They'd survived the first twenty-four hours. He wouldn't count that as a victory, but at least it hadn't been a total disaster. Em didn't talk that much when he was around, but at least she hadn't mentioned leaving. He didn't think he could stand that.

"How was your day?" he asked, knowing he probably shouldn't.

"Okay."

"What did Elvis think of Beverly?"

Her mouth curved up slightly. "He liked her."

"Elvis always had great taste in women. I think she's pretty fun."

"I like Jill."

He thought of the slender beauty next door. "I know."

"When we played dress-up tonight before dinner, she let me be the princess and she was my lady-in-waiting."

"That was nice of her." He shifted so he could stroke his daughter's hair. "I'm glad you're here, Em. I've missed you so much."

Her eyes widened, but she didn't speak. He waited, hoping she would say something. After a few seconds, he leaned forward and kissed her cheek.

"Sleep well, kiddo."

"Night."

He turned off the lamp and walked out of the room. A night-light glowed, illuminating his way. When he was in the hall, he stopped and rubbed the back of his neck. She still hadn't called him Dad or Daddy. She'd avoided addressing him as anything. Was she punishing him, or had he simply lost the right to be called that?

Not sure of the answer, he walked downstairs. The silence filled the space like a living creature. He stood in the center of the living room and wondered what happened next. How did he fix things with his daughter? How did he work his job, satisfy Hollis, heal the emotional breach and figure out what to do next?

Footsteps on the porch gave him a more immediate task. He crossed to the front door and pulled it open. Jill smiled at him.

"I know you didn't eat. I tried not to care, but I couldn't stand it, so I brought lasagna."

She stood with the single bulb adding a warm caramel cast to her dark hair, a foil-covered plate thrust out like an offering.

"I never could resist a woman with food," he said, pushing the door open wide. "Want to keep me company?"

"Sure. Is Emily in bed?"

"Yeah."

She gave him the plate and followed him to the kitchen. This house was similar to her aunt's, with a couple hundred more square feet and a bigger lot.

"Can I offer you anything?" he asked. "Beer, wine, Pop-Tarts?"

She laughed. "How about wine? I've only had one glass and that was about three hours ago, so I'm probably safe."

"Not looking for a repeat of yesterday?"

"I think not. I like to keep my passing out to a minimum."

"Probably a good policy."

He grabbed a bottle of cabernet from a small wine rack on the counter and opened it. When he'd poured them each a glass, he sat across from her and removed the foil. The delicious smell made his stomach growl.

"I knew you hadn't eaten," she told him.

"Em was full when I brought her home and it seemed like too much trouble to fix something just for me."

"Typical male," she murmured, and sipped her wine.

"That's a little judgmental."

"But true."

He ignored that and took a bite of the lasagna. Even if he hadn't been starved it would have been delicious. "Your aunt sure knows how to cook."

"Agreed. I had two servings at dinner." She leaned

back in her chair. "As did your daughter. Want to know how we got Emily to have some?"

He glanced down at the tomato sauce covering the lasagna and remembered his daughter dressed entirely in purple. "She didn't put up a fuss?"

"We played dress-up. Funny how the princess dress just happened to be red. She didn't change back into her regular clothes until *after* the meal."

"Pretty slick."

"You'll have to thank my aunt, not me. She's the one who came up with the idea."

He put down his fork. "I'm sorry she's so difficult."

"Emily? She's not. She's a sweetie."

"But she's dealing with some tough issues. The divorce. Being here for the summer."

"Of course. It's all been strange for her, but if the worst of it is a little manipulation of the adults around her by being picky with food, I think you're going to be fine. It's a pretty safe way to act out."

He hadn't thought of it that way.

Sometime in the past few hours, Jill had let down her hair...literally. It fell long and straight to the middle of her back. She had even, delicate features—wide-set eyes, a straight nose and a stubborn pointed chin. She'd been a cute kid, but she was a beautiful woman. He vaguely remembered her having a crush on him when she'd been fifteen or sixteen. If she trailed after him with those puppy-dog eyes now, he'd have a hell of a time resisting her.

"How was your meeting with the social worker?" she asked.

He tore a piece of garlic bread in half and handed it to her. "You don't want to know."

"That bad?"

"Worse. He's an uptight just-graduated idealist who doesn't think men in law enforcement make good fathers. I have to report to him every other week, take care of Emily and not have any run-ins with the law."

"That doesn't sound too difficult, unless you were planning to commit a felony or two."

"Not this week." He sipped his wine. "I know his job is to keep Em safe. I want that, too. I want her to be happy. What I don't like is dealing with Hollis." He shrugged. "I'll survive."

"Maybe you can catch him speeding and give him a ticket. That would be fun."

He grinned. "Good idea. I'll alert my deputies."

She nibbled on the garlic bread. "Do you really like it here? Are you happy?"

He didn't think in terms of being happy or unhappy. He just was. "I'm glad to be back. As you pointed out, this is a great place to grow up. I've always liked the town. Even when I was a teenager and raising plenty of hell."

"So this is a permanent move?"

"I'm running for sheriff in November."

Jill looked surprised. "An actual election?"

"Not much of one. So far no one else is interested in opposing me."

"Wow. So you're serious about sticking around."

"About as serious as you are about leaving."

"I thought you craved adventure," she said, leaning forward and resting her forearms on the table. "Aren't you the guy who joined the military to see the world?"

"It was a way out. I knew I wouldn't go anywhere here, except maybe to get into more trouble. Your father showed me that."

"He does like to save people, in his own meddling way. When he found out I'd left Lyle and been fired, he told me about the practice here."

"You could have told him no."

She laughed. "I suppose that's true. In theory. But he's very persuasive. Plus, I didn't have anywhere else to go. I'll manage until I land a job somewhere else."

"Go back to being a big-city lawyer."

"Oh, yeah."

He took the last bite of lasagna and pushed the plate away. "Let's go get comfortable," he said, picking up his glass and the bottle of wine.

"Sounds good."

Jill followed him into the living room, where they settled on opposite ends of the worn sofa. Scattered rugs warmed up the hardwood floor. She liked the oversize fireplace and the big windows. During the day, this room would get a lot of light.

"Nice," she said. "How did you come to be in this house?"

"It's a rental. I'll buy something after the election."

She still couldn't believe he was willing to settle down here on purpose, but apparently he was.

"We're destined to live next door to each other," she teased. "At least for the time being."

"Sounds like it. Of course, it's much more interesting now."

She almost fainted from shock. Was he flirting with her? Whoa. No need to check her pulse to see if it had zipped into the aerobic range—she could feel the rapid thumping in her chest.

His dark eyes brightened with humor. "Do you disagree?"

"What? No. Of course not."

She wanted to whimper with delight. She wanted to freeze-frame time and hang on to this moment forever. She wanted to yell to the heavens that Mac Kendrick thought she was interesting. Instead, she reminded herself that not only was her stay in town temporary, he had always been popular with the ladies. His flirting with her didn't mean much more than a knee-jerk reaction to being alone with a woman. Only a fool would take it personally. And a really smart woman might take advantage of the situation to soothe her recently shattered ego, as long as she kept things in perspective.

"You're very different from the teenager I remember," he said. "You were cute then, but you're amazing now."

Amazing? That worked. She resisted the urge to say *Tell me more,* and instead focused on an unpleasant truth.

"You didn't think I was cute. At least not naked."

He nearly choked on his wine. "What?"

"You didn't think I was cute naked."

He set down the glass and stared at her as if she were crazy. "I never *saw* you naked."

Now it was her turn to be shocked. "Of course you did. On my eighteenth birthday. You were home on leave and I hid out in your bedroom." She grimaced. "I wanted you to be my first time and you weren't interested. At least I'm assuming that's what the throwing up meant."

"Wait a minute." He shifted toward her on the sofa. "What are you talking about?"

Was it possible he didn't remember? No. He had to.

Refusing to be embarrassed about something that had happened a decade before, she met his questioning gaze.

"Do you remember being on leave?"

"Sure. I partied every night with my friends. A couple of times things got completely out of hand and I blacked out. Talk about being a dumb kid. But I would have remembered you naked."

"Apparently not."

Partying? She turned the idea over in her mind. Had that been it? Of course. It made sense. But at the time, she'd been crushed.

"I don't know if I should laugh or cry," she admitted.

"Why don't you tell me what happened and I'll help you decide?"

He was sitting so close she could feel the warmth from his body. If she moved just a little, they would be touching. The thought made her stomach clench and her heart flutter.

She set her wineglass on the end table. "As I said, it was my eighteenth birthday. I went out to dinner with my dad, then when he went to bed, I crept over to your house. Your mom was already asleep, so I tiptoed inside and waited until you got home."

She thought back to that long-ago evening. How scared and excited she'd been. How she'd thought that night would change everything. It had, but not in the way she'd imagined.

"You always teased me about being jailbait," she told him.

He reached up and fingered a strand of her hair. "That was to remind *me* as much as you."

"Really?" His words made her want to beam. "I don't care if you're lying, it's nice to hear."

"It's the truth. So there you were, waiting in my bedroom, which I still can't believe. What happened?"

She winced. "The one thing I never would have dreamed. You walked in, hit the lights and I dropped my dress to the floor. I wasn't wearing anything underneath. You took one look at me, ran into the bathroom and promptly threw up."

He stared at her incredulously. "No way in hell."

"Do you think I'd *make up* an embarrassing moment like that? You were the first guy to see me naked. I've been emotionally scarred ever since."

She could tell he didn't want to believe her.

"I would have remembered," he said.

"Apparently not. And all this time I've wondered what you thought of me and that night. I can't believe you don't remember it."

He took her hands in his. He had big hands, with long, thick fingers. Wasn't that supposed to mean something?

"I'm sorry," he said as he looked into her eyes. "I can't tell you how sorry. And speaking for the twenty-two-year-old I was back then, I'm damned disappointed to have missed the opportunity to take advantage of your gorgeous, naked self."

She smiled. "I was determined we were going to make love."

"I wouldn't have said no. Except for how I would have felt about your father."

"He actually never wanted to do it with you."

Mac grinned. "Thanks. That's not what I meant."

"I know. He was there for you and you wouldn't have wanted to repay him by deflowering his daughter."

"Exactly. But I might have worked past the guilt." His humor faded. "Are you okay? Are you really scarred?"

"I got over it."

"I'm sorry, Jill. It wasn't about you. Like I said, I was partying pretty hard."

"I know. It's fine."

She liked how her hands felt in his and the way he brushed his thumbs against her skin. She liked the regret in his expression and how the night was so quiet and they felt like the only two people in the world. She especially liked the heat in his eyes and the way he seemed to be moving closer. She swayed toward him.

"Want to consider a rain check?" he asked, his voice low and tempting, just before he kissed her.

Jill didn't have an answer, which was just as well,

because the second his mouth brushed hers all brain power ceased. There was only the moment and the man and the magic of what he did to her.

He teased her with just the right amount of pressure. No wimpy almost-kiss, no plunging right for her tonsils. Instead he moved back and forth, discovering, teasing, withholding just enough to make her want more before he offered it.

He smelled delicious and radiated enough heat to make her want to throw herself into his arms. One strong hand cupped her face, the other got buried in her hair. She sent up a brief prayer of thanks that she'd left it loose for the evening, then put her hands on his shoulders and gave into sensation.

Their lips clung. Instinctively she tilted her head. He touched the tip of his tongue to her bottom lip and sent shivers rippling through her body. She parted for him, both aroused and amazed that this was really happening. Her kissing Mac? Was it all a dream?

It had to be, when reality was him slipping inside, stroking her lower lip before deepening the kiss. Desire quickened her blood and made her breasts ache. She squeezed his shoulders, feeling the thick muscles tense under her touch.

He pulled back slightly and rested his forehead against hers. She opened her eyes and found him watching her. He was so close, he was almost blurry, but she didn't want to pull back. Not ever.

"You kiss like you mean it," he murmured. "You're the kind of woman my mom always warned me about. Sexy and dangerous."

It was a good thing that all her blood had rushed to her lower body to keep her grounded. Otherwise she would have floated away.

"You're pretty tempting, yourself."

"So what would have happened all those years ago, if I'd had the good sense not to get plowed at the party?"

"You tell me. I was doing the offering. Would you have accepted?"

He chuckled. "In a heartbeat. Even though your dad would have killed us both."

She'd never gotten past the humiliation of the moment to think how her entire life might have been different if Mac had made love with her. Based on his gentle but erotic kiss, she had a feeling the experience would have changed her forever. She would never have gotten involved with Evan, and without him, she wouldn't have been interested in the rat bastard lying weasel dog who was Lyle.

"I guess we'll never know how that one night could have changed things," she said regretfully.

He kissed her again, then stood and held out his hand. She took it and allowed him to pull her to her feet.

"Now for the mature portion of the evening," he said, still holding on to her fingers. "I have an eight-year-old daughter upstairs."

"Right. And I'm recovering from an ugly breakup, not to mention only passing through town." She smiled at him. "Plus there's that close personal relationship you have with my father."

"Hell of a way to repay him. Even if you are all grown up, he wouldn't appreciate me making a move on you."

"I know." So they were attracted to each other. So the kissing was spectacular. There were complications.

She wanted to say they were both adults who could work it out. Even more than that, she wanted to revel in the fact that she could actually believe Mac wanted her. Was that cool or what?

"I guess I should get home," she said.

"Thanks for bringing me dinner."

"No problem."

He walked her to the door where he cupped her face and kissed her so exquisitely her toes curled.

"See you soon," he murmured.

She floated home, carried along by the promise in his words.

CHAPTER FIVE

JILL FINISHED UP the filing Tina had left from the day before. She had a feeling that Tina might never find time for filing. Currently her assistant/secretary/receptionist had taken off to drive one of her children to a playdate. Then there were errands to run, but Tina had said she would return later in the morning. Jill wasn't holding her breath.

Had the situation been different, she would have replaced Tina and found someone interested in working at least some of the day. But what was the point in going through the trouble? Sixteen résumés were currently zooming through the U.S. mail, on their way to various law firms around the state. She'd made four calls that morning to network with fellow Stanford Law School grads and start putting out the word that she was looking. Interestingly enough, no one was shocked that Lyle had turned out to be a weasel bastard. Had she been the only one not to see the truth?

"I see it now," she told herself as she closed the file cabinet in the reception area and returned to her office. As Tina was gone and might or might not return and Jill had a ten-o'clock appointment, she was careful to keep her door open so she would hear her client.

Besides, nothing about Lyle could upset her good

mood. Not after last night. She grinned as she remembered the kiss and Mac's attraction to her. After what she'd been through, knowing he found her sexually appealing was more invigorating than sixteen hours at a day spa. She found herself humming "I Feel Pretty" under her breath, which was both embarrassing and fun. To think that Mac had been interested in her all those years ago, despite her lack of breasts, put a whole new light on her world.

"Okay, time to get serious," she told herself as she pulled out a blank legal pad. "Time to think about work and not sex or Mac.

But honestly, weren't they one and the same? And wasn't it amazing that kissing Mac had been way more exciting than kissing any other guy she could remember?

She glanced at the clock and saw Pam Whitefield was due any second. Talk about a blast from the past. Pam Whitefield—or Pam Baughman as she'd been before her marriage and subsequent divorce—was three years older than Jill and her best friend Gracie. Three years older and light-years ahead of them in experience; at least, she had been back in high school.

Pam had been one of those golden girls—beautiful, built and popular. She'd wanted to go places and do things, and she was interested in any guy who could take her there.

Her junior year of high school she'd decided that guy was Riley Whitefield—local bad boy with a rich uncle. Pam had seen the potential, if not in Riley himself, in his future inheritance. At least that had been Jill and

Gracie's theory. Gracie had loved Riley even more than Jill had loved Mac.

Ah, those times had been bittersweet, Jill thought. Two fourteen-year-old girls in love with older guys who wouldn't give them the time of day.

The sound of a door opening snapped Jill's attention back to the present. She braced herself to see Pam again—the woman never known for her gentle and loving spirit—and stood.

"In here," Jill called.

Pam Whitefield strolled through the reception area and entered Jill's office. Still the golden girl, Jill thought, taking in the perfectly coiffed gold-blond hair, the wide green eyes and the honey-colored tan. Pam wore a tailored suit that looked as expensive as the one Jill had on. Her perfect makeup emphasized her perfect features, which made Jill want to spit.

She reminded herself that people change—maybe Pam wasn't a bitch anymore. She deserved a second chance...didn't she?

"Jill!" Pam sounded delighted as she crossed the hardwood floor and shook hands. "How lovely to see you. And that suit. You look fabulous."

"Thanks. So do you."

Pam did a quick hair flip as she settled into the leather chair next to the fishing net. "I work to keep it all together. Some days it's a real trial."

Jill resumed her seat. "I don't believe you for a second. How are you?"

"Doing great. I've made some investments that have paid off well."

"Good for you."

Jill glanced at the other woman's left hand, searching for a ring. Pam and Riley hadn't lasted a year, just as Gracie had predicted. He'd left town, never to be heard from again, and Pam had stayed.

"So, what can I help you with?" she asked, not wanting to do the second half of the "how are things after all this time" exchange. What was she supposed to say to *that* question?

Pam sighed. "I'm having some difficulty with property I recently purchased and I want to sue the owner and her real estate agent for misrepresentation."

Jill picked up a pen. "What's the problem?"

Pam's mouth thinned into a straight line. "I bought the old Engel place. Do you remember it?"

"Sure. Big house up on the bluff. Great views. It was a little run-down when I was a kid."

"It's worse now. I got a decent price, but I paid more than it's worth based on its reputation."

Jill blinked. Reputation? She'd always thought the old house was butt ugly, but she didn't think that's what Pam meant.

She raised her eyebrows. "Can you explain?"

Pam sighed. "It's supposed to be an alien landing site."

"Oh, right. Sure. When we were kids we would dare each other to run up and knock on the door. Visitors from Mars or wherever were supposed to live inside and if they answered, they kidnapped you or something." She had the most amazing thought. "You didn't really think the place *had* aliens, did you?"

"I thought it had something. Everybody talks about it all the time. The owner even mentioned it in the sales brochure." She took out a cigarette and lit it. "The thing is, alien landing sites are very popular with tourists. I was going to open a bed-and-breakfast, but if it's not visited by aliens, it's just one more junky old house that needs refurbishing."

Oh, great, Jill thought. Just what she needed. *X-Files* law. This conversation made the hundred-year-old stone fence complaint seem almost reasonable.

"Are you telling me you paid more than market value for an old house based on the fact that you thought it was inhabited by aliens?" she asked, trying to sound calm instead of incredulous.

"Yes, and now I've found out there aren't any, and I want my money back."

"Okay, I'm not sure what sort of precedent there is for this kind of problem. I'll need to do some research. Also, do you still have the sales material? If the previous owner actually claimed the house had aliens, that will strengthen our case."

"I'll get you the information this week."

"Great." Jill outlined her hourly fee. "I'll need a five-thousand-dollar retainer."

She didn't usually ask for so much, but honestly, she was hoping to scare Pam off. It didn't work.

As she got her checkbook out of her purse, she flicked ash into a dish Jill wasn't sure was supposed to be an ashtray.

"This must be a real change for you," Pam said. She wrote out the check, then signed it.

"I'll admit I've never dealt with the problem of lack of aliens before."

"I didn't mean just that," Pam said, handing over the retainer. "I meant being back here." She stood, then glanced around the room. "What a nightmare. I never expected to see you back in Los Lobos. Everyone thought you were going to make something of yourself. I guess we were wrong."

She walked toward the door and waved. "I'll wait to hear from you."

Jill was too stunned by the insult to speak. So much for Pam having changed. The thought of the woman stuck with a ratty old house she couldn't use or sell eased some of the sting of Pam's parting shot. Of course, Jill was a good enough attorney that the odds of her having to keep the house were slim. Oh, well. She would take whatever bits of happiness she could find.

She ignored Pam's brief conversation with a recently returned Tina, not wanting to hear any other comments about her having a stick up her butt, and was surprised when Tina came in as soon as Pam left.

"You had a delivery," she said eagerly. "It's a beautiful plant, and Annie from What's in Bloom said it was from Gracie Landon. Is it really? Our own Gracie?"

"I guess," Jill said as she rose, not sure who "our Gracie" was. "We're still friends."

Tina, dressed in khakis and a tucked-in T-shirt, pressed both hands to her chest.

"I know I'm a few years older than you two girls,

but I just love that Gracie. She's a legend. People still talk about her and what she did to get her man."

Jill winced. Gracie would not be pleased to know her teenaged exploits in the name of claiming the love of Riley Whitefield lived on.

"She was pretty young," Jill said as she walked into the reception area and saw a beautiful tree with flowering things tucked in around it.

"It's a miniature ficus," Tina said. "The flowers in front are cut. They'll die soon, but the tree could last for years. There's a card."

She handed over the envelope, then waited expectantly. Jill felt obligated to read the note wishing her luck aloud.

"Imagine. Gracie Landon." Tina touched the leaves and smiled. "Remember the time Riley and Pam went parking up on the bluff and Gracie followed them on her bike and dumped a bag of crickets into the car?"

Jill remembered the incident all too well. While she'd had a massive crush on Mac, she'd been content to love him from afar. Not so Gracie. At fourteen she'd been stubborn about Riley being hers, and bitter about him dating Pam Baughman. She'd come up with scheme after scheme to separate the two, most of which Jill had quietly participated in.

There had been the crickets in the car, the potato in his tailpipe to keep him from being able to pick up Pam. Once Gracie had nailed all of Pam's doors and windows shut, trapping the teenager in her house so she couldn't make a date. Gracie had put itching powder in Riley's shorts the night of spring formal and had even thrown herself in front of his car and begged him to just kill her if he was going to keep dating Pam.

Gracie had declared to all who would listen that Pam didn't care about Riley at all—that she was just dating him because one day he would inherit old man Whitefield's fortune. No one had paid attention. Jill supposed that their divorce less than five months after the wedding had been a form of vindication, but for Gracie, the news had come too late. Heartbroken by what she'd seen as Riley's ultimate betrayal, she'd moved in with some relatives and had never returned to Los Lobos.

"Gracie's amazing," Tina said. "You haven't loved until you've loved like Gracie."

"In many quarters what she did would be considered stalking."

Tina looked shocked. "No. She was just a kid in love with a boy who didn't notice her. But she had a big heart and she loved with every inch of it. I admire that. So do most folks in town."

"I'll be sure to mention it," Jill said wryly. "She'll be thrilled."

"Are you going to call her right now?" Tina asked excitedly. "Oh, tell her hi from me. I'm sure she won't remember me, but I sure remember her. Gracie Landon. She sure knew how to love a man."

Jill picked up her miniature ficus tree and carried it into her office. The fish watched suspiciously as she set it on a small table by the window, then crossed to her desk and grabbed the phone.

"I'm calling to say thanks," she said when her friend answered.

"I know you have the black thumb of death," Gracie said with a chuckle, "but even you should be able to keep a ficus alive."

"I hope so. It was sweet of you to think of me."

"Are you kidding?" Gracie asked. "You're back in Los Lobos. You have my deep sympathy."

"How about instead of sympathy you come visit me? I could cry on your shoulder."

"Are things that bad?"

Jill glanced at the fish, then at the files on her desk. "It could be worse."

"Yeah, I could be there with you. Which is never going to happen. I have vowed not to return there ever. No matter what."

"So had I, and look what happened to me."

"Good point." Gracie sighed. "Seriously, how are you holding up?"

"I'm fine. There have been some interesting law cases. Guess who came in this morning?"

"I'm not sure I want to."

"Pam Whitefield."

Gracie laughed. "My first instinct is to say 'that bitch,' which tells me I may have some unresolved issues."

"That would be my vote. She's still snarky."

"But single, right? My heart beats faster knowing no one wants to marry her."

Jill laughed. "Yes. Still single. There's something

else. It seems your reputation hasn't died the death you would have liked."

Gracie groaned. "No. Don't tell me that. It's one of the reasons I've stayed away and convinced my entire family that it's really fun to come visit me in L.A. for the holidays."

"Yup, Tina, my assistant, just did five minutes on the Gracie legend. About how you haven't loved until…"

"Please be kidding."

Jill shook her head. "Sorry. I think this is bigger than both of you."

"I can't believe it. When I think about what I did to that poor guy. Riley must get hives every time he remembers me."

"I'm sure he's recovered."

Jill picked up a pen and turned it over. Should she tell Gracie what had happened with Mac? They didn't have many secrets from each other, but she wasn't sure about spilling something so intimate with Tina in the next room.

"I'll give you a call in a couple of days," she said instead.

"Please do. I'm knee-deep in wedding season. There are cakes everywhere."

Gracie had become a specialty baker whose wedding cakes were in high demand by the rich and famous of Los Angeles.

"Send me pictures," Jill said. "You know I love to keep up."

"Will do. You hang in there. Call if you need to scream or anything."

"Promise."

"Bye."

Jill hung up and leaned back in her chair. Just thinking about Gracie always made her smile. Those had been some wild, fun times. Even though Gracie had moved away the summer they turned fifteen, they'd stayed close friends.

She glanced at her watch, then at the closed door between her office and Tina's. She might as well ask now, while her assistant/secretary/receptionist was in a good mood. She wanted a ride to her car so she could move it from the baseball practice fields to the grocery store parking lot. She had a plan to park it by the cart return.

MAC SAT on the corner of the desk at the front of the conference room and took stock of his employees. The Los Lobos sheriff's office wasn't anything like the LAPD. While there wasn't the same level of crime in the two communities, there also weren't the resources for his department. He had ten full-time deputies, three part-timers, one detective, five clerical workers, and four dispatchers, including Wilma, who pretty much ran things.

Most everyone did a good job, some better than others. The only problem he'd found in the three weeks he'd been sheriff was a new deputy named D.J. Webb. D.J. had plenty of attitude but no experience to back it up. Not a combination that made Mac comfortable.

"The tourist season is a little busier than we expected," Mac said, "but we're handling it. With the

Fourth of July next week, we need to pay attention. The beaches will be crowded as will downtown. This is a time for families. So we'll pick up all the D&Ds and give them some time to sober up. Wilma, we have the extra space reserved?"

"You bet."

The drunk and disorderlies weren't his only problem. With the crowds came petty criminals, short-tempered drivers searching for parking and the occasional motel robbery.

"We need to remember to be friendly," Mac said. "Don't go looking for trouble—it will find you soon enough."

"What if there's a terrorist attack?" D.J. asked.

Wilma snickered and the detective grinned.

"I'm serious," D.J. said earnestly. "We're not prepared if a group comes in here with heavy firepower."

"We're more likely to be held hostage by a band of rogue sharks," one of the deputies said. "It's Los Lobos, D.J. Lighten up."

Mac felt the beginnings of a headache—one that would last the entire summer. "We're not a big terrorist target," he told D.J.

"Not so far as you know. We need to get into those federal databases and figure out what we should be doing."

"Thanks for sharing." Mac glanced around the room. "If that's it, check the board in the morning. I'll be posting a new schedule to get us through the holiday weekend."

People stood and left the conference room. Wilma

waited until they were alone, then patted his arm. "D.J.'s gung ho, but he'll grow out of it as he matures."

"I'm not sure I can wait that long."

The older woman grinned. "I know for a fact you were once young and foolish."

"That I'll admit to."

"Any stories you want to share?"

He laughed. "Sure. When I was seventeen I stole Judge Strathern's Cadillac on a bet."

"I hadn't heard about that. Did you get caught?"

"Of course. I was young and stupid, right? When the judge came to the jail the next morning I thought he was going to tan my hide. Worse, I was afraid my mother would lose her job—she was his housekeeper."

Wilma's eyes widened. "What happened?"

"He piled me into the front seat of that car and drove me to Lompoc prison where I spent the day in a cell with a very scary felon. By three-thirty that afternoon, I'd more than seen the error of my ways. On the way back to Los Lobos, the good judge talked to me about staying on the right side of the law and joining the military when I graduated from high school. He pretty much saved my ass."

"He's a good man," Wilma said. "As are you. Patience with D.J."

"I'll try."

"That's all any of us can do." She walked toward the door, then paused and glanced at him. "Jill seems a lot like her father in temperament, if not in looks."

Mac instantly thought of the very hot kiss they'd shared and how the aftereffect had kept him up half the night. Yeah, she and her dad didn't look anything alike. "They have a few things in common, but she's her own person."

"She's pretty, too."

"I hadn't noticed."

She laughed again. "You're not a good liar, Mac. Don't try to make your living playing poker."

"Never crossed my mind."

JILL RETURNED HOME at the end of day two in a slightly better mood than at the end of day one. Tina had not only continued to be pleasant, but she'd actually stayed and worked until nearly four. The only black cloud in her otherwise bright blue sky—except for the lying rat weasel dog and her lack of acceptable employment— was the BMW.

There hadn't been a scratch on it. Not a dent, not a hint of any contact at all. It still gleamed like a show-room special. She hoped that a couple of days in the local grocery store parking lot would take care of that.

She entered her aunt's home a little after five. "It's me," she called.

Bev came out of the kitchen to greet her. "Better?" she asked.

"Not half-bad. Except for being insulted by Pam Whitefield."

"No one likes her, so her opinion doesn't matter."

"I'll keep that in mind. Oh, I talked to Gracie. She sent me a ficus tree. She said even I shouldn't be able to kill it."

"I hope she's right."

Bev waited until she'd shrugged out of her jacket before leading the way back to the kitchen.

"How was your day?" Jill asked.

"Good. Emily and I had a terrific time. We spent the afternoon at the beach. Oh, speaking of which, you know it's nearly the Fourth of July."

"I'd heard a rumor, yes."

"Mac has to work so Emily will be joining us on our picnic."

Jill grabbed a diet soda from the refrigerator and popped the top. "Are we having a picnic?"

"Of course. It's what the holiday is about."

"Huh, and here I thought it was about celebrating our country's independence."

"That, too, but how could we celebrate without a picnic?"

"I'm not complaining. I'm sure it will be fun." Los Lobos was at its best during holidays of any kind.

"Good. Now read this." She held out a piece of paper.

Jill grabbed it and read the note twice. "Oh, man. Do I have to?"

"The mayor has graciously invited you to join the pier centennial committee meeting tonight. Don't *you* think you should go?"

No. Not even for money. "I'm not going to be here that long. I don't want to get involved in a project and then have to drop it halfway through."

Bev opened the refrigerator and pulled out a plastic pouch of marinating chicken. "I'm sure if you keep repeating that, eventually it will sound like the truth."

"Fine. I don't want to go. I've never been a fan of the pier and the mayor isn't my favorite person. He's smarmy and I think he looks up women's skirts."

"Have you seen him doing that?"

"No, but he seems like the type." Jill stomped her foot and felt like a two-year-old. "Jeez, I hate this." She looked back at the message her aunt had taken. "I'll go but only if I get two desserts. One before and one after."

"I'll even read your cards for you if you'd like."

Jill took a step back. "I'm not ready to know my future, but thanks for asking." She glanced down at her slacks. "I need to go change. I hate this."

"I know, dear, but it's for the best."

"That's what you used to say about going to the dentist."

"Was I wrong?"

CHAPTER SIX

MOST SIGNIFICANT EVENTS in Los Lobos took place in the community center and the committee for the pier centennial celebration was no exception. Jill experienced a slight case of déjà vu as she pushed open one of the heavy double-glass doors.

She'd attended Girl Scout meetings in this building, had decorated the largest room for various school dances. She'd had her first kiss out on the basketball courts on a rainy afternoon when she'd been seventeen. The boy in question—Kevin Denny—had quickly turned his attentions elsewhere, but to her that first kiss had been a huge deal.

Tonight she was less enthused about stepping into a piece of her past. For one thing, she didn't want to get assigned actual work involving the celebration. For another, she dreaded answering questions about why she was back, how she was doing and what she thought would happen in the future. There was also the twenty-eight-and-soon-to-be-divorced syndrome to deal with. Ah, to be home with a good DVD and a bowl of Ben & Jerry's.

Knowing that her aunt would give her "the look" if she returned early, she stepped into the building and followed the sound of voices to the second meeting doorway on the right. As she walked into the large room and glanced around at too many familiar faces, she felt a slight tickling on the back of her neck. She turned. Mac stood by the coffee urn. His dark gaze settled on her face and he gave her a slow, sexy smile that reminded her that just about twenty-two hours ago, they'd been kissing and she'd been thinking about giving in to a whole lot more.

In the sensible light of almost-twilight, she didn't know if she should go for a sophisticated I-do-this-sort-of-thing-all-the-time or if running for cover was the better option. Figuring there wasn't anywhere to go, she walked toward him and accepted the cup of coffee he held out.

"How did you get roped into this?" he asked.

"The mayor's office called and when I tried to whine my way out of it, Aunt Bev looked stern. I'm easily guilted."

"Apparently."

"What's your excuse?"

"I'm the sheriff. I have to be here."

"The joys of small-town life." She glanced around the room. "Quite a turnout. All the small-business owners, the city council and many concerned citizens. With luck there will be more hands than work."

Mac grinned. "Wishful thinking."

"I know, but a girl has to have dreams. Is our esteemed mayor here yet?"

Mac put his free hand on her shoulder and pointed

with the one holding his coffee cup. She liked how they were sticking together and how he touched her. She liked a lot of things. If Mac was the door prize for attending the meeting, she would consider this an evening well spent.

She looked where he pointed and saw Los Lobos mayor Franklin Yardley speaking with a young woman she didn't recognize.

Yardley had been mayor for as long as Jill could remember. Probably fifteen years. He was handsome, as tanned as George Hamilton and too well dressed for a town this small. He wore his gray hair short, in a modified military buzz. His eyes crinkled when he talked, giving the impression of good humor and affability. He had the practiced smile and easy manner of a successful used-car salesman. He'd always made Jill uncomfortable, especially at honors events during high school. Becoming a National Merit Scholar or winning a prize meant getting your picture taken with the mayor. In her opinion, he'd always held the girls a little too tight and she distinctly remembered him patting her butt after she received a scholarship to Stanford.

"Disgusting old man," she muttered under her breath.

"He's not that old," Mac said. "Fifty-two, fifty-three."

"Whatever his age, he gives me the creeps. Can we sit in the back?"

Mac chuckled. "Sure thing. Are we going to pass notes, too?"

"I'm ignoring the implication I'm acting as if I'm in high school. Sitting up front is the same as volunteering and my goal for tonight is to slip out unnoticed."

"Jill, honey, is that you?" a loud, female voice called from the doorway.

Jill winced as she turned and saw Pam striding toward her. "Oh, great. Here's another opportunity for her to insult me."

Mac leaned close. "What are you talking about?"

"She came by to see me about a legal thing today and nailed me good." She plastered a smile on her face and tried to act pleased. "Pam. Hi. So you're here, too."

"Of course. The centennial celebration of our beloved pier is going to be an event to remember. The Fourth of July is just a warm-up. We've already started a national advertising campaign. We only have six weeks to get things finalized." Her smile widened. "I'm sure we have something you can help with. Maybe stuffing information folders for the chamber of commerce. I know they need help with that."

Determined to have a witty comeback *this* time, she searched her brain as she opened her mouth. Just then Franklin Yardley called the meeting to order.

Pam waggled her fingers and sauntered off.

"Bitch," Jill said as Mac led her to the back of the room.

"Try to play nice with the other children."

"You heard what she said."

"I did. I also know that you're younger, more successful and a hell of a lot sexier. Did it ever occur to you she's acting this way because she's bitter?"

Jill felt her bad mood drain away. "No, but I like it."

EMILY HELD the deck of cards in her hand. Bev demonstrated how to shuffle and Emily did her best to follow directions.

"Just slide a few in front," the older woman said with a smile. "It's easy."

The cards felt big and awkward, but Emily did as instructed. The cards slid into place.

"Good," Bev told her. "Let's try it again." She winked. "We need a well-shuffled deck so I can beat you this time."

They were playing Go Fish, which was a little kids' game, but still fun. Emily shuffled two more times, then dealt out the cards. When one slipped and fell on the floor, Bev didn't say anything. She was nice that way, Emily thought as she put the card back in place. She never yelled or got mad. She never made Emily feel scared.

"You have other cards," Emily said as she sorted her cards by numbers. She already had two threes and two fives. That was good. "Cards with pictures and stuff on them."

"You're right. I do. My tarot cards."

"What are they for? Different games?"

"Not exactly. The cards can be fun. People use them at parties. Some people think they're special—that they can tell what's going to happen in the future or what happened in the past."

Knowing the future sounded scary, Emily thought. "Doesn't everyone already know the past? Weren't they there when it happened?"

"Sometimes. But they aren't always clear on the events. A lot of people think tarot is silly."

"Do you?"

Bev put down her cards and leaned forward. Her long red braid hung over her shoulder and nearly brushed against the table.

"I believe I have a gift. I can see things other people can't. Like you're a good reader. You read better than most kids you know. That's a gift, right?"

Emily nodded.

"Now you being able to read is something people can see. They don't have to take it on faith. But my gift is different. You can't see it or touch it. So while I believe, others don't."

Emily thought she understood. "Does Jill believe?"

Bev laughed. "An interesting question. My niece is one of my doubters."

Emily was shocked. "She thinks you're lying?"

"Not lying, just pretending."

"Are you?"

"No."

Emily tried to understand. "So the cards tell you what's gonna happen tomorrow?"

"Not specifically. They give me ideas. Good fortune,

bad fortune, that sort of thing. People come to me with questions and I try to help them find answers."

"Wow." That sounded pretty exciting. If Emily could know the future…she closed her mind to the question. There were too many dark places she didn't want go.

"There are responsibilities that come with my gift. Do you know what responsibilities are?"

Emily nodded. "You have to do the right thing and you have to think it up even if no one tells you. Like having a pet. I'd have to feed it and stuff, even if Mom didn't remind me. Or doing my homework without being reminded."

"Exactly. I have to be careful what I tell people. Some may make decisions based on our conversation and I don't want them making a mistake."

Emily could see how that would be bad. "Do you get scared?"

"Not very often, but it's happened. Also, I have to stay pure for my gift."

"Pure?"

Bev grinned. "It's like staying clean, but for grown-ups." She leaned close. "Emily, if you could know one thing about your future, what would it be?"

Emily shrank back in her chair. "Nothing. I don't want to know anything."

"Are you sure?"

She nodded so hard her hair slapped her cheeks. She didn't want to know. What if her mom left the way her dad did? What if her dad didn't love her anymore? What if she was left all alone with nowhere to go?

Her stomach got all tight and hard and she thought she might throw up.

Bev straightened and picked up her cards. "One thing I don't need tarot to tell me is how special you are. I'm really enjoying having you with me. I'm afraid the summer is going to go by really fast and then you'll be gone and I'll miss you. I guess if I'm going to miss you a lot and I've just met you, then your mom must be having a hard time right now. She's known you all her life."

Emily had wondered about that. "She said she would."

"Of course. You're a part of her day. She's missing you just like your dad missed you while he was apart from you."

Emily was less sure about that. "He never called or anything."

Bev nodded. "Sometimes that happens. And when they mess up, grown-ups feel very guilty, and then they don't know what to do to make it right. Especially with kids. How much should we say? How much will you understand? But now that you're with your dad, I know you can see the love in his eyes. I do."

Emily stared at her. "You do?"

"Uh-huh. Every time he walks into this house, his whole face lights up. He's so bright, he could be a lamp."

Emily giggled at the thought of her dad with a lamp shade on his head. "You're funny."

"Thank you." Bev held out her arms. "I need a hug. Is that all right?"

Emily grinned. "Sure." She stood and walked around the table, but as she got closer to Bev, something funny happened inside. Her chest got all sore and her face got hot and suddenly she wanted to cry.

Bev pulled her close and set her on her lap. "A nice big hug," she said, wrapping her arms around Emily. "I think I need one at least once a day."

Emily tried to talk, but she couldn't. She flung her arms around Bev's neck and burst into tears.

"It's all right," Bev said, her voice low and gentle. "You have yourself a good cry. Some days we need that as much as a hug."

Emily didn't know what was wrong. Why was she crying? Why did everything hurt so bad inside?

Bev continued to hold her, rubbing her back and kissing the top of her head.

"My brave little girl," she murmured. "This has been hard for you. But you're safe now. You're safe with me and you're safe with your dad."

Emily shook her head. "I'm not."

"I see. Because he's mean?"

"No." She sniffed, then rubbed her cheek against the softness of Bev's flowered dress. "Because he never came and found me. He was supposed to. He was supposed to find me."

"Of course he was. All dads are supposed to find their little girls. He broke the rules."

Emily raised her head and stared into Bev's face. "He did."

"I know. Don't you hate it when that happens?"

Emily didn't know what to say. She'd expected Bev

to tell her she was wrong. That she shouldn't expect her dad to come find her.

"I was mad," she admitted.

"I would be, too. You're still mad, aren't you?"

Emily opened her mouth, then closed it. Was she mad? Was that it? She nodded slowly.

"And even when your dad says he loves you, you don't know if you can believe him."

Emily nodded again. Bev *knew*.

"When you're mad at your dad it makes you scared, which makes you think about your mom. And you start to wonder if she's even missing you at all."

Tears filled her eyes as she nodded, then she collapsed against Bev. "What if they both forget about me?"

"Sweetie, that's not going to happen. How could anyone forget about you? It's only been a couple of days and I know I never could. But I understand what you feel. I understand."

They were the most precious words Emily had ever heard. She stayed in Bev's arms for a long time. When she started to feel better, she raised her head again.

"Are you going to tell my dad what I said?"

Bev straightened and raised her eyebrows. "Me? Betray a secret? Never! I'm shocked you'd even ask. Shocked and insulted."

Emily smiled. "You're funny."

"That, too. Shocked, insulted and funny." She smoothed Emily's bangs. "I won't tell him what you said, but I will tell him he needs to keep working on making you feel safe. Just like I'm going to tell you that you need to open your heart enough to think about forgiving him. If your dad wasn't trying, then I'd agree with you about staying mad. But he is trying and he loves you so much. Wouldn't it be sad to miss that because you keep turning your back on him?"

Emily wasn't sure exactly what Bev meant, but she got enough to know Bev was telling her not to be mean. "I'm scared. What if he goes away again?"

"What if he doesn't? Are you going to spend every day waiting for that?"

"I don't know."

"You need to think about it. And you can always talk to me. Or Jill." She grinned. "Or even your dad. I'm not so sure about Elvis. I don't think he gives very good advice."

Emily giggled. "He doesn't talk."

"No, but he has opinions about everything." Bev squeezed her. "Better?"

Emily nodded, then hopped down. She felt good. The tightness was gone and she found herself looking forward to seeing her dad when he got home. She wanted to see if he really lit up like a lamp when he saw her.

"NEED A RIDE?" Mac asked when the meeting ended.

Jill picked up the large box containing plastic bags printed with "Los Lobos means fun" and several hundred sunscreen samples, along with the other freebies she was supposed to stuff inside, and sighed.

"Thanks. I don't think I could walk home with all this." Her expression was an intriguing combination of amusement and frustration.

He grabbed the second box of supplies and led the way outside. "Why didn't you refuse when Pam volunteered you?"

"I don't know. I was caught off guard. Everyone else was doing something for the celebration and I felt guilty because I don't even want to be here. I can't explain it."

"Maybe it's best if you don't try."

She laughed as they stepped out into the night. "If I'm going to keep getting suckered into jobs like this, I'm going to have to do something about getting transportation. Either give up on trying to get Lyle's car dented or get a car of my own. But I really liked the idea of revenge. It's a big part of my new five-year plan."

He unlocked his truck and opened the back hatch. After loading in his box, he took hers. "I don't want to hear about your revenge."

"Don't be a stick-in-the-mud. I won't do anything illegal."

"That's how it starts. Then things get out of hand."

"Ha." She slid into the passenger seat. "I would like to take this moment to point out that of the two of us, you're the only one who has been arrested for stealing a car."

"That was a long time ago." Another lifetime ago. He'd been young and stupid and out for the thrill. In some ways, getting arrested had been the best thing that had happened to him—it had turned his life around.

He started the engine and pulled away from the curb. Jill leaned back in her seat.

"Aunt Bev is going to be so happy that I volunteered," she said. "Maybe I can get her to stuff the bags for me."

"You wouldn't do that."

Jill glanced at him and grinned. Her long dark hair swayed as she moved. "You're right, but I will take the boxes into work tomorrow and see if I can talk Tina into it. She doesn't do much work, anyway. This would be a change for her."

"And for a good cause."

He navigated the quiet streets. He liked seeing the warm glow of lights behind drapes and the bikes left scattered on lawns. This was his town, his responsibility. He wanted to do right by the people. Jill, on the other hand, counted the days until her escape. If she hadn't had a run-in with Lyle, she wouldn't be here at all.

"So if your soon-to-be ex is so horrible, why did you marry him?" he asked.

Jill shook her head. "Good question. I plead youth and ignorance. Maybe bad timing. We met in law school. Lyle was funny and nice and good-looking enough to catch my attention but not so good-looking that I had to worry he'd have a busload of women following him everywhere. Boy, was I wrong about that."

"Did he cheat on you before this last time?"

"Not that I know about. I'm willing to forgive some things, but not that. It's just too much of a betrayal. No, at first things were good. We were in a study group. He wasn't the smartest one there, but he did okay."

Mac turned onto their street. "Let me guess. *You* were the smartest one there."

She batted her eyes at him. "A lady never studies and tells."

"Figures. So you got him through law school and then what?"

Jill frowned. "You know, I was about to say I *didn't* get him through law school, but I think you might be right. I helped him with his homework and papers and we studied together for tests. My God, I never got that before."

He pulled in front of her house. "It's okay that you helped him."

"It's crazy. What was I thinking?" She unfastened her seat belt and angled toward him. "I got him his job, too. When I graduated first in our class, I had a ton of offers. There were a couple of law firms that really caught my attention, including the one I went with in San Francisco. Lyle wasn't getting many offers and he used to talk about how sad it was going to be for us to be apart. By then we were dating."

Sleeping together, Mac thought, but he kept that to himself. Lyle had probably been bright enough not to be so drunk the first time he saw Jill naked that he threw up. Mac nearly groaned when he remembered what she'd told him. Talk about bad timing.

"He went on about us getting married," she continued. "About how great it would be. On my last interview, I told the senior partners I wanted them to hire Lyle, as well."

She grimaced. "A pretty ballsy move, but I was young, I thought I was in love. They agreed, and he got the job. Then he got me fired."

Mac unfastened his seat belt and turned toward her. "Any more information on how that happened?"

"No. I sent e-mails to a couple of people. My former assistant is doing some investigating. I brought in more money than any other associate. More than a couple of the partners. I did a good job, my clients were happy and well represented…."

"Do you think Lyle did something."

"Yeah. Or said something. Lying weasel rat bastard."

Her energy made the air crackle, and her intensity only added to her appeal. She was a hell of a woman and not one he should be thinking about. Not only did they want different things, but once again he was forced to remind himself that sleeping with the man's daughter was a piss-poor way to thank Judge Strathern for all his help. Plus he needed to spend his free time focusing on reconnecting with Emily.

But he couldn't resist reaching out and gently wrapping a strand of her hair around his finger.

"What happens if you find out Lyle did something?" he asked.

"I'll go break his kneecaps." She leaned toward Mac. "Want to help?"

"It violates the terms of my custody agreement. Plus I'd have to arrest myself afterward."

"We don't want that. I guess I'll have to come up with a different kind of punishment."

Mac wanted to tell her that Lyle had already suffered the greatest loss—he'd lost Jill. Obviously the lying weasel rat bastard hadn't known a good thing when he'd seen it. But Mac knew.

He wanted her. Funny how long it had been since he'd wanted a woman. Not just in bed, either, although he wouldn't turn that down. He wanted to hear her laughing at his jokes, sharing her opinion on everything. He wanted to talk about politics and the possibility of an afterlife. He wanted to know if she opened presents on Christmas morning or Christmas Eve. He contented himself with staring into her dark eyes and wanting her mouth on his.

"Tell me what you're thinking," she whispered.

"Not even for money," he said with a chuckle.

"Where's the fun in that?"

"There's not going to be any fun."

She pouted. "Why not?"

"I can give you a list of reasons, but here are the two most pressing. I'm going to guess your aunt and my daughter are looking out the window right now."

"Emily's only eight and will get bored."

"And your aunt?"

She leaned closer. "Let her get her own guy."

A ready-and-willing Jill was more than he could resist. He tangled his hand in her hair and shifted so he could kiss her.

She responded instantly, her warm, soft lips moving against his. Her fingers curled into his upper arms. Their breath mingled and he figured he wouldn't mind doing this for the rest of the night.

As he moved his tongue across the seam, she made

a noise low in her throat, then parted for him. He wel-
comed the invitation and swept inside.

She tasted of mint and coffee. Heat swirled
around them. He shifted so he could kiss her jaw,
then he licked the soft skin under her ear. She shivered and breathed his name. From there it was a
short journey down the velvety smoothness of her
neck to her collarbone. The V of her T-shirt offered
possibilities, but none he could take advantage of at
the moment. With the console jutting out between
them, he couldn't get close enough, and he growled
with frustration.

"What?" she asked as she raised her head. Her eyes
were nearly black in the faint glow of the streetlight.

"I want you closer."

"Me, too."

She pushed against the seat and promptly banged
her head against the roof of the truck.

"I'm horrible at this," she said with a laugh. "Jeez.
Are we too old or what?"

Instead of answering, he kissed her again. A soft but
demanding kiss that had her melting in his arms.

"Oh yeah," she breathed. "This is good."

He was hard and ready. It had been a long time
since his last close encounter. Too long. But his need
for Jill was about more than just being without. Still,
his daughter was waiting, her aunt might be watching
and this wasn't the time.

He cupped her face. "I need to ask for another rain
check."

"You're piling them up."

"I may collect all at once."

"That would be interesting."

"Ready?" he asked, reaching for his door handle.

"As I'll ever be."

NEARLY A WEEK LATER, sometime close to midnight, two long, black limousines drove into Los Lobos. Mr. Harrison saw them as he put out his cat for the night. Mrs. Zimmerman heard them drive by as she muted the *Tonight Show* during a commercial break. And the night clerk at the Surf Rider motel nearly had a heart attack when they pulled into his parking lot.

Six men in dark suits stepped out of the vehicles and made their way to the reception desk.

The clerk, Jim, a college student majoring in chemical engineering, felt his knees begin to shake. He was going to die. Right there. And no one would know for hours.

"M-may I help you?" he asked as the men pulled open the glass door and stepped into the reception area.

"We have a reservation," one of the men said. They were all big men, with dark hair and distant eyes. "Under Casaccio. Six rooms for tonight, all close to-gether, then two rooms for the next week."

Jim pushed the registration card toward the man and handed him a pen. "If you'll just sign the register?"

"Not necessary," the man said. "I'm Mr. Casaccio. You can call me Rudy." He passed over a fifty-dollar bill. "I appreciate your understanding."

"Of course. Sure. Great."

Jim shoved the reservation card back into the file and

quickly programmed six keys. It was only when he'd given the men directions and they'd left that he dared to pick up the fifty and tuck it into his jeans. As soon as he got off work, he was going to take that money and get seriously drunk. It wasn't every day that a kid like him faced men like that and lived to tell the tale.

CHAPTER SEVEN

JILL STARTED her second week in Los Lobos by wearing her hair—straight, of course—in a braid instead of up. Yes, it was more casual, but it was also easier and didn't give her a headache by the end of the day. Determined to maintain the facade that she was indeed practicing actual law, she still wore a suit, although she was briefly tempted by summer silk slacks and a loose shirt.

She arrived at her office promptly at eight-thirty and started coffee. After going through the mail dropped through the slot in the door on Saturday, she went over her open cases and made notes for the coming week.

There was still the question of what to do about Mr. Harrison's fence problem. Moving it seemed out of the question. After over a hundred years of tacit agreement on placement, no court would side with the old man. But she hated the thought of sending him away unhappy.

Jill was less concerned about Pam's mood, but her natural inclination to give a hundred percent had her searching case law for something on aliens.

Not that she *wanted* to help Pam, she thought, as she leaned back in her chair and stared at the fish on the far wall. They stared back.

"Don't think about her," she told herself. "Think about something pleasant."

Mac instantly came to mind. She hadn't seen him in a few days and they hadn't had a repeat of that hot kiss in the car in over a week, but just the memory was enough to make her toes tingle. He was a perfect distraction—and a temptation. At least she had the comfort of knowing she'd had great taste in men back in high school. Of course, things had taken a bad turn with the rat fink lying weasel dog.

Tina arrived about nine-fifteen and walked into Jill's office.

"You know it's almost the Fourth of July," she said by way of greeting.

"Yes. In a couple of days. Why?"

"I have family coming in. The kids don't have any activities this week. Dave's real busy over at the tire store. A lot of people get new tires before taking a driving vacation."

Tina's annoyance and impatience were clear. Jill couldn't figure out the cause. "Are you saying you don't want to work this week?"

The other woman practically rolled her eyes. "What do you think?" she asked in a sharp tone.

"Then go home."

Tina didn't look any more pleased at the instruction. "You're not going to pay me, are you?"

Jill raised her eyebrows. "For not working? No."

Tina huffed, then turned on her heel and left.

"Amazing," Jill murmured. She desperately wanted to replace the woman but kept telling herself it wasn't worth the effort. Not when she, Jill, would be leaving so soon. Patience, she thought. She could survive this with a little patience.

After flipping through more files and doing some research on the Internet, Jill got up for a quick potty break. Liquid in, liquid out, she thought with a grin as she made her way to the bathroom. Once inside the small room, she did her business and turned to wash her hands.

As always, a bright blue-silver fish caught her eye. It stared right at her as she went, then watched while she washed her hands.

"You're really getting on my nerves," she told the long-dead creature, took the hand towel and hung it over its pointed little face.

"Better."

As she walked back into her office, she sensed movement. Several men in dark suits stood by her desk. They turned as she approached. The taller of the men walked toward her.

"Your secretary wasn't at her desk. We let ourselves in."

"She's gone for the day."

"Good."

"I'M LATE," MAC SAID as he walked toward the front of the sheriff's office.

"I know, but this is too good to wait." Wilma trailed after him waving pink slips of paper. "We got a couple of calls from the usual crackpots, but Mr. Harrison never phones anything in. He's a sensible man and not too bad-looking if you like 'em old."

"Wilma, if there's a point, you have until I get to my car to give it to me."

"Fine." She thrust the papers into his hand. "Two long, black limos were seen driving into town late last night. Six men checked into the Surf Rider motel. The night clerk there is the grandson of a friend of mine, so I heard the whole thing from him." She glanced around and lowered her voice. "They were wearing dark suits and pinkie rings."

Mac didn't need this. The Fourth of July was in two days. D.J., his youngest deputy, still wanted to talk about more firepower to ward off terrorist attacks. A broken water pipe had flooded one of the big beach parking lots and city maintenance wasn't sure they'd have it fixed in time for holiday parking and he was late for his appointment with Hollis Bass.

"What's your point?" he asked as he reached his truck.

"The Mafia!" Wilma sounded more excited than horrified. "They're here."

Right. "Not every man who wears a pinkie ring is involved in organized crime."

"But these guys are."

"Fine. I'll deal with it when I'm done with Hollis. I'll call from the car."

"Okay. I'll make a few calls myself and see if I can find out where they are." She grinned. "Do you think they're in town to rub somebody out?"

MAC SPENT the short drive to Hollis's office thinking about all he had to do that afternoon and wondering how

Emily was. Ever since Bev had told him that his daughter still didn't feel safe with him, he'd been working on different ways to let her know how much he loved her. He thought things were getting a little better. She smiled more and responded to his teasing. They were talking more.

But how was he supposed to convince an eight-year-old that he wouldn't abandon her again? Not sure he was ever going to find that answer, he pulled into the parking lot and cut the engine.

After taking the stairs two at a time, he walked into Hollis's office and took a seat.

"I'm here," he said flatly.

Hollis smiled. "How are things going with Emily?"

As if he would tell this guy anything. "Great. She's adjusting well."

"Any behavior issues?"

He thought of the monochromatic food/clothing problem. Emily still required her meals to match her clothing. He and Bev were working together to find creative solutions to the potential difficulties. Thank God, it was summer and there were plenty of fresh fruits around. Berries had saved his butt more than once.

He studied Hollis—the man's small, round glasses, his prissy shirt, the air of "I know everything and you don't know shit" about him.

"We're doing just fine," he said.

Hollis nodded and made a few notes on his pad. "I'm happy to hear that. She's sleeping well and eating?"

"Sure."

"I see." Hollis scribbled some more. "I have something I want you to read." He bent down for something.

Mac expected an article of some kind, but the social worker handed him a book on anger management.

Instead of taking it, Mac leaned back in his chair and tried not to punch the little prick for presuming. "What makes you think I need this?" he asked.

"It's a by-product of what you do. Your high-stress job requires a lot of aggression without letting you act on it. Tension builds up and eventually explodes." He set the book on his desk and pushed it toward Mac. "I would like you to read the first three chapters by our next meeting."

Mac could feel an explosion coming on right this second. "Want to explain why you have such a thing against cops? Was your dad one?"

Hollis gave him a superior smile. "There's no reason for you to try to analyze me."

"This had to come from somewhere?"

"Why? The statistics speak for themselves. I'm trying to help you be a good father, a good citizen and a good person."

"You've taken on quite a job, then, Hollis," Mac said as he picked up the book. How dare this kid try to tell him what problems he had. The kid didn't know him from a rock.

But Mac was well and truly trapped. Hollis was his key to keeping Emily for the summer. If the social worker called the court and said he wasn't cooperating, his daughter would be taken away within hours.

He picked up the book and flipped through it. "I thought our meetings were going to be every other week," he said. "I just saw you last week."

"I know, but I'm allowed to change the schedule as I see fit. I'm thinking we'll go another ten days or so. And I will be checking on Emily in the next few days."

Perfect. With Hollis likely to turn up any second, Mac had no choice but to give in on the food issues. Hollis would accuse him of starving his daughter and it would be all over.

"Anything else?" he asked.

"That's everything. Have a good holiday," Hollis said.

Mac stared at him. He had about ten thousand tourists showing up in a town with a normal population of less than twenty-five hundred. There would be heat, surf and too much liquor. Yeah, it was going to be a peachy time.

"Thanks," he said as he stood. "You, too."

He left the room and walked to his truck, where he tossed the book on the passenger seat. What he really wanted to do was drive over the pages until they were dust. Instead he pulled out his cell phone and called Wilma.

"I'm done with my meeting and heading back to the office."

"You'll never guess," she said breathlessly. "I've

been getting calls for the past half hour. The Mafia guys are at Jill Strathern's office."

SURE ENOUGH when Mac pulled up in front of the small building with the Dixon and Son sign out front, he found a black limo parked in front. A little unusual for Los Lobos, he thought as he got out and walked toward the door, but hardly reason to assume that organized crime had come to town.

Too many people with too much time on their hands, he thought was he walked inside. When he heard voices, he called out a greeting.

"In my office," Jill said. "Come on back."

Mac walked through the fish-filled reception area and into Jill's fish-filled office only to come to a stop when he saw her drinking coffee with two men who looked like extras from the *Godfather* movies. Holy shit.

They were both dark, Italian looking, wearing expensive, well-cut suits and pinkie rings, and an air of menace.

The men stood. Jill pointed to the taller of the two, a man in his mid-fifties. "This is Rudy Casaccio and his associate, Mr. Smith. Rudy, this is Mac Kendrick, our sheriff and a friend of mine."

"Sheriff," Rudy said with a smile as he shook hands. "A pleasure."

Mr. Smith also shook his hand but didn't speak. He was much bigger than Rudy and several years younger, with massive shoulders and hands as big as hubcaps.

Mac didn't know what to say. He'd figured the reports had all been exaggerated and brought on by too many late-night movies. Obviously he'd been wrong.

The Mafia? Here? With Jill?

"Coffee?" she asked. "You can stay for a bit, can't you?"

"What? Oh, sure."

Rudy pulled up a chair. "Interesting office," he said as he motioned for Mac to take a seat. "I like the fish, but Jill isn't so sure. She says they smell."

"They do," she called from the storeroom. "I'm thinking of bringing in a few candles, but I'm not sure if stuffed-fish fumes are flammable. I'd hate to see the whole place go up in flames."

Mac accepted the mug she offered. She seemed perfectly at ease as she settled back behind her desk and picked up her own cup.

"Are you in town long?" he asked Rudy.

The other man smiled. "A few days. I wanted to come see Jill. When we spoke on the phone, she said she was fine, but I didn't believe her."

Stunned, Mac could only stare. "You're that close?"

"Jill is our attorney. She's the best. We had hoped she would make partner this year, but after what Lyle did…" His low voice trailed off.

Jill held up a hand. "We don't know if he actually did anything. Innocent until proven guilty and all that? Remember?"

Rudy shrugged, then put down his mug. "We should

be going. Nice to meet you, Sheriff." He rose and turned to Jill. "We'll talk soon."

"Absolutely. Have fun."

He left with the silent Mr. Smith. Mac turned to Jill.

"What the hell is going on? My office has been getting calls all morning with hysterical people telling us the Mafia has arrived. I thought it was joke."

Jill could see that Mac wasn't handling this well. "They're not the Mafia."

He put his mug on her desk. "What would you call them?"

"Businessmen who like to talk about having connections. The key word is *talk*. Rudy has far too many legitimate business interests to have the time or energy for anything else, but he likes to act menacing and it doesn't bother me."

Mac didn't look convinced. "So you're not involved in organized crime."

"Of course not. I'll admit Rudy is a colorful character, but he's not in the Mafia."

"Right. So how connected is he?"

"Oh, please." She laughed. "He's a sweetie. He's always been perfectly normal. He brings me a lot of nice *legal* business and he pays his bills on time."

"Did he offer to take care of Lyle for you?"

She pressed her lips together.

He swore again. "Tell me you didn't accept his offer."

"Of course not. Besides, he wasn't really saying he'd *do* anything."

"Are you willing to test that theory by accepting?"

Actually, she wasn't, but Mac didn't have to know that. "He feels badly for me. He knows how hard I worked and how much I enjoyed the different challenges."

"Are you working for him now?"

She leaned forward. "You can't seriously be worried about him being in town."

"I don't like it and you didn't answer the question."

"Technically, I don't have to, but for the sake of peace between friends, no, I'm not currently doing any work for him. I don't have the resources here to do a good job."

"That's something."

She hated seeing him worried for no reason. "Mac, relax. Rudy's going to stick around for a few days, take in the local sights, then head back to Vegas. I promise, he won't make any trouble. Why would he?"

"Because it's what he does."

"You don't know that for a fact."

"I know it in my gut. Would it do any good to tell you not to see him again?"

She shook her head. "Besides, talking about actual corporate law is way more thrilling than worrying about wills and fences."

He stood and paced the length of her office. She liked watching him move, although she felt a little guilty about the tension tightening his body.

"I saw Hollis today," he told her. "The little twit gave me a book on anger management. He said it was because all cops have anger issues. It made me want to beat the crap out of him."

"Which might have proven his point."

"That's what I thought."

He turned to face her. "I don't need these guys hanging around, Jill. You may think they're here to vacation, but I don't agree. Men like Rudy Casaccio can't help making trouble—it's in their blood. You may be passing through, but I'm making a home here for myself and Emily. I'll do whatever it takes to protect this town. No one is going to get in the way of that. Not Rudy and not you."

"Is MAC STILL ANGRY with you?" Bev asked a few mornings later as they loaded the picnic basket for the Fourth-of-July celebration.

"I don't know," Jill admitted. She hadn't seen him since he'd stalked about of her office. "I think he's wildly overreacting to the whole thing."

"He has a lot to deal with right now. His new job, Emily, the social worker."

"I know." She remembered Mac's complaint that Hollis had given him an anger-management book and wondered if he'd had any time to read it. Maybe when he got to the chapter on jumping to conclusions, he would be less crabby with her.

Technically, she hadn't done anything wrong, but she still hated that he'd left in a temper.

"Men," she said.

"They can be a trial," Bev agreed. Her long sundress swayed as she worked. As always, she'd pulled her wavy red hair back in a braid. "That's another reason I stay clear of them."

"I'm going to follow your example," Jill said with determination. "Lyle was a complete disaster. Mac is confusing. I don't need this pain in my life. I'm happy and successful on my own." Well, maybe not *successful* considering her current circumstances, but she had been before and she would be again.

"Where's the car?" Bev asked as she tucked sandwiches into the insulated picnic basket.

Jill carefully stacked frosted cookies into a plastic container. "The beach parking lot. You know, I'm beginning to think Lyle arranged for some kind of Gypsy protection on that damn car. It's been nearly two weeks and there's not a scratch on the thing. I left it by the shopping-cart return for three days. That should have done something. With the black paint, every little mark shows up. But is there even one? No. I really hate that."

"You're thinking the beach will be the answer?"

"I hope so. You know how the main parking lot curves and there's that one spot that juts out a little?"

Her aunt nodded.

"That's where I parked the car. I'm hoping a few people nick it. Does that make me a bad person?"

"Not at all. Lyle earned it."

"I know." She put the cookies beside the sandwiches, then reached for the bags of chips. "I haven't done much on my revenge plan. I can't ever think of anything good. I'd rather focus on my own life and getting that in order than trampling over Lyle."

"Maybe you're getting over him."

Jill nodded. "I am. I've also been thinking that there might not have been much to get over. I'm angry and humiliated, but I'm not emotionally devastated. Wouldn't I be if I'd loved him?"

Her aunt patted her arm. "Be happy that you're doing so well."

"You're right. I am. I had that phone interview yesterday. That was good. I think they're going to invite me in for a face-to-face."

"Would you like that?"

Jill considered the question. "I'm not sure they're the right firm for me, but I'm happy to be getting responses to my résumé. It's nice to be wanted." Especially after what had happened with her being fired and all. If only she could figure out what had gone wrong.

"Will your Mafia friends be at the beach today?" Bev asked.

Jill laughed. "First of all, they're not my *Mafia* friends. They're more like business associates. And second, Rudy doesn't strike me as a beach kind of guy. I can't imagine him in anything but a suit. But if he shows up, I'll be sure to introduce you."

Bev giggled. "It will be just like the *Sopranos*."

"I hope not. Mac would be furious if someone started shooting on his beach."

There was a knock at the door. Jill's heart gave an odd little flip. She wiped her hands on a dishcloth, then walked over and pulled open the door.

Emily stood on the front porch. She held a blanket in one hand and a canvas tote in the other.

"Sunscreen," she said glumly. "Daddy says I have to."

Jill looked past her to where Mac stood. As always,

the sight of him in uniform made her want to kick up her heels and suggest something naughty. Unfortunately, he was wearing sunglasses, so she couldn't see his eyes and figure out if he was still upset with her.

"He's smart," she told Emily. "Sunburns hurt like crazy. Come on in. We're packing the picnic basket." She eyed the girl's outfit…red from head to toe…and thought of the red-iced cookies. Either Bev had guessed right or she and Emily had discussed clothing in advance.

"The sandwiches will be a problem," she murmured as Emily skipped past her.

"Her bathing suit is white," Mac said. "Does that help?"

"You bet. We used white bread."

He stayed where he was, on the bottom step of the porch, his gaze shielded by his damn mirrored lenses. She closed the door behind her so they were both outside.

"Take those things off so I can know if you're mad at me," she demanded.

He whipped off the sunglasses and grinned.

"Better," she said. "Look. You have no right to be mad at me. I didn't do anything wrong. Rudy came here on his own, not by my invitation. So I know the man—that's not a crime. To the best of my knowledge, he's never committed a crime. If you're going to be a butthead about it all, I can't stop you, but I think it's really stupid."

He moved up one step and raised his eyebrows. "Did you just call me a butthead?"

"You bet."

He didn't seem angry at all. Intense, maybe, what with how he moved up another step and got a whole lot closer. Raw energy radiated from him. Sexual energy. She liked it.

"You're nothing but trouble," he said. "You're mouthy and completely naive about what Rudy may or may not do in this town. But I like you."

Her toes curled into the smooth wood of the porch and her stomach clenched. "Yeah?"

"Yeah. Even if you are a pain in the ass."

Then his arms were around her and his mouth was on hers. The short, hot, intense kiss stole her breath, along with her ability to reason. He straightened and she pressed a hand to her chest.

"Oh, my," she breathed.

He grinned and touched the tip of her nose. "I have to go."

"Okay. See you on the beach."

"I'll be the good-looking one."

That she already knew.

CHAPTER EIGHT

PERFECT BEACH WEATHER kept the crowd happy, Mac thought as he walked along the boardwalk fronting the main beach in Los Lobos. It was a little after eleven and already the parking lots were filling up and the lines for the vendors were five or six people deep. Minimal surf meant less work for the lifeguards. Even D.J. seemed to be having a good day, Mac noted as he saw his youngest deputy patrolling in the official dune buggy, stopping every now and then to chat with the sweet young things who instantly surrounded him. Maybe a bevy of beautiful women would take his mind off his need for more firepower.

Mac's teams had already patrolled the parks, and the smaller beaches. Fireworks would start promptly at nine-thirty, go for a half hour, then his men would be standing by to direct traffic so everyone got home quickly and safely. Two guys had drawn short straws, which meant they were stuck cruising the beach well into the night to take care of any problems that might arise from the folks who chose not to leave.

Mac paused at a vendor to buy a bottle of water. He twisted off the top and took a long sip.

"Morning, Sheriff," an older woman said as she walked by with her two children.

"Morning. Having fun?"

The youngest, a boy, maybe twelve, grinned. "You bet."

He continued to greet the locals and visitors alike, knowing he was responsible for them. A few months ago, he would have cringed at the thought of taking responsibility for one more life, but now it felt right.

He eyed the crowd on the beach and wondered if Emily was having a good time. Jill had mentioned introducing her to her assistant's kids so she could play with someone her own age. He was in favor of the idea. Em could use a break from the grown-ups. He appreciated Jill being willing to—

A familiar silhouette captured his attention. Mac watched as two men strolled toward him. They were both big, dark-haired and dangerous looking. Dammit all to hell, he thought grimly. He wouldn't have thought Rudy Casaccio the beach celebration type, but here he was. In shorts, no less, although Mr. Smith was dressed in a suit.

His good mood drained away as they moved toward him. Too bad getting on his nerves wasn't a good enough reason to run them in.

"Sheriff Kendrick," Rudy said pleasantly as he offered his hand. "Good to see you."

Mac grimaced. "I wouldn't have thought this was your kind of party."

Rudy shook his head. "Nor would I, but I find everything about your little town completely charming. We had breakfast on the boardwalk earlier and the food was delicious. You have a big crowd, yet everyone is so orderly."

"I'd like it to stay that way."

"Of course." Rudy smiled. "Mr. Smith and myself have no intention of making trouble. We're here for some much needed R and R. Besides, the day is too beautiful for anyone to think about making trouble."

He nodded and started walking. Mr. Smith trailed after him. Mac stalked off, his pleasure in the holiday ruined.

"WE'RE GONNA need a little flexibility here, kid," Jill said with mock severity. "What do you think?"

Emily stared at her with big blue eyes as if considering the question.

"It's a holiday," Jill added, not sure if she was about to make the situation worse or better. With the bright blue sky overhead and the scent and the sound of surf, it was difficult to imagine anything bad happening today. But if Emily didn't want to cooperate, things could go downhill pretty fast.

Bev leaned close to the girl and kissed her forehead. "When in doubt, go with your stomach."

The tension around Emily's mouth eased and her shoulders relaxed. "Okay, but you won't tell anyone, right?"

Jill knew what she was asking. For them not to tell her dad. She considered the question, then glanced at her aunt, who shrugged.

"If that's what you want," Jill said, hoping this didn't come back to bite her in the butt later. "Can we just say we agree to keep the secret, or do we have to stick ourselves with pins and spit?"

Emily giggled. "You can just tell me."

"Oh, nothing that boring," Bev announced.

She held out her pinkie to Jill. When the fingers were linked, Jill closed her eyes and intoned, "By the light of the sun I pledge my word."

"By the light of the moon, I am vowed," Bev said in a low, serious voice.

"Forever," they repeated together as they bounced their hands three times, then clapped their palms together.

Emily looked impressed. "Can you teach me that?" she asked Bev.

"Sure. Nothing to it. But let's eat up, first."

Jill handed over the plate she'd prepared. The one that could have given Emily fits, what with the sandwich—white bread—the barbecue chips—orange—the helping of fruit salad—multicolored—and a couple of spoonfuls of coleslaw—green and purple. The red-iced cookies had yet to put in an appearance.

Emily sat in her red shorts set and speared a grape, then chewed. Jill felt like doing the happy dance right there on the blanket. Of course, she'd just made a solemn vow not to tell Mac that his daughter *would* eat more than one color, which made her feel kind of crappy inside.

An emotion to be dealt with later, she thought.

"Good afternoon, ladies."

Jill turned toward the speaker and had to shield her eyes against the sun. When she was able to focus, she didn't know if she should laugh or try to bury herself under a couple of tons of sand.

Rudy Casaccio stood beside their blanket, looking very fit and dressed for fun in shorts and a polo shirt. The same couldn't be said for Mr. Smith, who hovered a few feet away and looked both uncomfortable and out of place in a dark suit.

"Rudy," Jill said as she scrambled to her feet. "What are you doing here? I wouldn't have thought you'd like this sort of thing." She motioned to the crowded beach as she spoke.

Rudy grinned. "Just checking out the local color." His gaze strayed to Bev. "So far I like what I see."

Jill's mouth dropped open. Was that her client coming on to her aunt? Was that her aunt blushing?

She was so stunned she wasn't sure what to say. Bev had always been beautiful with her gorgeous long red hair, her perfect skin and her petite but curvy figure. And Rudy wasn't half-bad. He was in his early fifties and Bev only a few years younger than that, so nothing about the situation should have grossed her out. But still...wow.

She cleared her throat. "We were just eating. Would you like to join us?"

"If you don't mind the company. We had a late breakfast, so we're not hungry, but everything looks delicious." He settled next to Bev and smiled.

Jill stole a peek at Mr. Smith, but the large man simply hovered a few feet away from the blanket. She sank onto her knees.

"Should I find Mr. Smith a chair?" she asked.

Rudy chuckled. "He'll be fine."

"He looks uncomfortable."

Rudy's dark eyes brightened with humor. "Good."

As Jill didn't want to understand Rudy's relationship with his associate, she didn't pursue the matter. Instead she offered a diet soda, then picked up her plate. Emily shifted closer.

"Who's that man?" she asked in a mock whisper.

Rudy smiled at the girl. "I'm a friend of Jill's. My name's Rudy. Who are you?"

"Emily Kendrick."

Rudy's eyebrows rose slightly as he put the relationship together. "Nice to meet you, Emily. Are you enjoying your holiday?"

"Uh-huh." She took a bite of her sandwich.

Bev cleared her throat. "How long have you been in town, Rudy?" she asked.

"A couple of days. Until her unfortunate change in circumstances, Jill was my attorney. When I learned she'd moved here, I wanted to come over and see how she was doing."

Bev's lashes fluttered. "That was so thoughtful of you. Where do you live?"

"Vegas."

"An exciting city," she said.

"You're right, but Los Lobos has certain charms." Rudy looked at Jill. "So who is this Gracie Landon I've been hearing about?"

Jill nearly choked on a bite of fruit salad. When she'd swallowed, she cleared her throat. "What? You've heard of Gracie?"

"Of course. There was that nice lady at the bakery, and the waitress this morning. We were talking about the history of the town and her name came up. Did Gracie really grind up a sleeping pill and put it in Riley's drink so he couldn't go on his date?"

Jill dropped her chin to her chest. "Gracie isn't going to like this."

"What? That she's a legend?"

"That no one seems to be forgetting what she did all those years ago."

Bev laughed. "We're all admiring her guts to go after what she wants."

"In some circles, what she did could have landed her in jail," Jill pointed out.

"No," Rudy said. "It was true love. How old was she?"

"Fourteen."

He looked at Bev. "The young know how to love with their whole hearts. I admire that."

"Me, too," Bev said breathily.

"She made Riley's life miserable," Jill said. "Not to mention his girlfriend's." Although she had much less compassion for Pam. The woman hadn't been very nice back in high school and time seemed to have left her much the same. Or, once a bitch, always a bitch, she thought with a smile.

"I hope I get to meet her," Rudy said.

It took Jill a second to realize he meant Gracie and not Pam.

"Sorry, she doesn't come back to Los Lobos, ever. In fact, she's convinced her entire family that it's much more exciting to visit her in Los Angeles during the holidays. I don't think she's stepped foot in town in about fourteen years."

Rudy looked disappointed. Jill took a bite of her sandwich. How weird was it having him here? She'd only ever seen Rudy in her office where he'd been dressed for success and surrounded by "associates." Here, on the beach, he was almost human. Although Mr. Smith hovering in the background wasn't the most comforting of sights.

She glanced at Emily, who had been listening with interest. "So I talked to your dad," she told the girl. "I have a secretary where I work and she has children. One of them is a daughter your age. I thought it might be fun to go hang with them for a while. What do you think?"

Emily nodded. "It's a good idea."

Jill patted her shoulder. "Poor kid, stuck with all us adults. We're pretty boring, huh?"

"You're not so bad."

"Wow. What a compliment. I'm honored. And touched. Really."

Emily giggled and popped another strawberry into her mouth.

Jill finished up her lunch, then slathered on another coating of sunscreen. Too many years in law school and then behind a desk had robbed her of her tan. Despite her dark hair and incredibly boring brown eyes, she had fair skin that punished her by burning if she wasn't careful.

Bev was still in conversation with Rudy, which freaked Jill out a little. She had the thought that it wasn't safe to leave her aunt alone with the man, which was crazy. Bev was a grown-up and this was a very public place. There were families spread out on the sand everywhere. Deputies patrolled everywhere—besides, she didn't think Rudy was really a bad guy, did she?

Jill realized she didn't have an answer. Her contacts with the man had all been professional as she worked with several very legal businesses. He'd always been honest and open and paid his bills on time. When Emily asked Bev for another chocolate milk, Jill leaned toward the man sitting next to her.

"She's my aunt," she said, her voice low, her gaze steady as she stared into his eyes. Although what she was searching for remained a mystery. Did she think some banner would wave through his irises saying *I'm really a good guy and I won't whack your aunt if she gets on my nerves?*

"I know," Rudy told her, and patted the back of her hand. "I understand about family. She'll be safe with me."

"I'm more worried about her being safe *from* you," she muttered, then had to change the subject when Bev finished with Emily.

Complications, she thought ten minutes later when Rudy invited Bev to go with him to get ice cream and she agreed. He stood, then held out his hand. He helped Bev to her feet as if she were a delicate flower. Worse, Bev giggled and smiled at him.

It wasn't just the older people connecting that made her uneasy. That was kind of weird, but she thought she might be able to deal with it. But this was her aunt. And Rudy. She would never have imagined him hooking up.

Bev was into serious psychic energy and staying pure—sort of—for her gift. Rudy was into… Jill frowned as she realized she couldn't answer that question.

"Did you know Gracie?" Emily asked as she polished off the last of her sandwich. "The legend one?"

"Uh-huh. We were friends. We still are. She lives in Los Angeles."

"She really liked a boy?"

Like didn't begin to describe it. "She did, but he didn't like her back and that made her sad."

Emily wrinkled her nose. "Boys aren't very nice. They play mean sometimes."

"That will change," Jill promised. At least she hoped it would for Emily. In her world, Lyle had played mean enough for two men. Why couldn't he have loved her as much as Gracie had loved Riley?

Jill reconsidered that. She didn't actually want stalker love—just someone to pay attention. And kiss like Mac, she thought with a smile. Even on the run, his kisses were plenty hot. But Lyle had been nothing but a mistake. If her life had been just a little different, she wouldn't have ever married him. It was the naked thing.

"Ready to go meet Tina's kids?" she asked.

"Sure." Emily put her paper plate into the trash bag, then scrambled to her feet.

Jill made sure the blanket was anchored and asked their neighbors to keep an eye on things. Then she took Emily's hand and started off in the direction of lifeguard station number three, where Tina said her family would be encamped.

Why was life complicated by getting naked? she wondered. The first time had been with Mac and he'd promptly thrown up. Now she understood why, but at the time, she'd been crushed. Then there'd been Evan. He'd been Mac's opposite. Slight, bookish, not nearly as handsome, but gentle. He'd made Jill laugh, had been tender and romantic. Practically the perfect boyfriend. They'd dated for nearly eight months before deciding to take things "to the next level."

She'd slipped off her clothes, he'd taken one look at her body and had announced he was gay.

Events like that had a way of changing a woman's perspective on the world. Then three years later Lyle had come along. He'd been interested in her sexually and hadn't had either an involuntary negative physical response or an epiphany leading to a major lifestyle change upon viewing her without clothes. She'd been so grateful, she'd decided she was in love with him.

Looking back the sequence of events was so clear, but at the time, she'd thought she really loved him. Worse, she'd worked hard at a marriage destined for failure. And she'd cooked for him. That *still* made her bitter. At least she didn't have to worry about being in love with him anymore. She didn't think her heart had ever been fully engaged. Which meant picking up the pieces wasn't too difficult at all.

EMILY RUBBED her hands against her shorts. "Do you think…?" she asked, then stopped, not sure what to say.

Jill tugged on a strand of her hair. "Do I think what?

That you'll have fun? Absolutely? That they'll like you? They'll adore you. That Tina will start to think I'm actually a person? That is less likely."

Emily laughed. Being around Jill always made her feel good.

"You two. In the shorts. Stop right there and put your hands up."

Emily spun toward the sound of her dad's voice and saw him jogging up toward them. For a second she felt happy and good and wanted to run to meet him. Then she remembered that she was mad and her insides got all scrunchy.

"Mac." Jill put her hands on her hips. "I'm sorry, but I don't have any time to be arrested today. It's going to have to wait."

"Ha. I have handcuffs right here."

Jill grinned. "Interesting," she said. "What's up?"

"This."

Her dad held out his hand. Emily saw a tiny little rhino sitting on his palm.

"It was in one of those grab machines. It cost me three bucks, but I got it. I figured Elvis could use a friend."

Emily didn't know what to do. She wanted to take the toy and thank her dad, but something inside of her was afraid. She looked from him to the rhino and back, then watched as his smile began to fade. Her tummy tightened and her face got all hot.

"You're kidding," Jill said, taking the tiny stuffed animal from him. She held it up and started to laugh.

"It's too sweet for words." She pulled Emily close and hugged her. "Don't you just love it?"

Emily felt the scary tightness start to fade. She smiled a little, then giggled. "It's cute."

"More than cute. Charming beyond words." Jill handed the rhino to her. "Your dad is pretty cool."

Emily glanced at her dad. He looked pleased. She tucked the baby rhino into her pocket and reached for her dad's hand. "He's okay," she said softly.

WEARY BUT SATISFIED, Mac made his way to his patrol car a little past midnight. The day had gone well. At last count there'd been nearly a dozen arrests, which was right in line for the holiday. Considering the crowds, he figured they'd gotten off lucky. There hadn't been any fights and the only injuries had been minor. That was the good news. The bad news was summer had just started. There would be a lot more busy days, especially for the pier centennial celebration. But for now, he was pleased.

Even Emily had had a good time. Bev had taken her home shortly after the fireworks and had promised to put her to bed, then stick around to baby-sit. Mac knew whatever he paid the woman wasn't close to enough.

The night was cool and clear. By the ocean, the temperature dropped with the sun, so he didn't have to worry about too many stragglers on the beach. D.J. had volunteered to make the last run of the evening, leaving Mac free to head home.

As he approached his patrol car, he saw someone sitting on the hood. He could only think of one person likely to do that and his blood quickened at the thought of Jill.

She smiled as he approached. "I thought maybe I could convince you to give me a ride home."

"Where's the 545?"

"I left it in the beach parking lot. I'm still hoping for a dent or a scratch or something, but that stupid car must be protected by fairies or Gypsies. There's nothing. Not a even a hint of body damage. I have to tell you, that's really pissing me off."

She shifted as she spoke and her long hair swayed with the movement. Too much heat and humidity had vanquished her attempts to straighten it and the loose curls jutted out in all directions. She wasn't wearing makeup, her shirt had a stain on it and she'd dropped her sandals on the asphalt by his tire. She looked sexy as hell.

He stepped close, sliding between her bare thighs, and settled his hands on her hips. His crotch pressed against hers and it didn't take more than a second or two for him to react to the contact. Her brown eyes crinkled with amusement.

"No one can ever accuse you of being subtle, Mac, can they?"

"Not my style," he murmured, before slipping one hand under her mass of hair to cup her neck while he dropped his mouth to hers.

She put her arms around his neck as she kissed him back. They didn't bother with gentle introductions, instead they eased right into deep, soul-stirring kisses that made every part of him hard.

She smelled of sun and sand and suntan lotion; she tasted of chocolate and wine. Their tongues circled and stroked and brushed and aroused. She raised her legs and wrapped them around his hips, holding him in place.

He pulled back and rubbed his thumb against her swollen mouth. "Liquor is illegal on the beach and at the park. I may have to run you in."

"I have no idea what you're talking about."

"I can taste the wine."

"Oh. All right. We smuggled a bottle in. So charge me." She grinned, then bit his thumb. "Will there be handcuffs involved? You mentioned them before and now I have a very particular image I can't seem to shake."

She was teasing, but now he pictured it as well. Her at his mercy. Naked. Him doing everything in his power to make her moan, writhe and scream…while coming, of course.

"My house is about ten minutes from here," he told her.

She rubbed her hands up and down his chest. "I actually know that, and while you're tempting me, this is where I get to be the sensible one and point out you have an eight-year-old daughter at your place or mine. I'm not sure where Bev took her."

"Only a minor problem."

She tilted her head. "I'm not convinced I could get naked with my aunt in the house."

He wasn't sure, either.

Just then a car turned the corner. Jill dropped her

legs and he stepped back just in time for Wilma to pull up alongside of him. She rolled down the passenger window. "We did good today. The judge would be proud."

Mac mentally winced at the comment. Judge Strathern, Jill's father, was pretty much the *last* person he wanted to think about right now. "Thanks."

"See you in the morning."

"Bye."

He watched her drive down the street. When she'd turned again, he looked at Jill. She shook her head.

"Hard to get wild in this town," she said as she jumped to the ground, then collected her sandals. "Okay, I'm ready for my ride home."

"Sure." He unlocked the car.

Jill studied him. "You're thinking about my father, aren't you?"

"He's a good man."

She muttered something that sounded very much like "I'm never going to have sex again, I just know it" as she walked around to the passenger side and slumped into the seat.

"I owe him," Mac reminded her. He got into the car and put on his seat belt. "He saved my ass more than once."

"I know, I know. When you were a kid, and just recently. It's who he is and what he does. Do you really think he's worried that you're going to sleep with me?"

"He wouldn't be happy."

"He's my father. Trust me, he doesn't want to think

about me being with anyone. It's not about *your* penis—he pretty much hates them all."

Mac chuckled. "That puts it in perspective." He decided, for the sake of peace between them, to change the subject. "Emily had a good time today."

"She did, and I'm glad. Tina's kids were great. Her daughter, Ashley, introduced her to several girls her own age and they all had a blast together. Tina, my assistant who hates me, even thawed a little. I think it was seeing me in the company of a child who obviously likes me. If Emily thinks I'm okay, I can't be all bad. At least that's my theory."

He navigated the quiet streets of the town. "I'm sure Tina doesn't hate you."

"Oh, right. She's bubbling over with love." Jill rested her head against the window and sighed. "Relationships are so complicated. Even the ones that aren't all that personal. So are you missing your ex-wife much?"

He glanced at her and did his best not to smile. "That was subtle."

"Hey, it's late, I was out in the sun all day and I had wine. I can't do subtle. So, do you miss her?"

"No. It's over between us. She's seeing some guy and I really don't care."

"Oh." Jill straightened. "Thanks for sharing. Not that I was interested or anything."

"Of course not."

"I'm leaving in a few weeks, so what's the point of getting involved?"

"You're right."

"Plus, we're both dealing with bad marriages." She

stared out the windshield. "Why would we want to jump into something else? I know I'm not eager to trust a man again after what Lyle did. Why did your marriage break up? I can't remember."

He was fairly sure he hadn't told her but didn't mind giving her the information. "I disconnected. Carly and I got married because she got pregnant. We weren't ever really in love, but we tried to make it work."

"Right," Jill said, as if she'd known it all along. "But you love Emily a lot. That's obvious."

"She's my best girl."

"So it's not that you're incapable of loving some-one."

He pulled up in front of his house and put the car in Park, then turned to look at her. "What exactly do you want to know?"

She gave him a bright smile. "Nothing at all. I'm making idle chitchat."

"Sure you are."

"Really. We're just friends."

He grinned. "Right. That's why I'm hard, you're wet and we both wish we could be alone for a couple of hours."

"So we're friends who want to have sex."

"Exactly."

CHAPTER NINE

JILL ARRIVED at her law office bright and early on the morning after the Fourth. She was only a little sunburned, which was great considering how long she'd been at the beach. The one truly perfect sunscreen she'd ever found was staying indoors and, as she hadn't had a cabana to carry with her the previous day, she figured a slight burn was a victory.

She stuck her key into the lock and was stunned to find the door was open. Had she forgotten to lock it when she'd left? Had she...

The door swung open and she saw Tina sitting at her desk, making notations in files.

Jill glanced from her watch, which read 8:26 a.m., to the woman in question.

"Good morning," she said as she entered, not sure how to ask what Tina was doing here. Tina rarely arrived before nine-thirty.

"Hi." Tina smiled at her. "Thanks for bringing Emily by yesterday. She's a great little kid. Ashley had so much fun with her that she keeps asking when we can get together again."

Jill wanted to turn around and see who was standing behind her because that had to be the reason Tina was being nice to her.

"Emily had a good time, too," she said instead. "So did I."

The two women stared at each other while Jill expected to hear scary movie music start at any second.

Okay, Jill thought as she smiled brightly. *Too weird for me.* She walked into her office. Tina followed her.

"There was a message from Mr. Harrison wanting an update on his fence case."

Jill nodded, but only because she was too shocked to speak. Tina was wearing a dress. Sure, it was a sleeveless summer sundress and she had on sandals and no stockings, but it was a real, live, honest-to-God dress.

Jill took the paper Tina offered. "I hate to have to call him back. He's not going to like what I have to say. Anything else?"

"Yes. A message was left just before I got in, from a Ms. Sullivan. She mentioned a law firm in Los Angeles and how they'd like to see you on Thursday." Tina frowned. "Are you doing some work for them?"

Jill grabbed the message and stared at it, then grinned. "No. This is about a job interview. Wow. That was fast. My résumé hasn't been out that long. Of course I'm pretty much what they want, which is great." L.A., huh? She could do the drive in about three hours. "Did she give a time?"

Tina's warm, friendly expression fell like a punctured balloon. Her eyes narrowed, her arms folded across her chest and she took a step back.

"You're looking for a job?" she asked, sounding both insulted and incredulous. "You work *here*."

Jill wanted to hold up her hands in a T to call a time-out. "This was always meant to be temporary. I thought you knew."

"Judge Strathern said you were moving back to town when he phoned me. I thought it was permanent."

Tina turned on her heel and stomped out of the office. Their common door slammed behind her.

Jill sank onto her seat. "What was up with that?" she asked aloud.

Could Tina actually be *angry* because she wasn't staying in Los Lobos? But Tina didn't like her. Okay, maybe having Emily around had made her assistant/secretary/receptionist feel slightly more friendly, but that wasn't an actual relationship. What did Tina care if she moved on?

Was it about keeping her job? Jill tried to decide if she should offer to write the woman a recommendation, although to be honest, she wasn't sure what she would say.

Tina has a lively personality. Although she hates to follow orders and rarely works more than two or three hours in a row, she would be a delightful addition to any office situation.

Hmm, maybe not.

Determined not to let the other woman's reaction spoil the glory of the moment, Jill called Ms. Sullivan and made an appointment for Thursday at eleven in the morning. She would take the 545 and see if the locals could ding up the car.

Next, she called Mr. Harrison.

"It's Jill Strathern," she said when the old man

picked up the phone. "I've researched the matter in question."

"It's a fence, girly."

She winced. "Yes, I know. If the construction had been more recent, we might have had a chance, but with the fence having been there over a hundred years, there's very little we can do about getting it torn down. My suggestion is that I contact your neighbors and work out a fair market price for the land on their side of the fence. You had said your major concern was not leaving the problem to be dealt with after you were gone and this would solve that."

She paused, waiting for Mr. Harrison to respond. There was only silence, followed by a click and then dial tone.

"Perfect," she said into the empty room as she hung up the phone.

While her day was slowly sliding into the toilet, she might as well go ahead and flush the damn thing. She stood and walked to the door Tina had slammed.

When she opened it, she waited until Tina looked up and scowled at her.

"What?" the other woman demanded.

"I'm going to be gone on Thursday. Would you please make sure I don't have any appointments and if I do, reschedule them?"

"Sure. Whatever. I have to go in a few minutes. Something with one of my kids."

"That's fine. If you would please take care of my calendar first, I would appreciate it."

Jill had a feeling she wouldn't see the woman again for the rest of the day.

She returned to her office, where she felt the fish eyes following her every move. When she reached her desk, she spun in a circle and glared right back.

"I never said I was staying, so don't try to say I did. I'm leaving Los Lobos. Get over it."

MAC WOULD RATHER have been almost anywhere than the Business Leaders of Los Lobos Committee for the Preservation of the Pier meeting—except maybe another one-on-one with Hollis. Jill had an appointment she couldn't—or wouldn't—reschedule so he didn't have any kind of distraction.

He sat in the back of the community center conference room and scribbled notes from time to time while Mayor Franklin Yardley turned what should have been a ten-minute update into nearly an hour of rambling.

"Now that the Fourth of July is over," the mayor intoned, "we can all concentrate on this historic and wonderful event."

He outlined the activities for the day, which culminated in a big fireworks show over the pier itself. Mac briefly wondered what wayward sparks would do to a hundred-year-old pier, then told himself not to sweat the details. His joy was to keep the good citizens and various visitors safe from any and all evils.

"We're expecting crowds at least fifty-percent bigger than we had here over the weekend," Franklin said from his place at the podium. His silver hair gleamed in the overhead light and there was a fresh coat of tan on his leathery skin.

"No one in this town has experience with an event of that magnitude."

Mac stifled a yawn. If they were using the beach as the main venue and the mayor's numbers were right, parking was going to be a bigger problem than crowd control. They could use the old drive-in on the edge of town, he thought, as he scribbled a few more notes. Then get folks to the beach using school buses. He'd have to get a cost estimate. The big expense wasn't the buses themselves. Rather, it was the insurance they would need. Still it would solve a lot of problems with congestion and—

"So I've invited in an expert," Franklin said, sounding way too pleased for Mac's peace of mind.

He glanced up just as the side door opened and a familiar if unwelcome man walked into the conference room.

Mac sat up in his chair and glared at both the newcomer and the mayor. What the hell was going on?

Franklin Yardley beamed at the committee members. "I'm delighted to introduce Mr. Rudy Casaccio. He's handled events much larger than ours and has graciously offered to act as a consultant."

Sure he had, Mac thought as he swore under his breath. The mayor had accepted, right after getting a nice fat, juicy contribution for his reelection campaign.

Rudy stood beside the mayor and smiled at the small crowd. He looked slick, Mac admitted. Great suit, easy stance. He was a man used to being in charge. Mac's gaze drifted to the ever-present Mr. Smith, who hovered just inside the room. A snap to be big man on campus when you're always protected by the big guns.

The meeting continued. Rudy gave a few words of advice, then offered to meet with the business leaders individually to discuss their needs.

By the time everyone got up to leave, Mac had about ground his teeth to stubs. He pushed through the crowd around Rudy and made his way to Franklin.

After grabbing the other man by the arm and dragging him into the corner, Mac got close enough to get his attention, then leaned in for good measure.

"Do you have any idea what you're getting into?" he demanded.

Yardley's brown eyes narrowed. "I know exactly what I'm doing, Sheriff, and I'd advise you to listen and learn. Rudy Casaccio can do things for this town that the residents have never dreamed of."

"Sure. Gambling at the lodge, drugs in the high school. It'll be great."

"Mr. Casaccio is a reputable businessman. He wants to *help* our town."

Which Mac read as helping Franklin himself.

"I can't quite get it," he said. "Why would someone like Rudy Casaccio want to help our little town?"

"He's a man of vision."

"Uh-huh. How much did he contribute to your re-election campaign?" Mac asked.

The mayor bristled. "Maybe you should worry less

about me retaining office. You have an election of your own coming up in a few months. If you don't have my endorsement, you don't have a prayer."

Mac knew he was right, but he didn't like it. "I suppose he gave money to the pier restoration."

"Yes. Twenty thousand dollars."

Great.

"Get with the program," Franklin told him. "We're all making Mr. Casaccio feel welcome. You've only been here a short time, but everyone thinks you're doing a fine job. It would be a shame to lose that support because you have something personal and unfounded against one of our leading citizens."

"Last I heard, he's not a resident."

The mayor shrugged. "We're all hoping that will change. And if you make trouble, there may only be room for one of you."

JILL SMILED at the young woman sitting across from her. She looked to be in her early twenties and more than a couple of months' pregnant. Kim Murphy met her gaze, offered a shy smile in return, then ducked her head.

"I was kind of surprised to get your call," the young woman said in a soft voice. "I haven't seen my grandmother in years. I didn't think she still remembered me."

"Apparently she did."

Kim bit her lower lip and gave Jill a wary glance. "I wanted to see her more, of course. But I...I just couldn't."

Jill wondered why. "Had she been ill?"

"I don't think so. It's just things are...complicated." She managed another one of those almost-smiles and returned her attention to her lap. "It's been six years since I've seen her. Not since the wedding."

Jill studied the young woman. Her long platinum-blond hair hung limply to her shoulders. Her arms were pale and painfully thin. The too-large maternity dress surrounded her like a very unattractive tent. Oh, well, what did she know about pregnancy fashions? Maybe this was the latest thing.

She pulled papers out of a folder and raised her eyebrows when she saw Kim's birth date. "You've been married for six years. Gee, you must have gotten hitched the day after you turned eighteen."

Kim raised her face a few inches and nodded. "Three days, actually. Andy and I started dating when I was just fourteen. He was older, of course, but he waited for me."

She said that as if it were a good thing. Jill tried not to wrinkle her nose or say anything sarcastic.

"That's great," she managed instead.

"He's wonderful." This time Kim's smile reached her shadowed eyes.

"Nice to know there are still some good guys out there." Unlike Lyle, the lying weasel rat bastard dog. "Okay, this is all going to be very simple. Your grandmother left you eight thousand dollars. You get the entire amount. My fee is being paid out of the rest of the estate. It will take a couple of weeks to process everything. I'll have some paperwork for you to sign, then I'll hand over the money. In the meantime you'll want to think about what you want to do with the inheritance."

Kim's delicate blond eyebrows drew together. "I don't understand."

"I'm suggesting a separate account for your inheritance. A money market, savings." She grinned. "You could start a college fund."

Kim pressed a hand to her stomach. "Oh. No, thank you. Andy wants to buy a new truck."

So like a man, Jill thought irritably. "But this isn't Andy's money," she said gently. "California is a community-property state, which means what the couple earns together is owned by both of them. However, an inheritance—money, property, whatever, only belongs to the person mentioned in the will. In this case, you. If you keep the money in a separate account and don't commingle it with say Andy's paycheck, it's all yours. Even the interest."

Kim's expression tightened until she looked like a rabbit facing the big bad wolf. She leaned back in her chair and shook her head back and forth.

"No. No, I don't want to do that. No. It's not right. Andy wants a truck."

Jill didn't like the tremor in Kim's voice. "What do *you* want?" she asked softly.

Kim swallowed. "Are we nearly done, because I have to go. I have an appointment." She looked ready to bolt.

"Sure. Just give me a second."

Jill handed her several papers to sign. As Kim leaned

over the desk, her dress slipped off one shoulder. Jill stared at a dark, ugly bruise. It looked to be in the shape of a large hand.

She swore silently. Please God, don't let this poor woman be battered, she thought grimly. Not here. Los Lobos might not be her idea of a good time, but she hated to think of really horrible things happening here.

"Anything else?" Kim asked as she straightened and her dress slipped back into place.

Jill had a couple dozen questions that she knew she wasn't going to ask. Not yet. She knew nothing about what was really happening. Maybe she was imagining Kim's fear and the bruise had nothing to do with her husband. Maybe not. But she would find out.

"That's it for now." Jill rose. "I'll call you when I receive the check. Once we finalize the paperwork, you're free to take it over to your bank."

Kim still looked wary. She said goodbye and hurried from the room.

Jill followed slowly, waiting until she was gone before heading for Tina's desk. It was Wednesday and her assistant/secretary/receptionist still hadn't recovered from her snit, but Jill wasn't willing to be put off by that.

"Do you know Kim Murphy?" she asked from the doorway.

Tina didn't look up. "A little. She and Dave are second cousins, I think. We don't hang with them much." She raised her head. "Why?"

"I'm trying to decide if I should get involved in something or not."

"Why bother when you're leaving?"

Jill sighed. As always, Tina made her feel special. "What do you know about their marriage?"

"Her and Andy? They keep to themselves."

"What's he's like?"

Tina frowned. "Big guy. Quiet unless you piss him off. He works construction."

Great. A large, physically strong man with access to power tools and a possible temper.

"Why all the questions?"

"Just curious. I have to go out for a while. I'll be back in a couple of hours."

Tina sank back into her seat. "I won't be here then."

Why was she not surprised?

JILL WALKED to the sheriff's office, which was about six blocks away. As she crossed the street, she made a mental note to pick up the car that afternoon so she could have it for her drive to Los Angeles in the morning.

Now that there was the possibility of leaving town, she found herself taken by the picturesque qualities of the restored downtown and the way everyone smiled in greeting.

She pushed open one of the two double doors of the sheriff's office and crossed to the counter.

The main reception area was big, with vinyl flooring, a bulletin board with Wanted posters and ads for garage sales. A long waist-high counter separated the visitors from those in charge, while a mini swinging door the same height offered entrance to the inner sanctum.

A tiny gray-haired woman manned the counter. "Can I help you?" she asked, then narrowed her eyes. "Wait. I know you. Jill."

"Hi."

"So, are you here on legal business?"

"I'm here to see Mac."

"He's in his office," the woman said with a jerk of her head. "Go on back. He's on the phone, but he won't be long."

"Thanks."

Jill pushed through the swinging half-door and walked toward the glass offices in the rear. As she walked around several desks, she saw Mac hanging up the phone. He didn't look happy.

"Trouble in paradise?" she asked as she walked through the open door.

"What? No. Nothing about work. That was Bev on the phone. Hollis Bass stopped by for the surprise visit he promised. The little sneak."

Jill thought about pointing out that Hollis was only doing his job. At the same time she wanted to ask *why* Mac was under such close supervision with his daughter. She'd wondered, of course, but hadn't wanted to pry. Based on Mac's annoyance, this wasn't the time.

"Are you going over there?"

"No." He picked up a pen, then put it down. "I'll wait." He glanced at the clock. "It shouldn't be more than a half hour, right?"

"I have no idea."

"I know. Sorry." He looked at her, then waved at a chair. "Have a seat."

"Thanks."

"Here on official business?"

"Yes and no."

He smiled. "As long as you're clear."

"I had a client come in today. Kim Murphy. Her husband's name is Andy. She's twenty-four, seriously pregnant. You know anything about him?"

"No. Why?"

"I think he might be beating her."

Mac swore. "You're kidding."

"I saw a bruise on her shoulder. It looked like a hand. I don't know. She was scared and nervous. Maybe I'm crazy."

"Maybe not." He pulled a pad toward him just as the phone rang. "Kendrick."

He listened for a couple of seconds. "That is not happening!" Pause. "I know. You're right. Are you sure?"

His grip on the phone tightened. "Thanks. Yeah. Okay. You, too."

He hung up and stared at her. "That was Bev again. Hollis just invited himself to lunch. I can't believe it." He crossed to the glass door and banged his fist against it. "What if Em is in one of her moods? What if she gets picky about her food? Hollis could decide I'm not doing a good enough job."

Jill wanted to tell him it would be fine, but she didn't know that.

"You want to go?" she asked.

He glanced at the pad of paper. "Yeah, I do. Let's pick this up later."

"Sure."

He stalked out of the office. Jill followed more slowly. When she reached the counter, she stopped.

"Wilma, you've lived here a long time, right?"

"Sure have," the petite woman said. "Since the earth's crust cooled."

"Do you know Andy Murphy?"

"Oh, I know of him."

Jill didn't like the sound of that. "Meaning?"

"The boy has a short fuse."

"Does he take that temper out on his wife?"

"No one has ever seen anything, if that's what you're asking."

Jill nodded. "I understand you can't accuse him of anything. Have there been any domestic violence complaints at all?"

"No, but if you ask me, there should have been."

CHAPTER TEN

MAC DROVE through town until he reached Bev's house. An unfamiliar eight-year-old Corolla had parked in the driveway.

Hollis, he thought grimly, and wished he could have stalked inside and thrown the kid out. Maybe tell him to never dare talk to Emily again. Except Mac knew that, however misguided, Hollis had Emily's best interests at heart. He parked in front of his own house and walked inside. After throwing a frozen entrée into the microwave, he paced back and forth in the kitchen until the timer beeped. He used a dish towel for a hot pad and ate standing up, all the while watching out the side window until Hollis finally left. Then he headed over to Bev's house and banged on the door.

"It's open," she called.

Mac walked inside.

"We're in the family room," Bev yelled.

"You should lock the front door," he said as he moved down the hallway. "It could have been anyone."

"But I knew it was you," she said as he entered the warm but messy family room.

Stacks of books sat on several of the tabletops, along with magazines and coloring books. DVDs and videos filled a small bookcase. A large Oriental carpet covered most of the hardwood floor. There were plants, sun-catchers and cut-open rocks filled with purple crystals scattered around.

In the center of it all sat Bev and Emily playing Disney Monopoly. They both looked up and smiled.

"We're fine," Bev said. "Want to join us? We just started."

"You can be Baboo," Emily said as she held out the small pewter piece. "I'm Snow White."

"Thanks," Mac said as he shoved his hands into his slacks' front pockets and felt more than a little foolish. "I just wanted to drop by."

"Of course." Bev's green eyes were knowing. She patted Em's arm, then stood. "Let me give your father a couple of messages," she told his daughter. "Give me two shakes of a lamb's tail and I'll be right back."

"A lamb's tail?" Emily burst out laughing. She rolled onto her side and continued giggling. "You don't have a lamb's tail."

"I could surprise you yet," Bev said as she walked to Mac, then led him into the kitchen.

"We're fine," she said as soon as the door closed behind them.

"He stayed for lunch." Mac tried to keep the accusation out of his voice but wasn't sure he'd succeeded.

Bev shook her long red hair, then pulled a scrunchy from her pocket and fastened her hair into a ponytail.

"It was noon, we were hungry. Should I have thrown him out?"

"Yes."

Her steady gaze never left his face. He sighed and leaned against the counter.

"I know, I know. Better to keep your enemies close," he muttered.

"Or not make them enemies at all. I know Hollis is a threat to you, but you don't have to be adversaries in this. I think he's willing to meet you more than halfway."

"Sure. Just as soon as I get a different job."

"What?"

"Hollis believes that cops make bad fathers."

Bev pressed her lips together. "That's completely stupid. I like him a lot less now. Still, the visit is over and it went well. He talked to Emily. Asked her about school and her friends and life here. You barely came up at all." She squeezed his arm. "He wasn't trying to set you up."

"Good to know."

"He's not the devil."

"As long as he's in a position to take my daughter from me, that's exactly who he is."

Bev nodded. "I see your point. What happens now?"

"Hell if I know. I guess he files a report and I go back to work."

"For what it's worth, my sense of things is this will all work out."

"Is this you getting a message from the beyond? Because if they're giving out information, you want to go ahead and ask about some lotto numbers?"

"My gift doesn't work like that and you know it."

He chuckled. "Too bad. At least then it would be practical."

"It's plenty practical now."

"If you say so." He bent over and kissed her cheek. "Thanks, Bev. For everything."

She waved him off. "Go say goodbye to your daughter."

He did as she suggested, then returned to his car and drove into town. He had one more stop to make before returning to the office.

The front door of Dixon and Son was unlocked. Mac stepped inside the fish emporium but Tina wasn't at her desk.

"You back there?" he called.

"Yes. Mac? Is that you?"

"In the flesh." He walked through the reception area into Jill's office. She sat behind her desk, a large law book open in front of her.

"I came to apologize for running out on you," he said as he pulled out the chair by the netting and sat down. "I couldn't get Hollis out of my head."

"Makes sense." She closed the book. "Really, you don't have to apologize."

"Don't cut me any slack," he said seriously. "You were trying to tell me about a guy beating up his wife. That should have had my full attention."

Jill raised her eyebrows. "You sound serious."

"I am. This town is important to me. I'm still figuring out how to care about it and Em, and keep everybody happy." He grimaced. "Everybody except maybe the pier committee."

"What have they done to annoy you?"

He thought about Rudy Casaccio in the meeting and felt his temper flare. "Don't get me started on that. Just tell me what's going on with your client."

"I don't know," she admitted. "Kim came in to see me about a will. Obviously I can't go into details."

"Right. Attorney-client privilege. What *can* you tell me?"

"That she was young and scared and acting as if her husband beat the crap out of her on a regular basis." Jill shook her head. "No, that's not true. I'm jumping to conclusions. She was skittish." She hesitated, as if she wanted to share something of her conversation with Kim but couldn't. "My impression was that if she had anything of her own—anything *he* couldn't touch—that there would be hell to pay."

"You mentioned bruises." He pulled a pad out of his shirt pocket and started taking notes.

"On her shoulder. It was big and in the shape of a man's hand. Maybe I'm overreacting."

"Maybe not. I'll check it out."

She leaned forward. "Be careful. If he's beating her…"

"Hey, I'm the cop here, right? I know how to do this."

She smiled. "Of course. You're right. I worry because I'm good at it. Everyone needs a skill."

"I'll send a cruiser and have someone talk to the neighbors. Maybe I'll send Wilma to talk to her. Everyone seems to open up to Wilma. But if Kim won't file a complaint then there's nothing we can do unless we catch him in the act."

"I know." Her mouth twisted. "That's why I never went into family law. Too many ambiguities and way too much pain. Give me a cold, faceless corporation any day."

He knew what she meant, but he also knew she was whistling in the dark. "You can't escape people," he said. "Believe me, I've tried."

She tilted her head. "Want to tell me about it?"

"Nope."

"I figured you wouldn't. Want a fish instead? I'm thinking of giving away a select few. You could have your pick."

He glanced around at the array covering the walls. "No thanks. I'm not into fish or antlers."

"Me, either, but look where I ended up."

"WHAT DO YOU MEAN you have dinner plans?" Jill asked as she watched Bev try on her third dress in as many minutes.

Her aunt stood in front of the full-length mirror and turned to look at her back. "Does this make my butt look big?"

Jill glanced down, then shook her head. "You look great, but you're not answering my question."

Bev stared at her in the mirror. "I would think you're bright enough to grasp it all at once. Rudy invited me to dinner, I said yes and now we're going out."

Jill heard the words, but she couldn't believe them. "This is like a date?"

"Try not to sound so incredulous. I'm still on the front side of fifty."

"I know. You're a beautiful, vital woman, but a date?" With Rudy? "What do you really know about him?" she asked, mindful of a very interested Emily sitting cross-legged on the bed.

"That he's a charming man who knows how to make a woman feel like a goddess."

A goddess? Jill couldn't remember ever feeling like that. She ignored the spurt of envy that cut through her.

"Aside from that," she said. "I thought you didn't date. Because of your gift."

As a relative nonbeliever, she knew it was low for her to throw that in her aunt's face, but she didn't have many other options.

"Dating is allowed," Bev said primly. "Yes, this is the one."

"The one" turned out to be a black sleeveless dress that fell to Bev's ankles. Huge red-orange roses swirled up the side of the dress and draped across her shoulders. With her flame-colored hair pinned loosely on her head, red-and-black dangling earrings nearly brushing her shoulders and her skin practically glowing with excitement, she looked sensual, beautiful and very much like a goddess.

"I hope I have a lot of your gene pool," Jill said by way of surrender.

"You do," Bev said with a smile. She twirled one more time, then paused in front of Emily. "Do you approve?"

"Uh-huh. You look as pretty as my mommy."

"Thank you. High praise, indeed. All right. I'm off." Bev grabbed a small black handbag and headed for the stairs.

Jill trailed after her. "He's not picking you up?"

"I didn't know if I would be able to get you at the office and ask you to come home early. I thought I might have to drop off Emily, and I didn't think either you or Mac would want her in the car with Rudy. Ta-ta."

Jill heard her footsteps on the hardwood floor, then the sound of the back door closing.

"I thought life would be simpler here," she said, and headed back for Bev's bedroom.

"She abandoned us," she told Emily, who giggled. "So what are our plans?"

"We have to eat dinner," Emily informed her.

"Want to go out?"

Emily nodded vigorously. "Maybe to a diner?"

"Absolutely. The one I'm thinking of has yummy milk shakes. We can take the car and park it downtown, then walk home." Because a few days in the beach parking lot had done absolutely nothing to get Lyle's car dented and she was really starting to get annoyed by the whole thing.

Jill changed out of her suit into shorts and a T-shirt. Then she and Emily left for a really greasy and fattening dinner.

"I heard Mr. Bass stopped by today," she said as she drove to the center of town.

"Uh-huh. He's a social worker and he said he takes

care of kids. I told him I didn't need anyone to take care of me. I have my mom and dad and you and Bev."

Jill liked being included in the list. "I'm glad you have a lot of people to take care of you."

"Me, too."

Jill was about to say something else when she spotted a familiar address. She recognized it from the paperwork she'd been filling out that afternoon, what with Mr. Harrison insisting on continuing the lawsuit.

"I need to stop here for a second," she said as she pulled to the side of the road and parked.

Two nearly identical houses stood about sixty feet apart. Both were old Victorians with decorative trim and gables and fussy railings. Not Jill's thing, but she knew they were popular. Big trees shaded large yards and, between the two houses, stood a massive stone fence. As the fence was perfectly centered between the buildings, she could see why it had been built there. Too bad no one checked the deeds first.

She saw a man moving a sprinkler to another part of the lawn of the house on the right. Impulsively she climbed out of the car and waited for Emily to join her.

"Who's that man?" the girl asked.

"Juan Reyes," Jill said.

"Is he a friend of yours?"

"Not exactly." Jill knew she was flirting with danger by speaking with Mr. Reyes, but she had to know about the people she might be suing on Mr. Harrison's behalf.

"Good evening," she called.

Juan waved. "Evening." He was of medium height and handsome, maybe thirty.

"You have a beautiful house," Jill said. "One of a pair."

Juan laughed. "Thanks. My wife and I fell in love with it about five years ago. We could never have afforded it on our own. We bought it with my mother-in-law."

"Really? She lives with you?"

Juan grinned. "Yeah, I know what you're thinking, but she's a really great lady. I like having her around."

Jill was impressed. She loved her father, but if they had to share a house, she would slowly go crazy. Or maybe not so slowly.

"I know your neighbor," she said, pointing to Mr. Harrison's house.

Juan's smile disappeared. "He's not happy having us living next door."

"Really?"

"Sure. He says the fence is too far on to his land. But it's a stone fence that has been there for years. We can't afford to move it. I offered to take out a second mortgage on our house and buy the land from him, but he refuses."

The front door opened and a pretty dark-haired woman called out. "Juan, invite the company inside."

"Oh, we're not company," Jill said quickly.

As she spoke, she inhaled the most delicious scent in the world. Emily tugged on her hand.

"Let's eat here," she said in a mock whisper.

"My mother-in-law is an amazing cook," Juan said. "Would you like to come inside and have a sample?"

"No. We have dinner plans already." She looked at the other house. It was dark and closed, except for a single light at the back.

"Does he live here all alone?" she asked.

"Yes. He has no family. I think it's sad that he only has energy to be angry about the fence."

"Have you asked him to dinner?"

Juan stared at her. "What do you mean?"

"If your mother-in-law's cooking is as good as you say and Mr. Harrison is alone and lonely, a family meal might go a long way to helping with negotiations."

She could see Juan weighing her suggestion. She was sure his neighbor had made his life hell and that Juan didn't want the crotchety old man in his house, but if it helped...

"I'll talk to my wife," Juan said. "Who *are* you?"

Jill winced. "Please don't take this personally, but I'm Jill Strathern, Mr. Harrison's attorney."

Juan took a step back as his expression hardened. "Are you trying to trick me?"

"Not at all. I just hate to see the two of you at odds over the fence. If you could be friends instead of ene-mies, neither of you would need me."

"She's very nice," Emily said loyally.

Juan smiled at her. "Thank you for telling me. Then it must be true." He looked at Jill. "I'll talk to my wife," he repeated, then hesitated. "If there's no lawsuit, then there's no money for you."

"In this case, I would be delighted to be fired."

"ARE YOU SURE ABOUT THIS?" Jill asked as Emily continued to roll curlers into her hair.

"Uh-huh. I saw it on TV."

"But I already have curly hair. I'm not sure curlers…"

Emily walked around in front of the chair and raised her eyebrows. "I'm in charge," she said with a certainty that, under other circumstances, would have made Jill laugh.

"Yes, ma'am."

Emily returned to her task, first brushing out a strand of hair, then rolling it in the curler. Jill was grateful that the humidity was low and her hair had stayed straight. If it frizzed, she might have to cut the curlers out.

"I like your hair," Emily said, her small hands tickling as she brushed against Jill's neck. "It's pretty and long. My mommy's hair is short."

"Like yours?" Jill asked.

"Sort of. Hers is darker."

The curse of getting older, or so Gracie complained. Natural blond hair got darker. Jill's had stayed pretty much the same brown color, which was probably the curse of being boring.

Emily tugged as she rolled up another strand and Jill tried not to wince. "We have pie to eat," she said by way of a bribe.

"Can we eat it during the movie?"

"Sure," Jill said in defeat, as they'd already arranged to watch the movie *after* playing beauty salon. She figured she might as well resign herself to a serious trim later in the week and relax.

"Dinner was good," Emily said. "I liked my hamburger."

"Yeah, those folks down at Treats 'n Eats know how to make a good burger." She wondered about stating the obvious, then decided to go for it. "You didn't seem to mind that your food didn't match your clothes. Does that mean you're not doing that anymore?"

Emily's hands stilled. A curler fell to the floor.

Jill turned and saw the little girl staring at her with big eyes. "Emily?"

"Sometimes I still want my food to match."

Not hard to figure out when. "With your dad?"

Emily nodded.

Jill sensed they were treading in dangerous territory. Should she let it go? But something inside of her told her it might help Emily to talk.

"Are you angry with your dad?" she asked quietly.

Emily sucked in a breath and tucked her hands behind her back. Then she slowly nodded.

Jill shifted in the chair so she could draw the child close and put her arms around her.

"It's okay to be mad," she said, hoping it was. But if adults couldn't control their feelings, was it reasonable to expect an eight-year-old to? "Is this about something he's doing now or before?"

"Before."

Jill drew Emily onto her lap and brushed her hair

off her forehead. "Want to talk about what happened or not?"

Emily shrugged. "Daddy was a cop before. He kept good people safe from bad people. But after a while he was quiet. He would sit in the living room and he wouldn't talk or play. Sometimes I'd go look at him because I was scared he'd disappear. You know, like a ghost."

"I can see how that would scare you," Jill said. "But he didn't become a ghost."

"I know. But Mommy got mad and she would yell and he would yell back and Elvis and I hid in the closet, but it was dark and we didn't like that, either."

Jill ached for the little girl with nowhere to go. "Their fighting wasn't about you," she said. "You didn't make them mad at each other."

Emily didn't look convinced. "One day Mommy and me went away. I waited and waited for Daddy to come that night, but he didn't. Mommy said he couldn't for a while. I didn't know if he was lost. I used to pray every night. And I wrote him letters."

Tears filled her blue eyes. Her lower lip quivered. "After a long time Mommy said he was coming to see me. That I got to spend the whole weekend with him and it would really be fun. But he didn't come."

The tears spilled onto her cheeks. Jill pulled her close and rocked back and forth.

"I'm sorry," she whispered, knowing that while Mac might have gone through a tough time, there was nothing, save death or serious injury, that excused disappointing his daughter.

"He didn't come the next time, either, and I stopped asking when he would see me. And then Mommy said I had to spend the summer here."

Jill felt more out of her depth than she'd ever been in her life.

"Did you and your dad ever talk about this?" she asked, wanting to help, but not sure how.

"Yeah." Emily sniffed. "He said he was sorry and that he'd never do it again."

"But you don't believe him."

Emily didn't answer.

Jill wondered if there could be anything worse than wanting to trust a parent and not being able to.

What could have happened to keep Mac from Emily? She'd seen them together and knew how much he loved his daughter. Nothing about this made sense.

"Are you having a good time here?" she asked.

"With you and Bev."

"With your dad?"

Emily shrugged.

Jill wished she had a psychology expert on call to help with this.

"When you're mad at your dad, do you feel funny inside?" she asked. "Sort of bad?"

Emily looked at her and nodded several times.

Guilt, Jill thought. It strikes at any age. "Do you think your dad loves you?"

Mac stood just inside the kitchen and held his breath. He hadn't meant to eavesdrop, but neither Emily nor Jill had heard him knock. Now he stood frozen in place, unable to move and desperate to hear his daughter say yes.

But there was only silence.

Inside he ached with the pain of what he'd lost. What he could only blame himself for and how much it had cost Emily. There was no excuse. There couldn't be.

If he could go back, he would change everything. Not an option, he reminded himself as he continued to wait.

"Maybe," came the whispered response.

"Maybe, huh?" Jill said. "I happen to know he loves you a lot. He told me and you know it's wrong to lie to lawyers."

"Really?"

"Uh-huh. So he had to be telling the truth."

Something hit the floor.

"I think that was one of my curlers," Jill said.

"We need to finish."

He heard a thump, as if Emily had jumped to the floor. Mac backed out of the kitchen and went home to wait a few minutes before claiming Emily. He needed to figure out how to handle what he'd heard.

How did he explain to an eight-year-old child that he'd been in such hell, it had hurt to keep breathing? That nothing had mattered, except her, only he hadn't known how to show that? How did he explain screwing up and hurting her? How did he make it right?

He had loved Emily from the moment he'd found out Carly was pregnant. Most men wanted a son, but he'd been delighted by his perfect daughter. He'd shared responsibilities, changing his shift to be home while Carly worked. Emily had been everything.

He'd lost her because he hadn't been able to face what he'd become. And in losing her, he'd destroyed the love they shared.

He would get it back, he vowed. He would prove himself to her. If only he knew how.

CHAPTER ELEVEN

JILL FOLLOWED the human resources director down the carpeted hallway and did her best not to do a little happy dance right there between the kitchen and the supply room. The Century City law offices weren't just beautiful, they were blissfully *familiar*. Even the smell was just right—a combination of leather, wood and musty paper with a hint of carpet freshener thrown in for good measure.

She liked everything about the location—the floor-to-ceiling windows, the graduated sizes of offices which clearly spelled out authority, the amazing law library, even the little man who'd gruffly directed her to visitor parking in the cavernous underground lot beneath the building. She liked how everyone wore suits and was busy doing things and that there wasn't a fish in sight. She didn't even mind that just like in San Francisco, she was sitting in the middle of active earthquake faults and that, should a decent-size tremor occur, the building was going to sway like a theme-park ride.

Jill shifted her Tumi briefcase, the one she'd bought herself on her last promotion, to her left hand and squared her shoulders as her escort paused in front of a large, carved double door.

"First names," the woman told her with a smile, "but Donald, never Don or Donnie."

"Thanks."

The HR director shook her head. "I'm the one who's grateful. You have an incredible résumé and you present yourself so well. We would be delighted to have you join us."

"Thank you." She put her hand on the door and pushed it open, then stepped into the privileged office of the senior partner.

The open office had been paneled in rich wood. The Oriental carpet underfoot had probably been handmade nearly a century before. Jill knew all about the dangers of navigating old rugs in high heels, so she kept much of her weight on her toes.

She crossed to the massive desk where Donald Ericsson rose and offered his hand.

He was a few inches taller than her, late fifties, with graying hair and thin features. He looked pleasant enough but there was plenty of steel in his gaze.

"I'm glad you came down on such short notice, Jill," he said. "Everyone has been very impressed with you."

"I've enjoyed meeting the team," she told him sincerely. Back-to-back interviews with *eight* employees had only exhilarated her. She could see herself working here, fitting in, climbing the law ladder. She had this fantasy—okay, it was completely crazy, but one day—maybe—she would like to be a judge. L.A. had about four billion or so, so there was definitely room for one more.

"Let's get comfortable," Donald said, motioning to a grouping of leather furniture in the corner of his office. "Would you like coffee?"

"No, thanks," she said as she walked across the rug. "I'm on cup twelve or so. If I had any more caffeine in my system, you could use me as an energy source."

He chuckled and waited until she was seated before lowering himself into a club chair. "What do you think of our law firm?" he asked.

"I'm so impressed, especially with the level of commitment you have from your associates and partners, especially in terms of satisfying your multinational clients. I worked with several Japanese companies when I was in San Francisco."

"I read that, and to be honest, Jill, that's what attracted us to you. We need more expertise in that area."

As he spoke, she nodded to show she was listening, but as her head bobbed, she caught sight of something shiny out of the corner of her eye. What on earth?

Carefully, slowly, she shifted in her seat and glanced to her right.

Oh…my…God.

No way. She returned her attention to Donald, but it was impossible to focus. This was *not* happening.

He chuckled. "You noticed her. Isn't she a beauty?"

"Yes. Amazing."

"She is. I harpooned her myself off the coast of Mexico about fifteen years ago. Bet you haven't seen anything like her before."

Jill didn't know what to say. The stuffed swordfish hung in a place of honor, right above the door. As for not seeing one like that before, she would be willing to swear that the one in her office was the twin or at least a sibling.

"Do you fish a lot?" she asked.

He grinned. "It's more of a passion with me. Some partners prefer to conduct business on a golf course. Give me a powerful boat, a couple of tanks of diesel and I say, let's take on the world."

"Sounds exciting," she said, trying not to giggle. Imagine coming so far only to find herself in a very upscale version of Dixon and Son.

EMILY CURLED UP in the kitchen chair, her knees pulled to her chest, Elvis on the table by her shoulder. Her dad chopped tomatoes for the salad and dumped them into the bowl.

Watching him was different than watching her mom, she thought. Mom made cooking look easy and fun. She talked and laughed a lot, letting Emily help. But her dad always scowled and seemed to work really hard at making everything come out. Everyone always talked about how great boys were and a lot of people said they were better and smarter than girls, but Emily didn't think so. There was a lot of stuff boys couldn't do at all.

"I'm not working on Saturday," he said, when he'd finished with the last tomato and reached for a red pepper. "I thought we could go sailing together."

She'd been about to point out that her shirt was more

orange than red, but the thought flew right out of her head. They'd seen boats today, when she and Bev had been at the beach. Boats with big, white sails racing across the water.

"On the ocean?" she asked, too excited to pretend it didn't matter.

He glanced at her over his shoulder and grinned. "I'm not sure we could get a whole sailboat in a pool, so we're pretty much left with the ocean."

"You know how?"

"I've captained a boat or two in my time. A lady named Wilma at my work owns a sailboat and she said we could borrow it. Sound like fun?"

"Yeah." She glanced at her pet rhino. "I guess Elvis shouldn't come. He could fall overboard and get lost."

"Good point. Even the small life vest would be too big for him."

She squirmed in her seat, thinking about how much fun sailing would be. "Can I make the boat go?"

"Sure." He finished with the pepper, then carried the salad to the table.

Emily had already set it, carefully putting out plates and napkins and forks. She and her dad each had a glass for milk.

He crossed to the refrigerator and pulled out the chicken dish Bev had given him earlier. It was wrapped in plastic and ready for the microwave. Emily noticed the red sauce that had been poured over the whole thing.

Looking at the sauce made her feel kind of bad.

At Bev's or when they went out, she ate whatever she wanted, but when she was with her dad, she still made sure her food matched her clothes. She didn't think Bev had told him, but she wasn't sure. Would he be mad if he found out? Would he tell her mom?

Emily didn't like thinking about that. She didn't like feeling funny inside. Maybe she should say something to him. Maybe...

"I like being in Los Lobos," he said unexpectedly. "I like my new job. It's different from what I did before."

"You mean because you were a cop and now you're a sheriff?"

He punched numbers into the microwave and pushed the start button, then turned to face her.

"That's some of it. Where I worked before was different. There were more bad people. I didn't like dealing with them. Do you remember how I worked a lot of hours?"

She remembered him being gone. She remembered him and her mom fighting about all the times he wasn't home. She nodded slowly.

"You were tired a lot. Mommy used to say we had to be quiet so you could rest."

He leaned against the counter. "Something bad happened at my work, Em. A man I worked with died."

She stared at him. No one had told her. She thought about his friends—the ones he'd brought home. The one she hadn't seen in a long time. "Uncle Mark?"

He closed his eyes briefly. "Yeah."

"Oh."

She didn't know what to say. She'd met Uncle Mark a few times and he'd always been nice to her. He was dead now, but she didn't really know what dead meant. Gone. Not coming back. Was there more than that?

"Were you sad?" she asked.

"For a long time. I couldn't stop thinking about what happened—how he'd died. I'd been there."

Emily shivered. She didn't want to see anyone die. It sounded too scary.

He folded his arms across his chest. "Deep inside, a part of me got real quiet. Like being asleep. I knew that if I woke that part up, I would think about Mark being gone and I'd get sad and I didn't want to. So I let it stay sleeping. But by letting that one piece be asleep, I couldn't really see what was happening around me. That's when you and Mom left."

Emily leaned back in the chair. She didn't want to talk about this. She didn't like the way she felt icky inside.

"It's okay," she mumbled.

"No, it's not. I'm sorry, Em. When I realized what had happened, that you were gone, I wanted to bring you back. But that sleeping part of me made it hard."

Her eyes burned and she bit hard on her lower lip. She didn't want him to say he was sorry. She wanted him to tell her how much he loved her. How he wanted to be with her every day.

"I'm all awake now," he said. "I'm glad we're together. I want things to be different."

She shook her head, not sure how to tell him they couldn't *ever* be different. Not if he hadn't missed her more than anything. Not if he didn't tell her how much he loved her.

She hurt inside, like a big hole had opened up in her chest. She felt scared and small.

"I want things like they were," she said before she could stop herself. She stood and glared at him. "I wish I could be with Mommy instead of you." Mommy, who told her how important she was all the time.

Her dad didn't say anything. She watched his face change and knew she'd hurt him real bad. So bad she got even more scared, and the hole inside of her threatened to swallow her up. She started to cry and, rather than let him know, she ran out of the room.

Her heart ached so much, because whatever she might have said, she knew that while she did want to be with her mom, she liked being with her dad, too. But he didn't know that anymore. And maybe now he was going to send her away.

JILL ARRIVED BACK in Los Lobos around ten. After her interview, she'd treated herself to an afternoon of shopping and then a nice dinner before driving north. While the BMW might not have been her idea of how to spend sixty-five thousand dollars, she had to admit it was a pretty fabulous road car. Cruise control was the only thing that kept her from zipping along at ninety.

Despite her bad parking in the Century City parking garage, the enchanted vehicle was still scratch-, ding- and dent-free.

"Talk about a miracle," she said as she turned onto her street and pulled up in front of the house.

As she parked, she noticed a shadow on the front porch. The shadow stirred and rose, becoming a man she instantly recognized. Talk about an adrenaline rush, she thought, as she stepped out into the night and headed for Mac. He was just the thing she needed as a pick-me-up after the long drive.

She'd pulled off her panty hose and kicked off her high heels before leaving Los Angeles. The grass was cool on her feet as she approached the porch.

"Are you lost?" she asked. "You live next door."

"I know. I wanted to hear how things went. You look good."

She glanced down at her suit, then dropped her panty hose and pumps on the stairs. "Clothes make the woman and all that." She tugged the pins from her hair and shook the strands free. "What's up?" she asked as she sat on the top step and patted the space next to her.

"Nothing." He sank onto the painted wood. "How was L.A.?"

"Interesting."

"Did you like the law firm?"

"The senior partner had a giant stuffed fish in his office. Am I being punished or what?"

He smiled. "You're kidding."

"Not even close. It stared at me through the whole interview. I have no idea what I said." She tugged down her hem. "I don't think you were sitting out here waiting for me to hear the particulars about my trip. What's going on?"

"Nothing. Everything. I'm trying not to get drunk."

"Speaking as someone who was recently in that condition, it sounds more fun than it is." She angled toward him. "Want to tell me what happened to make that seem like an option?"

He raised his hands to chest level, then let them fall. "Emily."

Jill sighed. She knew his daughter wasn't making things easy. Not that she knew enough about what had happened to judge.

"Want to talk about it?" she asked.

"There's not much to say. She told me she's sorry she's here and that she wishes she were with her mother."

Jill winced. "She loves you, Mac, but she's a little girl. Her world doesn't always make sense to her. I'm sure, as much as she's enjoying her time here, she's also bound to miss her mom."

"I believe everything you're saying. I know it's logical. I've even been thinking I should call Carly and ask her if she wants to see Em some Saturday. But I'm scared, too. What if Emily doesn't want to come back to me? What if she convinces her mother to never let me see her again?"

"Oh, Mac."

Jill took his hand and squeezed it. She couldn't think of any words to help him right now. He knew what he was saying was crazy, but that didn't lessen the impact of the words.

"I love her so much," he said quietly. "She's the best thing that ever happened to me."

"I know."

He was a good man, she thought. Nothing like Lyle, who refused to take responsibility for anything. Mac cared about Emily and the town and he believed in doing the right thing. Plus he was totally hot.

"What are you thinking?" he asked.

"That I had good taste even when I was eighteen and tried to get you to sleep with me."

He chuckled. "I would question your taste for wanting to be with a guy who was too drunk to notice you were naked. I can't tell you how much I regret that."

Her, too. "It was a never-to-be-repeated opportunity."

Or was it? Jill had a sudden flash of inspiration and she knew she had to act on it before she lost her nerve. She stood, pulled up her skirt to mid-thigh, then turned toward Mac and straddled his lap.

He looked more than a little startled, but he didn't pull back. "Want to explain yourself?" he asked, even as he rested his hands on her hips and settled her more firmly on his groin.

They were close enough to kiss. Her legs pressed against his. Heat filled her, making her want and need and melt.

"You can't seriously be confused about my intentions," she murmured as she put her hands on his shoulders. "Weren't you the one saying something about a rain check?"

As she spoke, she felt him get hard. It took all of three seconds. She rubbed against him, making them both breathe a little faster.

"We talked about this not being a good idea," he said, his voice low and strained.

She nipped at his jaw. "Did we? I don't remember." She leaned closer. "You need to let your thing about my father go. Trust me, you're not his type. He's deeply into younger women, if you'll excuse the pun."

Mac chuckled. "Thanks for the tip." He cupped her face and stared into her eyes. "I don't have a hell of a lot to offer anyone right now."

She rotated her center over his erection. "All evidence to the contrary?"

"You know what I mean."

"I do." She brushed her fingertips against his mouth. "I'm not looking for anything long-term, Mac, and neither are you. I know you're worried about your daughter finding out so I promise to be quiet and leave long before dawn. Maybe it's the night. Maybe it's all those unfulfilled desires from when I was younger. Maybe it's how you make me feel when we're together. Regardless of the reason, I want this. I think you do, too. Wouldn't a smart man simply shut up and kiss me?"

"Hell of a good idea," he said, and did just that.

The openmouthed kiss was hungry, hot and tempting. Jill let herself be swept away by the feel of his tongue brushing against her lower lip, then slipping inside. He moved his hands up and down her back before returning them to her hips, where he took control of the rhythm of her pulsing movements.

With his fingers rubbing against the fabric of her suit, he slowed her way down, but exaggerated the movements so she slid forward and back against his hardness. As she drew back, he pushed up, bringing him in direct contact with about two million of her favorite nerve cells.

She sucked in a breath, then clamped her lips around his tongue. In response, he surged against her.

Between her panties she felt herself go from damp and intrigued to wet and ready. Her breasts swelled, her nipples got hard and the need to be naked and making love right that second nearly overwhelmed her.

He broke the kiss and slid down her jaw to her throat. Soft, damp kisses made her skin pucker, her body tense and her head loll back. She moved closer to give him plenty of access, at the same time she shrugged out of her jacket and thrust her breasts forward as suggestively as she could.

She loved that the man got it in one. His hands moved from her hips to her waist to her rib cage. Higher and higher until he—

In the distance a car door slammed, then an engine started. Jill resurfaced long enough to realize they were on her front porch, under the light, in full view of anyone who wanted to watch.

Mac dropped his hands to her legs and squeezed. "May I suggest a change of location? My room?"

"You betcha."

She scooted off him and stood. After putting her jacket, stockings, shoes and purse inside the house, she took his hand and followed him across the two lawns and up the front porch into his house.

There were only a few lights on in the living room and hall. Mac ignored them and headed directly for the stairs. She tiptoed after him, trying not to make any noise or think too much about what they were about to do. She didn't want to risk getting herself out of the mood.

At the top of the stairs, he pulled her close and kissed her.

"I need to check on Em," he whispered. "Meet me in bed?"

"Sure," she said when he pointed to a half-open door at the end of the hall.

Jill made her way inside and clicked on a light. The room was fairly basic. Bed, nightstand, dresser, TV. She debated what to do next. Start getting naked? Make herself comfortable on the bed? Pull off just her panties so they could do it like animals?

Mac returned before she could decide.

"She's sleeping," he said in a low voice as he closed and locked the door behind him. A slow smile pulled at the corners of his mouth. "And here I had this fantasy about you letting me redeem myself."

"In what way?"

He crossed to her and pulled her hard against him. "If you'd been naked, I would have proven how much I wanted to make up for what happened last time."

"I thought about taking my clothes off, but it seemed a little forward."

"Next time," he breathed, and kissed her.

Next time? She let the delightful promise sink into her consciousness as she gave in to the seduction of his kiss. As he teased and delighted her mouth and tongue, she felt his fingers unfasten the button at the top of the zipper. The metal teeth gave way, then the skirt slipped to the floor. He tugged at the lace elastic of her panties, soon freeing her of them, as well. Which left her standing in her blouse and bra.

Gently he pushed against her until she took a step back, then another until they were up against the mattress. He turned so, when they sat, she was in front of him and he behind, her bare bottom nestled against his crotch. Unfortunately, he was still wearing jeans, but the proximity was nice.

"You're so beautiful," he murmured as he reached around her for the buttons on her blouse. "Delicate, feminine. Sexy."

"The last one is my favorite," she admitted as he pulled open the silk blouse but didn't remove it.

"You're a huge turn-on. You know that, right?"

Not even on a good day, but she was willing to be convinced.

He reached between her breasts for the catch on her bra. She'd never had a man do this from behind her, pressed against her back, both of them watching. She felt his chin on her shoulder, his breath on her cheek. The bra hook released and the cups slipped back to reveal her modest curves.

She was about to apologize for them when he groaned low in his throat and covered her breasts with his hands.

There was something in the way he touched her—sensually, almost reverently. As if her breasts had somehow made his day. Which she would have thought was crazy if she hadn't heard his intake of breath and felt his erection surge against her.

He rubbed his palms against her nipples, which was so delicious that she forgot to think, then he dropped one hand between her legs.

There was too much, she thought hazily as he slipped between her curls into the slick, hungry heat. Too many sensations, too many things to watch. He moved his left hand from breast to breast while the fingers of his right explored her, slipping inside, pulling out, then centering on that place right above her opening.

Her chest tightened as all her muscles tensed. He quickly moved her long hair aside and began to nibble on her neck. Thumb and forefinger teased her tight, sensitive nipples. Between her legs he circled around and around. Sensations met, grew, exploded until every part of her body was aroused and on fire and she could only breathe her way through the pleasure. Faster and faster and more and more until her eyes drifted closed and she gave herself up to the—

"Oh, Mac," she gasped as her body convulsed into orgasm. She clung to him, her hands reaching behind her to grab his hips as she spread her legs more and pushed against his touch, wanting more, wanting it harder and harder and…

The contractions claimed her again. She shuddered and breathed and lost herself in all that he did to her body. When the last waves had faded, she surfaced to find him still gently kissing her neck and rubbing between her legs.

"Wow," she murmured.

He chuckled. "I like wow."

As he spoke he stretched out on the bed, drawing her

down with him. She turned so she lay on top of him. Her hair spilled down around them both. He was still hard and despite what had just happened, she found herself rubbing against him.

His blue eyes darkened with passion. "I'd like to do that inside of you."

"Mmm, sounds good."

She straddled his hips, then pushed up so she could shrug out of her blouse and bra. He fumbled with his belt.

"Maybe I could get naked," he said as he unfastened his jeans.

"You do that."

He grinned. "You're going to have to move."

She liked looking down at him and feeling his hands bump the inside of her thighs as he pushed at the denim.

"Maybe I don't want to."

"If you don't, I can't be inside."

As if to demonstrate the plus side of actual entry, he slid one finger inside of her and rotated it.

She sank down, pushing him deeper. Her muscles quivered.

"Okay," she said, sliding off him. "Good point. Hurry."

He kicked off his shoes, then pushed down jeans, briefs and socks in one quick movement. "Top drawer," he said. "Condoms."

Yikes. Protection. She was still on the Pill, but this wasn't safe married sex.

Thank God, she thought as she pulled out the unopened box and broke the seal before pulling out a condom. Married sex hadn't been nearly this exciting and, what with Lyle and his chickie collection, not all that safe.

She turned back to find a very naked Mac lunging for her. He grabbed her around the waist and gently tossed her onto her back. She landed with a bounce and a giggle. She handed over the condom. He bent over and kissed her, not even watching while he slid on the protection, which she thought was a neat trick. Then he was between her legs and things went from funny to fabulous with the first thrust.

He filled her until she thought she might have to scream from how good it was. The feel of his body, the fierce possessiveness of his kiss, the slick friction as he slid in and out in a rhythm designed to make her faint.

It was good. It was better than good, she thought, as she grabbed his hips and drew him all the way in. Then she lost it in a release so unexpected and powerful that she was afraid she was going to pass out. Still, she hung on enough to keep climaxing until he stiffened and shuddered, then broke the kiss long enough to whisper her name.

MAC PUT HIS ARM around Jill as she stretched out next to him, her head on his chest. He felt good being next to her. Really good.

"Don't let me fall asleep," she said as she stroked up and down the center of his chest. "That would require too much to explain to both Emily and Bev."

"I don't think Bev would mind."

"Probably not. If anything, she'd want details."

He grimaced. "I don't want to know if you tell her."

She shifted so she could rest her chin on his chest and grin at him. "Shy?"

"Scared, as any rational male would be. Guys don't want to know how much women tell each other. We think it's weird and a little threatening."

"Afraid we'll compare?"

He chuckled. "Of course."

She sighed and her expression softened. "Oh, honey, you don't have to worry on that account. You would definitely come in first on my list."

"Yeah?"

She nodded.

He fingered a strand of her hair. "How long's the list?"

Her eyes widened, then slammed shut. "Let's not go there."

"Why not? Come on, Jill. You can't have played around that much. I happen to know I'm rebound guy after Lyle, but what about before?"

She opened her eyes. "All right, but first why don't we talk about how my father would feel if he knew what we'd done?"

He feigned being punched, then rubbed his chin with his free hand. "That one hurt."

"Poor baby." She kissed his cheek.

"Fine. We won't talk about your past," he said.

"No, we can. There's not much to say. You threw up the first time you saw me naked."

"I wish you'd quit bringing that up. I feel like a complete idiot."

"Good. Eventually we'll be even."

He touched her shoulder. "Seriously, Jill. I'm sorry. If I'd been sober enough to take advantage of you…" What? Would their lives have been different? He thought maybe they might have been.

"It's okay," she told him. "But Evan really cemented things for me."

He didn't like the sound of that. "Who's Evan?"

"My first boyfriend at college. He was sweet and sensitive and a lot of fun."

"I hate him," Mac grumbled.

"You shouldn't, at least not for that. The first time *he* saw me naked, he announced that he was gay. Apparently my body provided the revelation he needed to figure it all out."

Mac stared at her. She looked just hurt and embarrassed enough for him to know she was telling the truth.

"No way," he said, because he couldn't help himself.

She nodded. "Pretty amazing, huh? The first guy who sees me naked throws up. The second turns gay. Is it any wonder I thought I was in love with the only guy who didn't react badly to the idea of having sex with me?"

He rolled her onto her back and stared into her eyes. She couldn't be saying…it wasn't possible that…

"Lyle is the only other guy you've slept with?"

"Counting you? Yes."

He didn't know what to say. "But you're incredible. That's crazy."

"I know the odds of it are impressive, but there we are. My life." She picked at the edge of the sheet. "I think it's a breast thing. As in I don't have any."

"You have beautiful breasts." He loved them. Their perfect shape, the way her nipples got so tight. The soft skin, the color. Just thinking about them got him hard.

"They're too small," she said.

"Large breasts are overrated."

She smiled. "You're not a bad liar. I like that."

He moved close and rubbed himself against her. "Does that feel like a lie?"

She raised her eyebrows. "Actually it does not. All that for me?"

"You and your perfect breasts." He tugged at the sheet. "Now what does a guy have to do around here to get another shot at proving his point?"

She wrapped her arms around him and pulled him close. "Anything he wants."

JILL ARRIVED at her office shortly before nine. Despite her lack of sleep and sneaking home shortly after four in the morning, she felt alive, alert and perfectly fulfilled.

Last night had been spectacular. Mac was even more amazing in bed than she'd possibly hoped. He'd made her feel things that probably weren't legal, not that she was going to complain. As she unlocked the front door and stepped into the reception area, she found she didn't even mind the fish.

"Good morning," she said to the nearest one and patted its scaly back. "Everybody sleep well?"

Still smiling and happy, she made her way to the blinking answering machine and pushed the button. While the machine informed her she had two messages, she made a mental note to make sure she was available around eleven. Bev was coming by so they could take the 545 to the parking lot by the dump. Surely all the gravel there would do *something* to the paint job.

Thirty seconds later she didn't know if she should laugh, dance, or simply give up. What was it with her life?

Donald, the fisherman/attorney/senior partner, had called to offer her a job, and another firm from L.A. wanted to talk to her about an interview.

CHAPTER TWELVE

THE MORNING WAS PERFECT, and driving through town seemed like a great way to spend a piece of his day. Mac left the beaches and turned toward the center of town. It was almost eleven and already the temperature was near eighty. Hot weather meant plenty of customers at the vending carts by the boardwalk and lots of tourists too enchanted to head back to the big city.

The jails were empty, the court schedule light and there were very few clouds on the horizon. For the most part—life was good.

Except for Emily, Mac thought. In the past week he'd thought a lot about what he'd overheard when Jill had taken his daughter for the evening, and he was still at a loss as to how to win his daughter's trust. He loved her with every fiber of his being, but that wasn't enough. He vowed to keep trying to convince her he would always be there for her.

"Keep showing up," he told himself. She was eight—didn't actions speak louder than words?

Their day of sailing had been great. They'd laughed and she'd done a hell of a job steering the boat. But back at the house, she'd still insisted her food match her clothes. He was running out of ideas.

As he turned left, he passed the offices of Dixon

and Son. Tina stepped out as he drove by. She waved. He wondered what errands Jill's secretary had at that time of day and if she would bother returning.

Jill. Now that was one part of his life that worked. Good times, great conversation, lots of laughs, all in the package of an extraordinarily beautiful woman with plenty of smarts. Their night together had been one for the record books and he sure wouldn't mind a repeat performance. It would have to be soon, he reminded himself. Jill seemed to be getting job offers and interview requests three times a day. The odds were she would accept one and be gone.

He didn't want to think about that, so he turned on the street by the high school and pulled up by the football practice field. It was too early in the summer for the team to be working out, but he knew what they'd look like. Awkward and out of shape those first couple of weeks, he thought with a grin, remembering his own days playing football. He and Riley had thought they were God's gift to the sport, not to mention every female within a fifty-mile radius.

Life had been easier then. School didn't matter—it was just a place to be a star and pick up girls. He and Riley had kept count, both being young enough to be more into volume than quality. Then Mac had stolen the judge's Caddy and gone for the joyride that had changed his life. Riley hadn't appreciated the differences. The friendship had ended in harsh words and a couple of well-placed blows.

Mac rubbed his jaw and wondered where Riley was now. His name still stood in the center of town—Whitefield Bank and Trust, established in 1948. Riley's uncle still ran things there. If Mac was to guess, he would put money on the feud between Riley and his uncle being alive and well. Riley had never been one to forgive and forget.

Mac shrugged off the past and put the car in gear. As he drove past the front of the high school, he saw a crew of teenagers painting the fence of a house across the street. A sign stuck in the ground read Los Lobos Town Beautification Project. Call And See If Your Home Qualifies.

"What the hell," he muttered as he stopped the car. Beautification project? That was news to him.

He climbed out and greeted the teenagers, then walked to the front door of the house and knocked.

"Sheriff Mackenzie Kendrick, ma'am," he said when an elderly woman cracked her door. "How are you?"

"Sheriff." She beamed at him and waved him inside. "If this is my day to be courted by the city, then I have to tell you, I like it. First those young folks show up and ask if they can paint my fence. As if I'm going to say no. They swear it's all part of some plan and that they wouldn't even accept a tip." Her smiled faded. "You haven't come to tell me they were lying, have you?"

"No. Of course not. I'm asking about the project though. I hadn't heard of it."

Furniture filled the entryway, forcing Mac up against the half-open door.

"Me, either," the woman said. "Wait. They gave me a flyer. Let me get it."

She disappeared into an equally crowded living

room and returned with a neon-pink piece of paper. He scanned the text as a fluffy gray cat wove around his legs, depositing large clumps of hair on his slacks.

He reread the offer to paint fence, trim lawns and shrubs, all for free for those unable to afford it on their own, all in the name of making Los Lobos "the paradise we all know it to be."

That's a bunch of crap, Mac thought, not sure who could be behind it.

"Mind if I take this with me?" he asked.

"Not at all." The woman smiled again. "Now you be sure to let me know when you city folks want to work on my roof."

"I'll do that, ma'am," he said as he stepped over the cat and made a quick escape.

After brushing off most of the cat hair, he started his car. Was the mayor behind this? Did Franklin think he could buy votes by doing work for folks? Mac wouldn't be surprised, but he happened to know Franklin wasn't exactly rolling in money. Oh, sure, there was a trust fund, but it belonged to his wife, and Mrs. Yardley kept her husband on a short leash. She had a reputation for being both difficult and cheap. Not exactly a combination to make a man's life easier.

The thought of Franklin Yardley getting hell from his wife brightened Mac's day. He drove toward the office, stopping only to make a quick stop at the coffeehouse on the corner.

Once inside, his good mood faded as he saw Rudy Casaccio and Mr. Smith already in line by the counter.

As Mac watched, Rudy paid for two coffees with a twenty, then put the change into the tip jar.

"Oh, Mr. Casaccio," Jen Brockway said with a smile. "You're too kind."

"Are you kidding?" Rudy asked. "You don't charge enough here. You have the best coffee I've ever tasted and if Mr. Smith and I keep eating your Danish every day, we're not going to fit in our car."

Jen Brockway, nearly sixty and with a reputation for being surly and difficult, actually batted her eyes at Rudy. Right then Mac swore off Danish.

"Coffee. Black," he said as Rudy stepped aside.

"Morning, Sheriff," the other man said.

"Morning." What he wanted to say instead was *Get out of town,* but what was the point? Rudy wasn't breaking the law. Not yet.

Jen poured him his coffee and handed it over. He started to pass her a dollar, but she shook her head.

"No, Sheriff. Mr. Casaccio has started an account here. He's asked me to put all purchases by you and your employees on it." She smiled again.

All this happiness made Mac uneasy.

"Isn't that incredibly generous?" she asked.

Mac wanted to growl his protest. Instead, he did his best to look pleasant and appreciative. "It's mighty neighborly of Mr. Casaccio," he said in his best Nick-at-Nite Andy-Griffith voice. "But to keep things all aboveboard, I think it's best if we continue to pay for our coffee." He looked at Rudy. "We wouldn't want people getting the wrong idea about things, would we?"

Rudy had set down his coffee. Now he raised both

hands in a gesture of surrender. "Just trying to do the right thing," he said easily. "I want to be a good citizen."

"I'll do my best to keep that in mind."

Mac took his coffee and left. As he returned to his car, he thought about the beautification project. No way the mayor could get his hands on that kind of money... unless someone other than his wife funded him.

He swore and headed directly for the office.

"Wilma," he called as he walked through the front door.

The older woman looked up from her desk. "What?"

He jerked his head toward his office. When she'd followed him inside, he closed the glass door and handed her the flyer.

She read it, then let it fall to his desk. "I'd heard about this."

"Is Rudy Casaccio behind it?"

"From what I can tell, he's been dropping a lot of money in town." She shifted, then shrugged. "I'm sorry, boss. I know you don't trust the guy. The thing is he's made a lot of people very happy. Doing this kind of stuff and more. Some foster kid's dog got hit by a car. The family couldn't afford the surgery so they were going to put it to sleep. Rudy found out and paid for everything."

Great. Just what he needed. A do-gooder from the Mafia. "He has a plan," Mac said through clenched teeth. "I can feel it. Men like him don't change."

Wilma cleared her throat. "There's more," she said, "and you're not going to like it."

"What?"

"He's been dating Bev. You know—the lady you have taking care of Emily."

"HE HASN'T DONE anything wrong," Bev said in what Mac figured was a reasonable voice.

The thing was, he didn't want to be reasonable. Not where his daughter was concerned.

"He's a criminal, Bev," Mac told her as he paced the length of her front porch. "I don't want Emily around him."

Jill's aunt leaned against the porch rail. "I hardly take her with me on dates, if that's what you're asking. We've had lunch a couple of times and I've left Emily with Jill. I see him in the evening, when you have Emily."

She threw up her hands. "Why am I telling you this? My personal life isn't any of your business."

"It is when you date men like Rudy Casaccio."

Why didn't anyone get it? Why was he the only one to see the trouble coming?

"What do you want, Mac? Are you asking me to choose? I love your daughter and I'm enjoying my time with her, but I won't let you dictate how I live my life outside of my time with Emily." She smiled. "You're not my father."

"So you'd let him dictate?"

"No, but I'd probably pretend to listen more."

"Great."

Was he being unreasonable?

"What about that damn social worker?" he asked. "He's going to have a shit-fit if he finds out my child's baby-sitter is dating someone known to be involved with organized crime."

"Are you saying Rudy has a criminal record?"

"No." Mac had checked. "He's too smart for that."

"Does he have a record at all?"

"No."

"I see." She stared at him. "So you could be wrong about him."

"I'm not."

"But you could be."

He had a feeling in his gut and that feeling had never let him down. Sometimes he wondered if it was the reason Mark had died instead of him.

"What do you want to do?" Bev asked. "Find someone else to take care of Emily?"

The question made Mac want to squirm. He liked Bev. Even more important, she liked his daughter and was good for her. He knew Em had a good time with her.

Bev's green eyes darkened. "I would never do anything to endanger your daughter. She means the world to me."

"I know." Why couldn't Bev simply stop seeing Rudy? But he knew better than to ask. "Will you keep him away from her?"

"Yes. I promise."

There was something in the way she said the word, as if it were a vow she would keep with her life. The tight knot in his gut relaxed a little. Now if only he could get Rudy out of town.

"So I'VE BEEN THINKING this through," Mr. Harrison said as he leaned back in his chair and kicked at the fishing net in front of her desk. "You're right about the fence. It's been there a long time and it makes sense that the courts wouldn't make anyone take it down."

Jill blinked, then glanced around the room wondering if there was a hidden camera somewhere and she was about to be on a reality show.

"Okay," she said slowly. "So, what's the plan?"

"I thought I'd let my new neighbors buy that bit of land from me. You know, for a real fair price. Maybe they could make payments over a few years."

Delighted by the turn of events, Jill couldn't help smiling. "You've spoken with them?"

"A couple of times. Juan and his wife are good people. Whoee, can his mother-in-law put together a peach cobbler."

Under the privacy of her desk, Jill kicked off her high heels and wiggled her toes. "You're being very fair and decent about this," she said.

"They're young folks, just starting out. I don't want to make things hard for them." He stood. "So you'll draw up the papers?"

"Sure thing. By Friday."

"Good. Now don't go charging them a lot of interest. Let's tie the loan to the prime rate. That should stay plenty low. And spread out the payments so they're not strapped for cash."

"Absolutely." She slipped on her shoes and stood. "It's been a pleasure."

"You bet."

He shook her hand and left.

Jill waited until she was alone—because Tina was gone again—and did a little dance around the room. Yeah and double yeah for good food and neighbors willing to take a chance on an old man. She had to give Mr. Harrison credit, too, for not being too stubborn about the whole thing. Now if only her other cases would wrap up this easily, along with a couple of wills and Pam Whitefield's suit over the nonalien landing house.

"I'm not going to think about that," she told herself.

The phone rang, interrupting her celebration. She skittered over to the desk and picked it up.

"Jill Strathern."

"Hey, it's Gracie. How are things?"

"Good." Jill sank into the chair Mr. Harrison had vacated. "I solved one of most difficult cases this morning."

"Congrats. Any news on the job front?"

Jill told her about the fish offer from Los Angeles. "And you?" she asked. "What's going on in your world?"

"I'm going to be in *People* magazine."

Jill sprang to her feet and shrieked. "You're kidding? That's so great!"

"I know. It's a whole issue about weddings and there's going to be a page featuring my wedding cakes. Do you know what this means?"

"Fame, fortune and more orders than you can handle."

"Exactly." Gracie started laughing. "Isn't it the best? The phone is already ringing. I've had to redo my baking schedule and everything."

Jill knew how hard her friend had worked at her business. "You've earned this."

"I hope so. There's just this one thing…."

"What?"

"Vivian's engaged."

Gracie spoke as if her baby sister had just caught the plague.

"Why is that a problem?" Jill sank down onto the chair and groaned. "Oh, God. She's not marrying Riley, is she?"

"What? No. The groom is this guy she met in college. But here's the thing, Jill. Vivian has always wanted a hometown wedding. You know—the country club, white chairs on the lawn, the whole thing."

"Sounds nice. So what's the problem?"

"If she gets married there, I'll have to come home."

Jill tried not to laugh, but she couldn't help it.

"You don't sound very sympathetic," Gracie accused.

"Sorry. I know this is terrible and all…" She cleared her throat. "Honestly, I don't get the problem. It's been years, Gracie. Almost no one remembers what happened."

"Uh-huh. You said I was a legend."

"No, I said that fourteen-year-old girl was a legend. You're a different person."

"I am, but I don't like the idea of spending two weeks being tortured about my past."

"You won't be. Besides, it's not as if Riley ever came back. If he lived here, I could completely understand your reluctance, but no one's heard from him in years."

"Good point."

"And I want to see you."

"The wedding isn't until next spring. You'll be long gone."

"You got that right," Jill said. "But I can come visit."

"Good. I'll need someone to protect me from my past."

"Count on it."

They chatted for a few more minutes, then hung up. Jill moved around to her side of the desk and pulled out an envelope of papers that had arrived that morning. She scanned the property settlement Lyle had proposed and took great satisfaction in drawing a line through every page and writing "no" across them. Then she turned to her computer and started her own settlement schedule...starting with the car.

"THIS IS ALL your fault," Mac said as he leaned against the porch railing.

Jill thought he had to be kidding, but one look at his stern, accusing expression told her he meant it.

She pushed against the porch with her bare foot and relaxed into the swing.

"What did I do?" she asked.

He glanced past her to the screen leading into the living room. Emily was in the family room at the back of the house, watching a Disney movie, but still he lowered his voice.

"They came here because of you," he told her. "Why don't you send them away?"

"They're not doing anything wrong. Mac, has it occurred to you that you're overreacting about Rudy and Mr. Smith? They just want to be a part of the town."

"Why?" he asked her. "What's so great about Los Lobos?"

"I thought you liked it here."

"I do, but I have specific reasons. Why would two guys from Las Vegas find this hick of a town charming? What's going on?"

"I don't know. Rudy says he likes that it's quiet. I know he likes Bev, she likes him. That should be allowed."

She leaned forward and ignored how sexy Mac looked in jeans and a T-shirt. Like her, he was barefoot. If only he could be naked all over.

"What exactly are they doing that's so bad?" she asked. "Tell me one thing."

"Rudy gave money to Yardley's reelection campaign."

She winced. "Okay, a case could be made to question his judgment, but it's not against the law or anything. So Rudy is helping old ladies with fence painting and he's given a ton of money to the pier restoration? Isn't that good?"

Mac's dark gaze pinned her in place. "People don't change. Rudy is what he has always ever been and eventually it's going to come out. Someone will get hurt."

Jill wanted to have him sit next to her, hold her hand and tell her how amazing their night together had been. She wanted him to whisper the time and place of a rendezvous so they could be together again. She wanted to talk about the stars or kissing or even politics. Just not this.

"You've changed," she pointed out. "Look at how you're worried about Emily and making things right with her."

"I've always loved my daughter," he said. "I have my priorities back on track, but I'm not any different than I was." He walked forward and crouched in front of her. "What about you, Jill? Have you changed? Are you thinking that you want to settle in Los Lobos permanently?"

"Not even on a bet," she said, then realized his point. "But I don't want to change."

"Does Rudy?"

"I don't know. We haven't talked about it."

"So you don't know for sure his motives are altruistic?"

"I…" She pressed her lips together. "No. I don't know."

He stood and returned to the railing. Silence stretched between them. Why on earth were they fighting about Rudy? She searched for a more bonding topic.

"How was your meeting with Hollis?" she asked.

"That little prick. I'm reading this book he gave me

on anger management. That's bad enough, but every time he asks about it, I want to squash him like a bug."

She couldn't help laughing. "Oh, right. So he doesn't have a point about your temper."

He crossed to the swing and sat down next to her. "Do I have a temper?"

Interesting question, she thought, as she recalled their time together. "I've never really seen you angry. You were annoyed a few minutes ago about Rudy, but not really mad."

"Hollis hasn't seen it, either. He assumes, because I'm a cop, that I have a lousy temper. Bastard."

She slid closer and rested her head on his shoulder. "It's just for the summer," she reminded him. "Think about why you're doing all this. You can stand him for a few more weeks."

He took her hand in his and laced their fingers together. "A lot of things are just for the summer. You doing okay?"

She'd been so caught up in the feel of him touching her that she almost missed the question. "Okay about what?"

He smiled a slow, sexy smile that made her tummy clench and her thighs burn.

"Oh, that," she whispered.

"Yeah. *That*."

"I'm good with it."

"Me, too. It's just there was only Lyle, then me."

"I didn't want Lyle to be the only one," she said. "I had some bad luck along the way."

"Yeah, me and the gay guy. You're so smart about everything else, Jill, but I have to tell you, except for me, you have lousy taste in guys."

She chuckled. "You think?"

"Oh, yeah. I should probably give you some pointers. Only I don't want to share."

He leaned close and brushed his mouth against hers. Need swept through her like a tornado, leaving her shaky and aroused.

She wrapped one arm around him, pulling him against her, and put her heart and soul into the kiss. In a matter of seconds they were both breathing hard.

Mac drew back first. Fire flared in his dark eyes. Need tightened his jaw. He looked like a man in some serious pain.

"Emily," she said into the silence.

"Yeah. Just down the hall."

"But if she was at a friend's house..."

"In a heartbeat."

She smiled. "Me, too."

TWO DAYS LATER Mac went looking for Rudy and found him dining with Mr. Smith at Bill's Mexican Grill. The timing probably sucked because he'd just come off another frustrating meeting with Hollis, but he couldn't help himself.

"How are the fajitas?" Mac asked as he pulled out a chair and settled into it.

Mr. Smith glanced at Rudy, who shook his head.

"It's all right," Rudy said. "The sheriff is always welcome. What can I do for you, Mac?"

"You really want to know?"

Rudy waved over the waitress. "Mandy, would get the good sheriff here something to drink. Beer? Margarita?" He pointed to his own frosty, salt-rimmed glass. "They do make a great margarita."

"I'm fine," Mac told the waitress and she left.

Rudy shook his head. "You're acting as if you don't want to be friends, Mac, and I don't understand why. I'm a successful businessman looking for a getaway place. Los Lobos is very appealing. You should be proud."

"I'd prefer you settled somewhere else."

"I know that."

Rudy sipped his drink. While Mr. Smith wore a suit, Rudy had traded in custom tailoring for upscale resort wear.

"I could be good for this town," Rudy said. "Bring in a little money, spruce things up."

"No thanks. We don't need your kind of help, or the strings that go with it."

"Jill was right," Rudy said regretfully. "You don't think a man could change."

Mac felt as if he'd been sucker punched. The blood rushed from his head and the room seemed to tilt.

"What?"

"She was telling me this morning that you didn't believe a man such as myself could change." Rudy shook his head. "I have to tell you, Mac, I'm wounded to my soul. I thought we could be friends."

Mac swore silently. Was that the way it was with Jill? She might be his friend and lover, but she was Rudy's lawyer, and being a lawyer came first with her? Why else would she have shared their private conversation with a scumbag?

"Watch yourself," he told Rudy. "You don't want to step out of line in my town."

Rudy took a bite of rice and chewed. When he'd swallowed, he said, "Is it your town, Mac? I'm not so sure. The mayor and I are real tight, and the residents seem to like what I'm doing. It seems to me that you're the one out of step. Don't you have an election coming up in a couple of months? And don't you need this job to keep custody of your daughter? It seems to me you should be worrying more about making nice than trying to throw around your weight."

Rage poured through Mac. How the hell did Rudy know so much about his life? Had Jill told him? What kind of information would she consider part of her responsibility as Rudy's attorney?

Damn them both.

"If you so much as forget to come to a full stop, I'll haul your ass into jail," Mac said in a low voice. "Do you hear me?"

Rudy looked at him. "You're not a man who gives up, are you?"

"No. And I'm not letting you win this one."

"I'm not sure you have a choice, Mac. Just remember, you have no idea what you're getting involved with. I'll win because I was meant to win."

"Not in my town."

CHAPTER THIRTEEN

JILL IGNORED THE cast on Kim's arm for as long as she could, but when the young woman was barely able to sign the papers releasing the money, she found herself unable to stay quiet.

"What happened?" she asked, nodding at Kim's arm.

"What?" Kim stared at the plaster that ran from the base of her fingers up to her elbow as if she'd never seen it before. "Oh. I, um, fell and slammed my wrist against a stair." As she spoke she nervously tucked blond hair behind her ear, then fumbled with the papers. "Where do I sign?"

"Here." Jill pointed to the spot.

Kim positioned the pen against the loop of the cast by her thumb and scrawled her name.

"Is the baby all right?" Jill asked.

"What?"

"You said you fell. Is the baby all right?"

"Oh." Kim placed her left hand on her stomach. "Yes. She's fine."

"You know you're having a girl?"

For the first time since walking into her office, Kim didn't look afraid. Her whole expression relaxed as she smiled. "Yes, they told me when I had the ultrasound."

"Is your husband excited?" Jill glanced at her notes. "Most men want a boy. Does Andy?"

The fear returned, striking Kim like a bolt of lightning. She shrank back in her seat and swallowed hard. "He, um, he doesn't know. He said he wanted it to be a surprise. I wasn't supposed to ask. You're not going to tell him, are you?"

Jill felt her insides turn over in an uncomfortable combination of pity and anger. She stood and walked around her desk, then crouched in front of Kim.

"You don't have to do this," she said quietly. "Kim, he has no right to hurt you or make you afraid. He's your husband and he's supposed to love you, not terrorize you."

Jill fingered the paperwork on the desk. "You don't have to put this money in your joint checking account. You can take the cashier's check and walk out of here right to a woman's shelter. It's enough to give you and the baby a fresh start. I could drive you there right now. No one would have to know where you are."

Kim pulled back as far as the chair would let her. She shook her head and held up her free hand in a sad gesture of protection.

"I don't know what you're talking about. Andy is a wonderful husband. He loves me."

Jill stood. "He loves you so much he breaks your bones. There's affection to stand by. What happens when the baby is born? He doesn't want a girl, does he? Is he going to blame you? Wonderful husbands don't beat their wives, Kim. They don't make them afraid."

Kim looked away. A single tear rolled down her cheek. "You don't understand. Andy needs me."

Yeah, because where else could he act like a bully? Jill thought grimly.

"What about your needs?" she asked. "What about spending the rest of your life afraid?"

Kim looked at her. "I'm not afraid."

But the fear was there—a tangible beast between them. Jill knew all the psychological theories as to why women stayed, but she'd never been able to wrap her mind around understanding the dynamics. To her it was just plain sad.

"Please, Kim," she said softly. "If not for you, then for the baby. What if he starts beating her?"

Kim turned away, one hand cupping her belly. "He loves the baby as much as I do."

"I see. Will he love the baby the same as he loves you? With his fists?"

Kim stood. "I have to go now. Are we done? When can I get the money?"

Jill didn't know what else to say. Short of kidnapping the woman, she'd run out of options. "It will be transferred the first part of next week. I'll call and let you know when."

Kim picked up her purse. "So I don't have to come back here again?"

Jill hesitated, wanting to make up an excuse to see Kim again, but she knew there wasn't any point. Until Kim was ready to leave, no one could help her.

"Here's my card," she said, pulling out a business card from Dixon and Son. She wrote her aunt's home number on the back. "If you change your mind about anything, call me. It doesn't matter what time. I'll come get you, no questions asked."

She held out the card, but Kim wouldn't take it. Finally Jill tucked it into the other woman's purse. Kim stared at her for a long time.

"He loves me," she said at last. "I'm his world. Why can't you see that?"

"You're his punching bag, Kim. Why can't *you* see that?"

Kim turned and ran from the room. Jill watched her go and knew she'd blown it big time. Dammit all to hell, she thought and picked up the closest law book and hurled it across the room.

She reached for another one, then sank into the chair Kim had vacated.

Tina stepped into the room. "What happened?"

Jill didn't bother looking at her. "Kim was here with a freshly broken wrist. She's what, eight months' pregnant and the bastard is still using her as a punching bag. I don't get it. I seriously don't get it. I can understand the fear, but I told her I'd take her away. Sure, he could find her in Los Lobos, but not if she were in L.A. or San Francisco or even Dallas. She doesn't have to be with him. The inheritance gave her money, so why did she stay?"

Tina didn't say anything. Jill stood and walked around to her side of the desk. She was about to sit down when Tina spoke.

"You care."

It was the last straw. She glared at her secretary.

"Of course I care. What did you think?"

With that, she grabbed her purse and left.

Once on the sidewalk, she wished the car were there. At this point she didn't care about scratches—she would happily deface it herself. Maybe that would help her feel better. How could Kim live like that? How could anyone? She found herself uncomfortably torn between compassion and anger.

Once on the sidewalk, she didn't know where to go. Home? A bar? A quick glance at her watch told her it was barely after ten in the morning. Okay. Maybe not a bar.

Mac, she thought, and started walking toward the sheriff's station. Maybe he could do something about all this. Surely one of the neighbors had seen something or heard something.

In the distance between her office and his, she made and discarded several plans. Everything from kidnapping Kim until the woman came to her senses to having Andy spend some quality time with the anal-probing aliens.

She pushed open the glass door at the sheriff's office and saw Wilma at the counter. "Hi. Is he in?"

The gray-haired woman shrugged. "He's in, but I wouldn't want to see him if I were you. He's not in a very good mood."

"That works for me," Jill said. "I'm pretty pissed off myself."

She walked to Mac's glassed-in office, knocked on

the open door, then stepped in. He was on the phone, his back to her.

"About ten-thirty," he said as he turned slowly. When he saw her, he frowned. "I'll make sure he's there. Uh-huh. Thanks."

When he hung up, he surprised her by not getting up or acting the least bit pleased to see her. They'd seen each other the day before last and things had gone well. Very well.

"Mac?"

"I have a meeting in a couple of minutes. Is there a problem?"

He sounded all business and slightly hostile. She grabbed the door and swung it shut, then moved closer to his desk. "Yes, there's a problem. I want to report a man for beating his wife."

"Did you see the attack?"

"No, but I saw the results."

"What does she say?"

"What most victims in spousal abuse say. 'He loves me.'"

"So you're alleging he beat her."

Her temper flared to life. "Dammit, Mac. Don't play that game with me. We both know what's happening. Why won't you do something?"

"Take it to Wilma. She'll give it to one of the deputies." He reached for a folder on his desk.

She slapped her hand down on top of it and leaned toward him. "I'm taking it to you. What's going on? Are you mad at me?"

"Mad? No. Of course not. I'm annoyed at myself, but that's nothing new."

"I have no idea what we're talking about."

"Not a problem, because I don't have time for a conversation." He stood. "If you'll excuse me?"

"No, I won't. What has happened in the past couple of days to make you act like this?" She mentally raced through the possibilities. "Did you have a run-in with Hollis?"

"No."

He moved around the desk and loomed over her. She told herself he was simply trying to physically intimidate her and while it was working, she wasn't about to let him know.

"But I did have an interesting conversation with your client."

"Which one?"

His blue eyes darkened with temper. "Rudy Casaccio. You know. The one you're always claiming is misunderstood. I hadn't realized the two of you were so close."

He sounded furious and she didn't have a clue as to why. "You don't want me talking to Rudy?"

"Not at all. Talk away. I don't give a rat's ass."

"Okay, look. I'm completely confused. Why are you so angry?"

He narrowed his gaze. "Because I thought I was having a private conversation with my lover and I found out instead I'd been speaking to the defendant's counsel."

"What?"

"Rudy. You told him I didn't think people could

change. What else do you tell him, Jill? What other little secrets do you share?"

"I don't…we never…" She didn't know what to say. Fury bubbled up inside of her until she wanted to bodily throw Mac through the glass door.

"We spoke," she said, her teeth grinding together. "You're right. I mentioned you were concerned about the town in the context of trying to find out how long he was staying and what he was going to do while he was here. He reassured me, and that's when I mentioned you would be difficult to convince because you don't believe people change. That's all."

"Sure. Great. It's all clear now."

"Don't," she said, raising her voice. "Don't patronize me. I would never betray a personal confidence. Your feelings about what the world will and won't do didn't feel like a secret. If I was wrong, I'm sorry."

"Don't be. I get it now. Rudy is your ticket out. How many millions in billing does he bring into a law firm? Two? Three? When you land somewhere, you bring him with you. That's got to be pretty hard for any law firm to resist. In the face of that, how can anyone else matter? My mistake for not seeing that. No wonder you're spending all your time kissing his ass."

"That is so unfair." She planted her hands on her hips. "I refuse to apologize for wanting to return to my real law career and handle something serious and important."

"Important, huh? What? Finding a legal loophole so a corporation doesn't have to pay taxes? There's a profession to be proud of."

"Now you're insulting what I do for a living?"

"Just clearing the air, babe."

Her fingers curled into her palms. "Don't you dare call me babe."

"Hey, why not? We're tight. Aren't I your local source of entertainment? Be sure to stop by before you head out to your next big career move. We can do each other before you go. Because hey, the sex was great."

All the color drained from Jill's face. She opened her mouth, closed it, then turned on her heel and left.

Mac watched her go. The second the glass door closed behind her, his anger and energy spilled away, leaving him feeling slimy and spent.

What the hell had he been thinking? Why had he wanted to hurt Jill? A voice inside whispered, because he'd been hurt, but that didn't make any sense. He'd known the rules when he'd gotten involved with her. That this was temporary—fun between friends. Nothing about that had changed. So why did he feel like shit inside?

He walked into the main office, then to the front desk.

"Jill say anything about a wife beater?" he asked.

Wilma handed him a piece of paper with two names. "Want to tell me what happened?" she asked.

"Nope."

THIRTY MINUTES LATER Mac parked in front of a small bungalow-style house. The place couldn't be more than eight hundred square feet, with a narrow, cracked cement walk leading from the sidewalk to the front door.

The paint had long since faded to a pale gray and the screens were torn, but every inch looked unnaturally clean. Even the splintering flower boxes by the front window were pristine, if empty.

He walked to the door and knocked. After a minute or two, a young woman answered. He introduced himself and asked if he could come in for a few minutes.

Kim Murphy might be twenty-four, but she looked sixteen and incredibly pregnant. She'd been pretty at one time; now she just looked scared. The kind of scared that came from a lifetime of living in fear of her life. Her eyes were wary, and her mouth quivered at the corner.

"Andy's not here," she said, her eyes darting between him and the patrol car parked in front, as if expecting to see her husband bolt out of the back and hurtle toward her. "He doesn't like me letting anyone in."

"We can talk right here," Mac said quietly, going for a calm and safe tone.

She bit her lower lip, then held open the door. Apparently her fear of Andy knowing someone had come inside was less than her fear of a neighbor seeing Mac lurking at her front door.

The tiny living room was as spotless as the front of the house. The throw rug had been vacuumed down to the backing. The sofa was covered in plastic, as was the only chair. He figured they could do emergency surgery on the dining table he saw to the left.

"You keep a very tidy house," he said as he settled

on the plastic-covered sofa. "Your husband must be very proud."

"Andy likes things clean," Kim said as she brushed at the plastic on the chair, before perching on the edge. "I like to make him happy."

Her expression was so earnest, so eager to please. Mac wanted to grab her and forcibly take her with him. Did she know what was going to happen when her neat-freak husband found out how messy a baby could be? Had she considered the hell she was getting into?

He studied her face, searching for clues. They were there—a tiny scar by her right temple, a barely notice-able drooping at the corner of her left eye. The cast, of course. He would bet there were others—that her body would be both a road map and a testament to her husband's temper.

On the way over, Mac had tried to think of the best way to talk to Kim. Now, in face of her youth, her pain and her pregnancy, he went for the truth.

"It's getting worse, isn't it?" he asked, careful to keep his voice low and as nonthreatening as he could make it. "At first he just slapped you around some. But now it's worse. Your eye, the scars on your legs, the broken arm."

Her breath caught. "I—I don't know what you're talking about."

"I know you love him," he said as if she hadn't spo-ken. "Of course you do. He's your husband. And he's always sorry and you know in your heart that if you could just stop making mistakes, everything would be great between you. Because he used to be so sweet.

Right? Back when you first started going out, wasn't he the best?"

Her mouth curved up and she nodded. "He was wonderful."

"But not anymore. And here's the thing, Kim. He's not going to be happy with the baby. Babies don't stay quiet. They don't keep to schedules and they don't clean up after themselves. Andy is going to be very, very angry. And when he puts you in the hospital, who is going to take care of your child?"

Her eyes widened. "He's not like that."

"We both know he is. This situation is escalating. After he puts you in the hospital a few times, he's going to turn on your child. Then he'll be beating the two of you and eventually someone is going to wind up dead."

He stared at her, willing her to believe him. "We can stop this right now. I can arrest him and hold him in jail long enough for you to get away. There are places you can go where he'll never find you. Never. Do you understand?"

A single tear leaked out of her eye and rolled down her cheek. "You have to go," she said, not looking at him. "You have to go, because sometimes Andy comes home for lunch and if he found you here…"

There would be hell to pay, Mac thought. More than hell.

"Kim, please."

She stood and walked to the door. "Just go."

Mac did as she requested. Feeling useless and angry

and as if he'd only made things worse, he walked to his car and watched her carefully close the door.

JILL RETURNED to her office and was surprised to find Tina working at her desk. She resisted the urge to snap and instead nodded as she stalked past.

"You have a one o'clock," Tina called. "He should be here any second."

Perfect, Jill thought, wondering how she was going to keep her temper in check. She still didn't understand what had happened with Mac. Okay, she could see how he might have misunderstood her conversation with Rudy, but why wouldn't he let her explain? And how dare he insult what she did for a living? That was hitting below the belt.

She still wanted to slap something. Or throw something. The fish offered a tempting target but, before she could figure out who would fly across the room best, she heard the front door open and a man speaking to Tina.

Later, she promised herself as she sat behind her desk and drew in several calming breaths. She had a second to glance down at the note by the appointment— "wants to sue neighbor for theft"—then Tina showed the man in.

He was tall, beefy, late forties, with the permanent tan of someone who makes his living outdoors.

"Mr. Wolcott," she said. "This is Jill Strathern."

Jill rose and held out her hand. "Mr. Wolcott. A pleasure."

"Call me Bob," he told her, and smiled. When he'd taken his seat, he glanced around. "Great office."

"Um, do you fish?"

"Sure. Not like this though. What a beaut."

He pointed to a particularly large, ugly fish of indeterminate origin. As Jill didn't want to hear about the wonders of catching so many prize specimens, she pulled out a pad of legal paper and picked up a pen.

"I understand you're having a problem with a neighbor."

"What? Oh, yeah. That bitch. She lives down the street from me and has always wanted my dog. You know," he raised his voice to a falsetto. "If Bucky ever has puppies I really want one." Mr. Wolcott grimaced. "The dog's name is Buck. Who the hell calls a dog Bucky?"

Jill told herself to remain calm. This wasn't as it seemed. Bob was having trouble coming to the point. There was no way he'd come to see her about his *dog*.

"Your neighbor down the street?"

"Sissy Dawson. What the hell kind of name is Sissy? Probably why she can't keep my dog's name straight. She's a real bitch."

"So you mentioned."

He placed both of his massive hands on the desk. "She kidnapped Buck."

Now they were getting somewhere...or not. "Your dog?"

"Hell, yes. Damn bitch held him for three days.

When he came home, he was real whipped if you get my drift."

Jill did not. Was there a drift? Could she please be on it and out of this town?

"Bob, I'm not following you. Your concern is that your neighbor kidnapped your dog for three days, then returned him?"

"Right."

"What exactly do you want to sue her for? Kidnapping?"

He brightened. "I hadn't thought of that. Sure. Kidnapping, but mostly theft."

Jill had a bad feeling she didn't want to know, but she had to ask. "Theft of what?"

"Buck's sperm. She was always after me to have him mate with her damn dog and I refused. So when her dog went into heat, she kidnapped him and locked those two together for three damn days. She could have killed him."

Twenty minutes later Jill showed Bob to the door after promising to research the problem. On her way back to her desk, she glanced up at the giant swordfish and wondered if there was any way to throw herself on the pointy part.

This couldn't be happening. Not any of it. Life hadn't gotten that unfair, had it? She had horrible law cases, was unable to help the one battered, pregnant person who really needed her, had a crummy ex-husband and furious ex-lover and assistant/secretary/receptionist who still hated her. If she didn't know she would regret it later, she would pick up the phone and call Rudy to ask him to take care of the lying rat fink weasel dog that was Lyle.

Just then the phone rang. Tina, of course, had left for the day. Jill grabbed the call herself.

"Jill Strathern," she said.

"Oh, hi, Jill. I'm Marsha Rawlings," the woman said, then rattled off the name of her San Diego law firm. "Honestly, I can't believe your résumé. Please, please tell me you haven't already accepted another position."

"I haven't."

"Wonderful. We would love to talk to you as soon as possible. I see there's a private airfield just outside of Los Lobos. How about if we send the company plane to get you first thing in the morning? Would that work for you?"

Jill looked at the fish, the empty reception area and her notes on the dog-sperm theft case.

"It would work perfectly. What time?"

CHAPTER FOURTEEN

JILL LEFT HER OFFICE a little after three. Tina had barely put in any time and Jill wasn't in the mood to deal with more clients. While she figured the odds of someone coming by with a case more amazing than dog-sperm theft were slim, she didn't want to tempt fate more than necessary.

As she rounded the corner to her street, she saw Mac's truck parked in front of his house. The sight of the familiar pickup made her uncomfortable. She still didn't know what had happened between them. He couldn't possibility believe that she'd told secrets to Rudy. Or that she would ever betray Mac.

But telling herself that his temper wasn't her problem didn't seem to be working. She wanted to talk to him and make things right, and even reminding herself she was excited about her interview in the morning didn't make her feel any better.

She walked up the front steps and entered her aunt's house.

"It's just me," she called, knowing that if Mac were home then Emily would be with him.

"Jill? You're early," Bev yelled from upstairs. "I was lying down. I'll be there in a second."

"Okay."

Jill kicked off her shoes and set down her purse. After wandering into the kitchen, she poked around a plate of cookies and picked up a frosted one. Clamping it between her teeth, she got a glass and poured milk, then sat at the kitchen table.

She hated feeling this out of sorts. Nothing was horribly wrong, but nothing was right, either.

"I blame my father," she said.

"For what?" Bev asked as she bustled into the kitchen. "Oh, good. You found the cookies."

Jill took another bite. "They're great."

"Emily and I made them this morning. That girl is a whiz in the kitchen. I wonder if I should let Gracie know she's going to have some competition."

Jill smiled. "Interesting thought."

Bev smoothed the front of her sundress and patted her braided hair. Jill watched her bring the plate to the table, then pull out a chair.

"You look especially nice this afternoon."

"Do I?" Bev looked away. "I didn't do anything special. I'm barely wearing any makeup."

Maybe, Jill thought, studying her more closely, but there was a definite glow in her cheeks and a gleam in her eyes.

"What about your father?" Bev asked. "How is anything his fault?"

"What? Oh, he's the one who convinced me to temporarily fill in at the law firm here. If I'd stayed in San Francisco…" What would she be doing, exactly? Fighting Lyle for the condo? Living in a hotel and licking her wounds? Plotting revenge?

"I was supposed to have a plan," she said, then drank some milk. "I was supposed to be figuring out ways to make Lyle's life a living hell. What happened to that?"

"You got busy and found more important things to do with your time."

"I guess. But what does it say about my marriage that a month or so after the fact, I barely think about the guy?" She held up her hand. "Don't feel you have to answer the question." She reached for another cookie. "I shouldn't have married Lyle. I never loved him."

"He was what you needed at the time."

Jill wrinkled her nose. "Let's not think about what that says about me. Yuck. I have another interview tomorrow."

Her aunt squeezed her arm. "I know that's what you want, even though the thought of you leaving makes me sad. I've liked having you around."

Jill stood and bent over her aunt, then hugged her. "You've been wonderful. I can't tell you how much I appreciate you taking me this summer. I've had the best time."

"I'm glad to hear that."

Jill sank back in her seat and sighed. "Nothing turns out like we thought, huh? Maybe I *should* let you read my cards and give me a hint or two about the future."

Bev stood and crossed to the sink, where she began rinsing dishes. "I'm not sure that's such a good idea.

At least not today. I'm not feeling all that in tune with the cards."

Before Jill could ask why, she heard footsteps upstairs.

"Is Emily here?" she asked. "I saw Mac's truck next door and thought he was with her."

"He is. He came home a couple of hours ago."

"Then who..." She pressed her lips together, suddenly not sure she wanted to hear an answer. After all, there weren't that many choices and she didn't like any of them.

Her string of not-so-great luck continued less than a minute later when Rudy came downstairs and walked into the kitchen. To Jill's amazement, he moved over to Bev, took her in his arms and kissed her. *Seriously* kissed her. Jill thought she might have seen a bit of tongue before she gathered herself together enough to look away.

Rudy? Here? Now? Upstairs?

"You're sleeping together?" she blurted before she could stop herself.

Rudy straightened and grinned. "You aunt is a very sensual woman."

"Didn't want to know that," Jill said as she put down the cookie and tried not to get anything close to a visual of what they'd been doing.

She risked a glance at Bev, who looked both flustered and pleased. "So what about staying pure for the gift?"

Bev sighed. "I never thought I'd say this, but my feelings for Rudy are more powerful than my need to stay pure for my calling."

"You're kidding?"

Rudy winked. "Hey, I'm Italian. You know what that means."

Actually, she didn't and was happy to keep it that way. "Tell me you at least waited until Mac took Emily home."

"Of course." Bev sounded shocked. "She's just a child."

"Good. Wish we could all say the same about me." She stood. "Look, I'll go and get out of your way."

"No need," Rudy said, slipping an arm around Bev's waist and pulling her close. "I'm taking her back to my place. We'll grab some dinner or something."

It was the "something" that gave Jill the willies. "Okay, then. I guess I'll see you…tomorrow?"

Bev leaned against Rudy and sighed. "I'll be back in time to take care of Emily."

"Great. You two have fun."

Jill ducked out of the room and headed for the stairs. When she reached her room, she carefully closed the door, threw herself on the bed and covered her face with a pillow. Only then did she allow herself to scream.

Rudy and Bev having sex? Why oh why did she have to know that? It wasn't that she begrudged them any happiness. Bev had always chosen to be alone and that seemed to make her happy. If now she wanted to be with a man, Jill thought it was fabulous. She wasn't sure she would have chosen Rudy as the guy, but it also wasn't her decision.

No, her discomfort didn't come from their relationship—it was much more primal than that. Bev was the closest thing to a mother Jill had known since she was Emily's age, and thinking about the woman who'd raised her doing it with anyone was a serious violation of the ick factor.

She tossed the pillow away and sat up. "What if I'd come upstairs without calling out?" she asked herself. "I might have seen something."

The thought made her shudder. She supposed children never really wanted to hear about their parents being sexual creatures. No doubt there was a biological reason for that and she should just let it go.

She could hear them moving around, probably packing for the big sleepover. Jill moved to her closet and quickly changed into shorts and a T-shirt. She pulled the pins from her hair and brushed it out, then slicked on sunscreen. A walk on the beach would help clear her head.

When she was ready, she plopped down on the bed to give Bev and Rudy plenty of time to make their escape. She touched the phone, wondering if she should check in with Gracie, then pulled her hand away. As much as she loved her friend, the person she most wanted to speak to was Mac, and he'd made it clear he had no interest in talking to her.

MAC PUT DOWN the latest issue of *Car and Driver* and watched as Emily turned the page in her book. She read silently, completely engrossed in the story. A couple of strands of hair fell into her eyes and she brushed them away without looking up from her book.

She was so precious, he thought, his heart aching with love for her. Despite the problems he had with her, the past few weeks had been damned amazing.

He studied the shape of her cheek, her slender shoulders, then grimaced at the purple T-shirt she wore. Purple and blue days were always a bitch. Em might be eating regular food with everyone else, but she still insisted on matching colors with him. He supposed it was a form of punishment—one that he'd earned.

He leaned back on the sofa and rubbed the bridge of his nose. She was so young, he thought sadly. Too young to have experienced all she had. To think *he'd* been the one to hurt her.

He'd never wanted that to happen, mostly because he knew how horrible it was. He'd only been a few years older than Emily when his father had disappeared from his life. His mother had complained his father was a bastard and no one should be surprised that he'd finally run off. But Mac had been. Didn't every kid want his or her dad to be perfect?

He swore silently and looked at Em. Isn't that what she'd wanted for him? Damn it all to hell if he hadn't let her down. He'd made so many excuses for his own father, had waited and waited for him to come back. Had Emily done the same?

She put down her book. "What's wrong?" she asked. "You have a funny look on your face."

"I'm okay. I'm just thinking about some things."

"Like what?"

He crossed to her chair and crouched in front of her. Such small hands, he thought. She was so young and defenseless.

"I'm sorry, Em," he said, and squeezed her fingers. "More sorry than I can tell you."

She frowned. "'Bout what?"

"Before. When I went away."

She closed her book. "You didn't go away. Mommy and me did."

"Okay. You went away and I didn't come after you. I'm sorry about that. I should have. I love you so much. You're my best-ever girl and I didn't come find you."

She shifted in her seat and drew her knees to her chest. "I know," she said in a very small voice. "I wanted you to find me."

"I got lost when I should have been looking for you and it took me a long time to find my way. And all that time you were waiting and wondering where I was. You probably wondered if I even loved you anymore."

Her eyes widened, but she didn't speak.

"I do," he said into the silence. "I love you, Emily. You're the best part of my life. I've loved you since before you were born and no matter what happens, I will always love you."

Her blue eyes seemed to see down to his soul. Was she looking for proof? He wished he could offer something other than his word. Time, he told himself through the ache. Time would help her see he could be trusted.

A single tear rolled down her cheek. He brushed it away with his finger.

"If I could go back to those days, I swear I'd come look for you. You matter so much to me. I think you're special and wonderful and the most amazing daughter any dad could ever be blessed with. I'm so proud of you all the time."

She made a noise in the back of her throat, then flung herself at him. He caught her against him and pulled her close. Thin arms wrapped around his throat, nearly strangling him, but he didn't mind. Em had been keeping her distance all summer. He planned to enjoy this hug for as long as it lasted.

"I love you so much," he whispered into her ear. "Thank you for spending this time with me."

"Oh, Daddy," she said with a sniff.

His chest tightened. *Daddy*. How long had it been since he'd heard that?

He held her and rocked her. After a few minutes, he moved so he sat on the chair and she curled up on his lap. Still she clung to him. He stroked her back and kissed the top of her head. Finally she raised her tear-stained face and looked at him.

"I love you, Daddy," she whispered.

The last band around his chest eased and he drew in a deep breath.

"I love you, too, kiddo."

She swallowed. "Are you going to get lost again?"

"No. I've found my way. When you go home to be with your mom, we're going to work out a schedule so you and I can see each other a lot. We'll talk on the phone and send cards and do e-mail. What do you think?"

"I'd like that a lot."

She leaned her head against his shoulder. He rocked her back and forth and thought about how empty the house would be when she was gone. She would leave a big hole in his heart.

"You must miss Mom a lot," he said. "You haven't seen her in a long time."

She straightened and looked at him. "I'm okay," she told him.

Em had never been much of a liar and this wasn't any exception. He tucked her hair behind her ears and smiled.

"You know what? I think maybe it would be okay for you to see your mom for a weekend this summer. I know she'd like that a lot."

"For real?" his daughter asked.

"Sure. As long as you promise to come back."

She grinned. "Daddy, you're the one who got lost, not me. I can find my way back just fine."

Words to live by, he thought.

"Then I'll trust you completely," he said. "Are you getting hungry? Ready for dinner?"

"Uh-huh." She slid off his knee and stood. "What are we having?"

"Funny you should ask. I have a couple of surprises for you."

"We're having ice cream?"

He ruffled her hair. "Did I say they were good surprises?"

"Oh. So what's for dinner?"

"Meat loaf." He took her hand and led her toward the kitchen.

"You didn't make that," Emily said. "Bev and I made the meat loaf this morning."

"I know, but she gave me a special gravy. It's purple."

His daughter looked doubtful. "Does it taste funny?"

"You're going to have to let me know. *I'm* not eating it."

She started to laugh. "Why not?"

"Purple gravy. Yuck. What's next? Orange bacon?"

She giggled some more.

He led her to the refrigerator. "I want to show you this." He opened the door and pulled out a bowl of Jell-O.

She stood on tiptoe and stared at the bowl for a long time. Finally she looked at him. "What is it?" she asked in a whisper.

"It's Jell-O. Purple Jell-O. I made it this morning when I saw what you were wearing."

Her expression remained doubtful. "What's inside?"

He leaned close and whispered, "Broccoli."

Emily jumped as if he'd bitten her. Her eyes widened. "You can't put vegetables in Jell-O."

"Sure you can. I just did it. See." He shook the bowl and the contents wiggled. He had to admit the combination of grape Jell-O and broccoli turned his stomach, but he wasn't the one with the color rule.

"I'm sure it's yummy," he said cheerfully. "We can put the gravy on it."

She put out her hands. "I don't want any."

"What? No purple broccoli? No purple gravy?" He put the bowl on the counter and began to tickle her.

Em laughed and began to squirm, but he noticed she pushed to get closer, not to get away.

"What are you saying?" he demanded loudly? "You won't eat purple food?"

"No!" she said with a shriek and grabbed his hands. "No purple food." She grinned. "Just regular food, okay?"

He touched the tip of her nose and knew they were going to be fine. "Okay."

JILL WALKED UP from the beach nearly three hours after she'd left the house. She felt windblown and was sure her hair looked like a perm experiment gone bad. That was just on the outside. On the inside…she wasn't sure *what* she felt. Confused mostly. About her life, her career, Mac. Especially Mac.

Telling herself he shouldn't matter was one thing, but believing it? Not gonna happen. She'd had a crush on him forever and, in the past month or so, they'd become friends. More than friends. They'd slept together. She didn't do that with just anyone.

Jill was pretty confident she wasn't in love with Mac, but she felt something. And when he'd turned on her like a rabid dog for no good reason…

She still didn't want to think about it.

A quick glance at her watch told her there was still plenty of time for a chick movie fest and a Ben & Jerry's marathon. As she'd skipped dinner, only half the calories would count. If she remembered correctly there was Cookie Dough *and* Cherry Garcia in the freezer and what could be better than that?

As she crossed the street toward Bev's place, she didn't even look toward Mac's house. Whatever he was up to, she didn't care. If he wanted to—

"Jill?"

She froze in the middle of the street, torn between walking toward him and running away. Unfortunately, her long walk had left her legs sore, so running wasn't really an option—not unless she wanted to risk permanent injury.

She sauntered toward the sidewalk, trying to look both unconcerned and uninterested.

"Hey," she said, then shoved her hands into her back pockets.

"How's it going?" he asked as he stepped off the porch.

She started to answer, then realized she couldn't speak. Not rationally, at least. The man was barefoot. Was that fair? Mac was sexy at the best of times, but with a worn T-shirt and shorts and barefoot, he was practically illegally attractive.

She stared down at the grass. "I took a walk on the beach," she said.

"Dealing with some things?"

"A few."

"Was I on the list?"

She raised her head and glared at him. "You didn't deserve to be."

"You're right." He moved toward her. "I was a complete jerk and totally out of line."

She made a show of looking behind her before tapping her chest. "Was that directed at me?"

"Yeah."

He stopped a few feet in front of her. Not within touching distance, but close enough to get her hormones singing a happy jingle.

"It's all the pressure," he said, his blue eyes locked intently on her face. "Dealing with Emily, my job, the town. Then Rudy shows up and everything goes to hell." He held up a hand before she could speak. "I'm not saying he's done anything. Maybe you're right. Maybe he's not here to make trouble."

"You don't believe that."

He smiled. "I'm trying to apologize. Maybe you could wait until I'm done to argue with me."

"Oh. Good point. Okay, go on."

"That was pretty much it. I'm sorry. When I heard you'd talked to him, I overreacted."

"You think?" She tilted her head and shrugged. "I didn't confide in Rudy. I didn't think I'd betrayed a confidence. And just for the record, he's not currently my client. At the rate things are going, he may never be again."

"I thought you had a lot of interviews."

"I do, including one tomorrow. But I'm beginning to think I'm cursed or something. The senior partner at that L.A. firm had a giant fish on the wall. Who knows what I'll see tomorrow."

Mac grinned. "Antlers?"

"Maybe." She shuddered. "I don't know what's going to happen, but I do know I want us to stay friends."

"Me, too." He held out his arms. "Am I forgiven?"

She nodded and stepped into his embrace. He was warm and strong and everything about touching him felt right. Jill gave herself over to the feeling of safety and home. Her eyes slid closed and she—

Home? Where had that thought come from?

She quickly stepped back and tried to smile. "So, how are things otherwise?" she asked, aware she was talking too quickly. "Not to get you mad at me again, but the whole world is weird at my place." She lowered her voice. "Bev and Rudy are having a sleepover."

Mac winced. "I could have gone all night without knowing about that."

"You only had to hear about it. I practically walked in on them. Bev is like my mother. I mean, ick." She held up both hands. "Don't worry. She's already promised to make sure Emily and Rudy aren't in the house together. You don't have to panic."

"I can't help it where that guy's concerned."

"I know. We'll have to agree to disagree. You think you can wait until he screws up before you get mad at him?"

"Maybe." He put his arm around her. "Want to come in and have some wine or something?"

To be honest, the "or something" was pretty tempting.

"Hi, Jill."

She looked up and saw Emily standing at the screen door.

"Hey, girlfriend," Jill called. "How are things?"

"Good. I like your hair."

Jill fingered the curly frizz. "I walked on the beach for a while. This always happens."

"It's pretty."

"Thanks."

Emily looked at her father. "Can we go get ice cream, Daddy?"

"Sure, kiddo. Put your shoes on."

Jill grinned as Emily raced away. "So you two are getting along."

"Very well. We talked about some things today. She ate broccoli."

Jill was pleased. "So the food-matching thing seems to be over."

"Thank God. I was running out of ideas." He put his arm around her. "Want to come with us for ice cream?"

Be with Mac and his daughter or spend the evening alone? Not much of a choice. "Sure thing."

"Good. I have an idea that will make you very happy."

"Oh?" She scooted a little closer. "What might that be?"

He groaned. "Unfortunately, it's not that." He gave her a swift kiss on the mouth. "You've got to know being close to you kills me, right?"

She felt the heat and the need ricocheting between them. "I have a fair idea."

Emily burst out of the house before she could say anything else.

"What's your idea?" Jill asked.

"That we take your car over to the high school parking lot."

"How is that exciting?"

He grinned. "They start a new class of driver's training tomorrow. You could park right in the way."

Jill bent over and hugged Emily. "Your daddy is a very smart man."

"I know," the little girl said, and took her hand. "What kind of ice cream do you want?"

Emily grabbed ahold of her father with her other hand and started walking. Jill kept step with her and did her best not to look at Mac. This was all too weird, she told herself. They weren't a family.

Did she want them to be?

"Jill," Emily said as she tugged on her fingers. "What do you want?"

"Maybe one of everything."

CHAPTER FIFTEEN

"YOU'RE DOING WELL," Carly said quietly as Emily raced out of the room to grab Elvis.

"We've had our ups and down," Mac admitted. "In the past few days it seems we've come to an understanding."

"More than that. She's wearing multiple colors. If you knew how many times I tried to get her to eat normally."

"She held out for a long time," he admitted.

Carly sat on a kitchen chair. Her perfectly neat, perfectly straight hair suited her attractive features. In her tailored shorts and polo shirt, she looked like what she was—a successful executive on vacation. She was, in theory, everything he could possibly want. So why couldn't he stop thinking about a curly-haired, impulsive, mouthy attorney who could make a man want to sell his soul for just one kiss?

"Em can be stubborn," Carly said with a smile. "I know she gets that from you."

"I'm not the only one," he told her. "You can get your back up about things."

"Maybe sometimes." She leaned toward him and grabbed his hand. "How's life?"

"Good."

"Mommy, can I bring a book?" Emily called from upstairs.

"Sure. Go ahead and pick one."

He heard the thunder of little feet as his daughter raced across the room to her bookshelf.

"This could take a minute," he said.

"That's okay. We don't have any firm plans. Maybe hang out on the beach, catch a movie. That kind of stuff."

"She'll enjoy it. She's missed you."

Carly nodded. "I've missed her, too. The house is quiet without her."

"I know."

His ex-wife squeezed his fingers. "How are things going with the social worker?"

"Hollis?" Mac felt his jaw clench. "He's a prick."

"As long as you're playing nice."

"I try. He thinks all cops make lousy fathers."

She frowned. "That's crazy. I'm sorry, Mac. I didn't want to make this more difficult for you."

He shook his head. "Don't sweat it. I'm the one who screwed up, not you. You gave me plenty of chances. Now I have to prove myself. I'm more than up to the task."

"I appreciate that, but if this Hollis guy gets unreasonable, let me know. I'll set him straight."

He released her hand. "I don't need you to fight my battles."

"You never did. You were always so self-sufficient." She folded her arms on the table. "That guy I'm seeing? It's getting serious."

Mac nodded, then braced himself for a physical reaction to the news. There wasn't any, except for some jealousy that if Carly married the guy, he would get to see Em on a daily basis.

"Is he one of the good guys?" he asked.

She nodded. "He's terrific. I'm going to tell Em about him. Just casually. But I wanted you to know—in case she's upset." She glanced at him, then down at the table. "We're not getting married or anything. It's too soon to talk about that, but I wanted you to know."

"I appreciate the heads-up." He touched her chin so she had to look at him. "I'm fine with it."

"I knew you would be. It's not as if we were a great love affair."

Mac knew she was right. What had started out as a casual relationship had turned serious when Carly had gotten pregnant. Mac had done the right thing and proposed. Together they'd done their best to form a family, but neither of them had ever been in love with the other.

"I cared about you," he said.

"I know. You were willing to be a husband and a father. I thanked you for that, didn't I?"

"Yeah. A lot. You didn't have to. I wanted to marry you."

"Because of Emily."

"Does it matter why?"

She smiled. "No. It doesn't. I'm glad I have her and I'm glad we were together. I hope you'll find someone to make you happy. It wouldn't kill you to settle down—fall in love, get married again."

He held up both hands. "Not this week. I have a full schedule already."

"Then soon."

"Maybe."

Her gaze narrowed. "You're still punishing yourself, aren't you? Jeez, Mac, you need to let it go."

He thought maybe she was right, but this wasn't the time to have that conversation.

"Am I going to have to come back in a couple of months and give you a stern talking-to?" she asked.

"If it makes you happy."

"It just might."

"Then have at it."

JILL WALKED into her office shortly after ten in the morning. As it was Saturday, she hadn't planned to come in at all, but she'd felt too restless to stay home and watch time crawl by. Her glow from her fabulous interview in San Diego had faded. There was plenty to keep her busy. It wasn't as if Tina did anything like filing or even organizing paperwork.

So she would take the morning to catch up, while waiting for Mac's "all clear" phone call, at which point she would dash over to his house and indulge in a couple of hours of very exciting, very hot lovemaking.

While the logical part of her brain was happy that he felt comfortable enough with Emily to let her spend the day with her mother, her hormones and pretty much every part of her covered with skin was delighted to have another chance at a close encounter with a man who could take her clear to another dimension.

Anticipation added a little spring to her step and made her hum as she sorted through files. At this point, she doubted she would much mind doing research on the dog-sperm case.

She paused, file folder in hand. "Scratch that," she said aloud. "I *do* mind about the dog sperm. It's just too weird."

She could understand if the woman wanted Bob to pay support for the puppies, but she didn't. Who cared if Buck had donated sperm? He wasn't a prizewinner. Besides, it sounded to her as if Buck had enjoyed his time with the in-heat dog. Was he complaining?

"Not my decision to make," she reminded herself. "If the client wants to sue, then I need to take the case seriously."

She winced as she pictured herself in court, arguing the case, and had a momentary wish that she hadn't been fair and levelheaded when it came to the property settlement with Lyle.

She'd nearly finished with the filing when the phone rang. Thinking it might be Mac telling her it was time, she reached over Tina's desk and grabbed it after one ring.

"Law offices," she said in what she hoped was a sexy voice.

"Oh, good. Someone's there. Hi. I'm looking for Mr. Dixon."

The official-sounding woman on the other end of the phone didn't sound the least bit like Mac. Darn and double darn, Jill thought.

"Do you wish to speak to him regarding a legal matter or is this personal?" Jill asked.

"Legal. I'm calling on behalf of one of his clients."

Good. Not a long-lost family member looking for a favorite uncle or godfather. "I'm afraid Mr. Dixon passed away about three months ago. I'm Jill Strathern. I'm handling his practice." For now...on a very temporary basis. "If you would like I can help you or I can collect the information and send it on to another attorney."

"Oh." The woman sounded flummoxed. "I can't imagine needing another attorney. I assume you can handle a will and any probate."

"Of course."

"Good. Then I'm phoning to inform you that Donovan Whitefield has died. Just this morning."

Jill walked around the desk and sank onto Tina's chair. Old man Whitefield? Riley Whitefield's rich uncle?

"I'm sorry. Are you a member of the family?"

"No," the woman said. "I'm Mr. Whitefield's housekeeper. The family will have to be notified." She sighed. "Actually there's only Mr. Whitefield's nephew. Everyone else is gone."

"I can get in touch with him right away. Have arrangements been made?"

"They're all in the will. I need you to tell me what they are so I can take care of things. There's no one else."

No one but paid staff? Jill grimaced. "I'll get right on it and get back to you. Give me a couple of hours."

"Yes, of course."

Jill took the woman's name and number, then hung up. Old man Whitefield dead. It didn't seem possible. He was as much an institution in this town as the bank he owned. And Riley was his only living relative.

Not good, she thought as she rose and headed upstairs for the files in storage. From what she remembered, Riley and the old man had never been close. They'd become estranged years ago and she didn't think he'd been back since. Had Donovan left everything to his nephew, or some charity?

Jill searched for a few minutes before she found the right files, then she carried everything downstairs. She carefully read the letters, Dixon's notes and then the will itself. When she'd finished, she leaned back in her chair and stared at the fish on the far side of the room.

"I don't even know what to say," she admitted. "It's a whole lot of money and a whole lot of strings. A man could strangle on them all."

She thought about what she remembered about Riley. Gracie had loved him for years. He'd been good friends with Mac until they'd had a falling-out. Together they'd ruled high school—two young gods, one dark, one light, both bad to the bone.

Mac had changed, she reminded herself. Maybe Riley had, too. Maybe he wasn't the brooding, dark-haired loner who could cause a woman to go up in flames with a single glance. Maybe he'd become respectable—even boring. Maybe he was married with three kids, a dog and an SUV.

She looked at the phone number handwritten on the inside of the file and shook her head. Looked like she was about to find out.

MAC DROVE toward Jill's office. He'd received her note that she would be at her office until he was ready. Well, Em had left with her mother, Mac had cleared up a few problems at his desk at work and now he was ready. More than ready, he thought with a grin. Parts of him were damn impatient.

He checked his watch. Carly had promised to have Em home by seven-thirty, which meant even leaving an hour as a buffer, he and Jill had eight hours together. While it didn't sound like nearly enough time to do all he had planned, it was a start. With a little luck, by this time tomorrow they would both be grinning like fools and walking funny.

He stopped at the corner and checked before cruising into the intersection. A car turned left in front of him into the barbershop parking lot. Mac kept going straight about twenty feet, then he pulled to the side of the road.

The sixth sense that kept cops alive had just twitched to life. The barbershop parking lot had been full. It was Saturday. Artie, the barber, never worked on weekends. Instead he stayed open late two nights a week.

Mac swore under his breath, then checked the mirrors before hanging a U-turn and heading back the way he'd come. He pulled into the crowded parking lot behind the building and watched as two men took the back stairs up to the second floor.

Mac knew what was there—a big empty room where

a couple of the smaller lodges met. The place could also be rented for parties and civic functions.

He told himself it was probably nothing. Just a meeting he hadn't been told about. Jill was waiting—his dick was hard. This wasn't the time to go investigate. Still, he found himself parking, then climbing out of his truck and heading up the stairs. Telling himself it was nothing didn't make that damn twitching go away.

He pushed open the door and felt his temper explode. Tables had been set up at the far end of the room. An equal number of men and women sat playing cards. A makeshift bar did a steady business in the back. The current racing odds covered a dry-erase board up front, there was an honest-to-God roulette wheel spinning away in the center of the room and a craps table next to it.

He didn't want this to be happening. Dammit all to hell, he hated being right.

"Morning," he said loudly into the crowd. A few folks glanced up. Several swore. In three seconds, he had the whole room's attention.

He strolled toward the bar and nodded at the man behind it. "I don't suppose you can show me a liquor license."

"Uh, I don't have it with me."

"Of course not."

He glanced around and didn't see Rudy. Had he called in a few employees to handle things here? A small-time gambling operation wouldn't be much fun for a man of Rudy's talents.

"Who's in charge?" Mac asked as several of his

citizens began to quietly collect their winnings and stand.

"Me." A small man in a dark suit approached. "Hello, Sheriff. Good to see you. Can I get you something?"

Mac reached for his radio. "Wilma, we've got ourselves a situation."

The little man in the suit blanched. "Sheriff, that's not necessary, is it? These are good people, just having a little fun."

Mac knew he could arrest them all, but what was the point? They hadn't started the trouble. That honor lay elsewhere.

"Where's Rudy?" he asked.

"Mr. Casaccio doesn't discuss his plans with me."

"Fine. You and your staff are going to stay right here. The rest of you." He glanced at the crowd gathering by the door. "Take it slow down the stairs. I don't want any pushing."

While they left, he called for backup. When D.J. arrived along with one of the other deputies, Mac arrested Rudy's employees and left D.J. in charge of taking them in.

Los Lobos wasn't that large, he told himself as he drove away. He would be able to find a long black limo, then have a little chat with the owner.

Two streets over he saw the vehicle in question in front of Bill's Mexican Grill. Mac pulled in behind, close enough that the limo couldn't get out, then walked toward the restaurant.

It was still early for the lunch crowd, especially on a Saturday. He had no trouble spotting Rudy, although the gangster's companion didn't make him happy. Mayor Franklin Yardley sat across from Rudy.

As Mac approached, the two men glanced up. Rudy shifted toward the wall of their booth.

"Sheriff Kendrick, join us."

"No, thanks."

He kept his gaze on Rudy, watching for any kind of reaction. But Rudy was too smooth and practiced for that. He raised his eyebrows expectantly.

"What is it, Mac?" the mayor asked.

"Ask your friend."

Rudy swirled his glass of iced tea and looked pleasantly baffled. "I have no idea why you're here."

"The room above the barbershop is being used for gambling. I thought I'd find out what you know about it."

"Nothing at all," Rudy said smoothly.

Franklin frowned. "Sheriff, are you accusing Mr. Casaccio of something?"

Mac glared at him. "You got that right. Your friend here is bringing his dirty business to our town. Don't you get that? He's out for a buck and he doesn't care who or what gets destroyed in the process."

Franklin frowned. "Those are pretty serious accusations. Do you have any evidence?"

"His employees are running the place."

Rudy sipped his tea, then picked up a tortilla chip. "Interesting. Except for Mr. Smith—" he nodded at the small table next to the booth where the suit-clad bodyguard sat over a plate of enchiladas "—and the driver of my car, I have no employees in town. I'm here strictly on holiday."

Annoyance grew into anger. Mac turned to the mayor. "You can't be blind to this. Your town is being overrun by organized crime. Sure, now it's just a friendly game of poker, but then what? Can't you see this is already escalating?"

"Sheriff, you're accusing one of our leading citizens of some fairly serious charges. Do you have any evidence?"

Mac stared at the two of them. Was Franklin so deeply in Rudy's pockets that he refused to see the truth? Or did the man seriously think Rudy wouldn't destroy Los Lobos?

As for evidence, Mac knew there wasn't any. The people they'd arrested would claim to have never met Rudy Casaccio, much less worked for him. No doubt a very experienced, very expensive lawyer would show up to get them out on bail and when the time came for trial, the judge would dismiss all charges. He'd seen it happen before, but he never thought it would happen here.

"I'll find a way to nail you for this," Mac said.

Rudy sighed. "And here I'd wanted to make a sizable contribution to your campaign. Aren't you running in November?"

"I don't need money from you."

"Sometimes we don't know *what* we need, Sheriff. Just remember, I'm always willing to be a friend."

"No, thanks." Mac glanced at Franklin. "You're making a big mistake. He's taking you places you don't want to go, and if you can't see that, you're a bigger idiot than I thought."

With that, he turned on his heel and stalked out of the restaurant. Temper fueled him until he wanted to punch something. Anything. Dammit all to hell, this could *not* be happening.

Too angry to drive, he left the car by the restaurant. Let Rudy have to call the station to get it moved so he could get his limo out.

Two blocks later, Mac wasn't any closer to calming down. Why was he the only one who saw the truth about Rudy? Everyone else thought he was God's gift to Los Lobos. Jill was his friend, the mayor was his slave and even Bev was dating the guy. It didn't make sense. Was he the only one who—

"Hey, you. Sheriff."

Mac turned toward the man on the corner. He stood across the street from the sheriff's office. Medium height, sandy-blond hair and mean-looking. Mac clenched his fists. He was more than in the mood for a fight.

"Is there a problem?" he asked, his voice thick with menace. Anyone with a brain would know to back away. This guy only moved closer.

"Yeah, there's a problem. You're the problem." The man approached, stopping less than a foot in front of Mac. "Where do you get off bugging my wife?"

"What?"

"You heard me."

Mac had heard all right, but it didn't mean anything. "What are you talking about?"

"You went to see my wife the other day. She didn't

tell me because she thought I'd be mad, and she was right about that." The man leaned in close. "Keep your stinking hands off her."

Mac could only think of one woman he'd visited in the past few days. "You're Kim Murphy's husband," he said. "Andy."

"That's right."

Mac turned his back and headed for the office. "I don't have time to deal with you and your crap."

He heard Andy run up behind him. "Come on, you coward pig," Andy yelled. "Don't walk away from me."

Mac couldn't believe it. He stopped and turned to face Andy. "You don't want to do this," he said.

"I sure do. Where the hell do you get off talking to my wife? She's mine, you hear?"

"She's your *wife,* not your possession, you disgusting piece of shit. You have no right to treat her the way you do. If you're looking for a fight, go beat up on someone your own size."

Andy's eyes brightened with temper. "You volunteering? Because I'm happy to take you on."

Mac shook his head. "You and what army? You're a bully. You wouldn't dare hit someone who would fight back. You might get hurt. You're the kind of man who gets his kicks beating up on defenseless women. You're disgusting."

Color darkened Andy's face. "She's my wife, which is the same as saying she's my dog. I'll do anything I want to her and you can't stop me."

Mac felt his control slip. He tried to grab it, then

figured what the hell. He punched Andy square on the jaw. The man staggered a few steps and shot out his fist, but Mac avoided it easily. Two more well-placed blows and the whole thing was over. Andy knelt on the asphalt, holding his nose and groaning. Mac stood over him, untouched and knowing he'd just made a really big mistake.

Seconds later the front doors of the sheriff's office banged open and everyone on duty poured into the street.

"What happened?" Wilma asked. "You got in a fight?"

Mac glanced from his bleeding knuckles to Andy's battered face. His stomach balled into a knot.

Andy staggered to his feet. "He jumped me. He can't do that, even if he's the sheriff. He just beat the crap out of me and I want him arrested and thrown in jail."

CHAPTER SIXTEEN

JILL HAD BARELY FINISHED her brief conversation with
Riley Whitefield when the phone rang again.

"Law offices," she said.

"Jill? It's Wilma. You need to get down here right
away. Mac was just in a fistfight and the guy wants to
press charges."

Still clutching the phone, Jill stood and grabbed her
purse. "What? Wilma, you're not making sense. *Mac*
was in a fight?"

"Oh, yeah. He cracked the guy good. I'm not saying
he didn't deserve it, but he sure doesn't need the trouble.
Not now."

Jill wasn't sure which "he" they were talking about,
but she decided it didn't matter.

"I'll be right there. Don't let Mac leave until I get
there."

"Don't worry. He's not going anywhere for a while.
We have to figure out how to keep from arresting him."
With that, the older woman hung up.

"Arresting him?" Jill repeated as she raced to the
front of the office and quickly locked the door. "They
can't do that."

Arrest Mac? Not only would that seriously impact
his ability to do his job, what about the custody issues

with Emily? There were some basic requirements put in place by the courts and one of them was to stay out of trouble. Getting arrested could fall into that category.

She had the BMW with her, so the trip across town took less than ten minutes. She parked and rushed inside to find the place in bedlam. Deputies were standing around talking about how Mac had done the right thing. Mac sat on the corner of a desk with a bag of ice wrapped around his knuckles. Wilma hovered over him, clucking like a mother hen, and in a back office, a man gestured wildly while blood trickled from his nose.

"Not good," Jill muttered under her breath. She might specialize in corporate law, but she knew enough about how the world worked to suspect Mac was in a truckload of trouble.

"What happened?" she asked as she pushed through the deputies and approached Mac. "Are you okay?"

He looked at her and she was relieved to see he wasn't hurt. Well, except for his knuckles.

Mac's dark blue eyes seemed filled with pain, but not the physical kind. "I'm completely screwed," he muttered.

"Not necessarily. He punched you first, right?"

Wilma shooed the deputies away, while Mac shrugged and said, "I'm not sure he got a punch off."

The girly part of her was pleased her man was such a good fighter. The lawyer part winced.

"Tell me what happened. Start from the beginning."

Mac explained about Andy approaching him and how he'd told him to stay away from Kim.

"He said she was his wife, which was the same as saying she was his dog and he could do anything he wanted."

"Then he threatened you," Jill said, trying to get it all straight.

"No, he threatened me before. I punched him after the dog comment."

"But he did threaten you."

"Sure."

"At least that's something."

Mac glanced back at the rear office where Andy held a cloth to his nose. "Someone get him out of here. Take him to the hospital."

D.J. moved closer. "You think that's a good idea, boss? Should we just take him home and let him cool off?"

Jill knew what the deputy was thinking. A trip to the hospital meant paperwork, which could later be used as evidence.

Mac narrowed his gaze. "Take him to the hospital now. Then have someone drive him home. We'll get his car to him later. In the meantime, send someone to his house to get Kim out of there for a few hours. She can't be around when he's released from the hospital. He'll want to take his pain out on someone and I don't want that to be her."

"I'll take care of Kim," Wilma said as she collected her purse from her desk drawer. "I used to know her mother before she moved to L.A. I'll go over for a visit."

"See if you can convince her to spend the night

somewhere else." Mac removed the ice and flexed his hand. "Otherwise he's going to beat the crap out of her."

Jill was afraid he was right. "You didn't have a choice," she said.

He glared at her. "Sure I did. There's always a choice. But I had a hell of a morning and then this guy showed up, looking for a fight. So I gave it to him."

"He deserved it."

"You think that's what the district attorney is going to say on Monday morning when Andy wants to press charges? I don't."

Jill wanted to stamp her foot in frustration. "So Andy gets to treat his pregnant wife like a punching bag, even break a few bones and that's fine, but when you teach him a lesson, you get in trouble."

Mac stared at her. "It's not that simple."

"I know. It's just not fair." She moved close and took his hand in hers. The knuckles were split and swollen. "You clocked him good."

"I had a lot of practice when I was a kid. I guess that's something a guy doesn't forget how to do."

"I'm sorry," she said as she touched his shoulder. "Can I do anything?"

"Get me the name of a good lawyer."

"You think it's going to go that far?"

"I haven't a clue. But I do know the second Hollis Bass finds out, there's going to be hell to pay."

Jill's eyes widened. The social worker. She'd forgotten about him. "He already thinks cops make lousy fathers and that you have an anger-control issue."

"Thanks for reminding me."

"Oh, Mac, this could be bad."

"I know." He turned away and stared out the window. "The thing is, I have no one to blame but myself. I should have walked away. Now the joint-custody agreement is at risk. And for what?"

She felt sick to her stomach. "Is there anything I can do?"

He smiled, but not in a humorous way. "I think you've done enough already."

She didn't like the sound of that. "What do you mean?"

"Just that your out-of-town friend, the one who is only here looking for a good time, seems to have brought his old ways along."

Oh, God. What had Rudy done? She braced herself. "Meaning?"

"I closed down a tidy gambling club this morning. It was very nice. Bar, craps table, the whole thing. Of course no one working there claims to know Rudy, but you and I have been around the block a few times. We know who's responsible."

He turned cold eyes on her. "Unless you want to convince me that I have it all wrong and that Rudy has changed."

She didn't know what to say. She couldn't think, couldn't speak. This wasn't happening.

"It's a real bummer, too," Mac continued. "Because Rudy offered me a sizable contribution to my campaign. Not that I expect to be running. What with the mayor in Rudy's back pocket, I would say my chances of reelection are close to zero." He stood. "Good to know that Rudy's a changed man, because I'd hate to meet up with him when he was still breaking the law."

With that he walked toward his office. Jill watched him go. She felt cold inside. Cold and sad. She and Mac were to have spent the afternoon together. Hard to believe that everything could change for the worst in such a short period of time.

JILL ARRIVED at her office on Monday shortly after nine. She felt as if she'd been run over by a big truck. Everything inside of her hurt and she couldn't say why.

Okay, lack of sleep had something to do with it. She'd spent most of the previous night pacing. And maybe not eating contributed to her situation. She hadn't been able to choke down a bite since Saturday morning.

Adding to her being out of sorts was the fact that she hadn't seen Mac, either. While she'd spent most of Sunday spying out her front window, she'd never seen his truck or his sheriff's car parked in his driveway. Had he and Emily left town? Had Mac's ex-wife found out about the fight and taken the girl away and had Mac disappeared who knows where?

Rudy was also missing in action, which annoyed the hell out of her. When she'd returned home Saturday, she'd found a note from her aunt saying she and Rudy had taken off for San Francisco for the rest of the weekend, and that Jill wasn't to worry. Jill had paged Rudy, but he hadn't bothered getting in touch with her.

He'd probably figured out that she was very unhappy with him. How dare he tell her he was just in town for some R and R, only to set up an illegal gambling operation. She might not want to spend the rest of her life in Los Lobos, but by God she wasn't going to stand by and watch Rudy destroy the town.

Plus, he'd betrayed her. As much as she wanted to, she couldn't ignore that hard truth. She'd known Rudy for nearly three years and, in all that time, he'd been completely aboveboard with her. There hadn't been a hint of illegal activity. The businesses she dealt with were squeaky-clean enough to be models of what to do to stay on the right side of the law.

Had he been playing her for a fool? Okay, so she wasn't technically his lawyer anymore, but hadn't he told her he would bring his business to her when she got settled? She'd been counting on that three million in billing to put a smile on her new employer's face. It looked as if that wasn't going to be happening. It had been one thing to represent Rudy when, to the best of her knowledge, he'd been completely legit. Now that she knew firsthand about illegal activities, she didn't want to have anything to do with him.

She got out of her car and walked to the front door. Okay, technically she didn't know *firsthand*, but she knew Mac wouldn't lie, which meant—

The door was open. Jill had a brief thought that someone had broken into the office before she realized she could smell coffee and hear someone humming. Had Tina decided to show up at a decent time?

Jill stepped inside. Sure enough her assistant/secretary/receptionist was already behind her desk and hard at work. Papers spit out of the computer printer, the copy machine zipped back and forth fast enough to make the entire stand shake and, surprise of surprises, the "to be filed" box was empty.

"Morning," Tina said cheerfully as Jill carefully stepped into the office.

Had aliens descended and abducted Tina, only to put a perky look-alike in her place?

"Morning. What time did you get here?"

"Eight. My husband's staying home with the kids this morning, so I thought I'd get an early start."

Jill didn't know what to say. As she crossed toward her own office, she noticed several packing boxes and—her breath caught in her throat—fish filling the boxes. Fish that were no longer on the walls. There was a serious absence of fish.

"You're taking them down?" she asked, trying to sound casual and not at all as if she wanted to break out some rusty cheerleading routines and root for the home team.

"Yeah. I called Mrs. Dixon yesterday and she's ready to have us take them down and bring them to her."

"Fine by me," Jill said as she walked into her office and came to a complete stop.

Here there were almost no fish and the netting was gone, too. Aliens, she told herself. It had to be aliens. Or a cult.

She put down her purse and returned to the reception area. "Okay, I'm still leaving. I have a couple of interviews lined up and I've already turned down two offers."

Tina smiled. "I know. It's really a shame you have to go. You've done so much for the town."

Her smile was sincere, her pupils weren't dilated and there weren't any scales or horns sticking out anywhere Jill could see. So what was up?

"Oh, you have a FedEx package on your desk."

"Thanks." Jill walked back into her office, then returned to stand by Tina's desk. "Okay. I can't stand it. You're being nice. What is it? Do you want a raise?"

"Well, sure. I wouldn't say no." Tina smiled. Then her humor faded. "But that's not the reason. I heard what happened. You talked to Mac and he gave Andy a taste of his own medicine. Someone should have done that years ago."

So that's what this was about. Revenge on a bully. Jill thought about mentioning that Mac was in some serious trouble for what he'd done. He could lose his job and his daughter.

"The whole town is talking about it," Tina continued. "Everyone is really happy."

"It's too bad no one bothered to intervene before," Jill told her. "Andy's been using his wife as a punching bag for a lot of years."

Tina sighed. "I know. It's just..."

"Right. No one wanted to get involved."

Mac had, she thought glumly. But in the wrong way.

"I'll be in my office," she said.

"Oh, you have an appointment at nine-thirty. Riley Whitefield will be in to talk about his uncle's will."

That was fast, Jill thought as she moved toward her

desk. It had been a long time since she'd last seen Los Lobos's favorite bad boy and the guy who had broken Gracie's heart. She wondered how time had treated him and what he would say when he found out about the terms of his uncle's will.

"I DON'T HAVE A CHOICE," John Goodwin said. It was only nine in the morning, but the Los Lobos district attorney had already discarded his suit jacket, loosened his tie and rolled up the sleeves of his long-sleeved white shirt. "I'm sorry, Mac."

"Me, too." Mac slouched in the chair and reminded himself he'd started the trouble with Andy Murphy and it looked as if he was going to have to see it through.

"I'm not saying I don't agree with you," John told him. "I do. I think Murphy's a bastard. But with his wife unwilling to press charges and no one else coming forward as a witness to the beatings, my hands are tied. He wants to file charges and I can't ignore that. I'll go as slow as I can. We'll need to do a thorough investigation. But the best I can do is buy you time."

"I appreciate that."

John, a big bear of a man, slapped a file on his already overflowing desk. "You'll need a lawyer. Get a good one. I can give you some recommendations."

"Thanks. I know a few people." He was sure Jill would have opinions on who would do a good job. For a second he thought about contacting Judge Strathern, but he didn't want to disappoint the old man by telling him what had happened. The judge would hear in time—he seemed to hear everything. But later was better than sooner.

"I want you to fight this," the D.A. told him. "You're a good man and good for this town."

"Tell that to Andy Murphy."

"He doesn't get a vote in this."

Mac glanced around the office and thought about what would happen when word got out. Hollis wasn't going to be happy.

"Seems to me he's getting a vote all right. He's calling the shots." Mac rose. "Not that I didn't earn it. I hit him and now I have to deal with the consequences." He'd given in to his temper and now he had to pay the price.

"I'll do what I can," John told him. "But I also have to do my job."

"I know and I appreciate the support. Let me know when the hearing is."

RILEY WHITEFIELD APPEARED to be one of those men who got better with age. He'd been a dark, dangerous teenaged boy who wore black T-shirts tucked into his jeans, motorcycle boots and a gold hoop earring. At seventeen he'd been sexy enough to get any girl he wanted; at thirty-two he'd moved on to women, but Jill was willing to bet they were just as available.

He walked into her office exactly on time. The jeans and T-shirt had been replaced with slacks and a long-sleeved shirt, the gold hoop with a small diamond. But there was still smoldering sensuality just under the surface and the promise of ten kinds of fabulous sin in his eyes.

"I'm sorry about your uncle," Jill said as she stood and motioned to the chair in front of her desk.

Tina mouthed the words *great butt,* then fanned herself with one hand as she closed the door with the other.

"Donovan and I weren't exactly on speaking terms," Riley said as he took a seat. "I haven't seen the bastard in nearly ten years, so don't expect me to be sorry he's gone now."

He'd filled out, she thought as she took in his broad shoulders and muscular chest. Time had been more than kind to Gracie's crush. What on earth would her friend say when Jill told her that Riley had been in her office?

The man in question frowned slightly. "I know this is going to sound like a line, but do I know you?"

"I'm a ghost from your past," she said with a smile. "I'm the judge's daughter. Jill Strathern."

His expression remained blank.

"Gracie's best friend."

That got his attention. Riley stiffened. "Gracie Landon? You knew her?"

"Unfortunately, I was her partner in crime." Jill held her hands palm up. "Let me just say how sorry I am for everything we ever did to you."

"Gracie was creative. I'll give her that. And persistent." He glanced around the room as if expecting her to jump out of a closet. "What's she doing these days?"

"She makes amazingly beautiful wedding cakes. Some of them were just featured in *People* magazine, which was fabulous. She's been inundated by orders from the rich and famous."

"Good for her. Does she live in town?"

Jill had to admit she sort of liked seeing the sexy and brooding Riley Whitefield look nervous.

"Los Angeles."

"Ah."

"She never visits."

Riley visibly relaxed in his chair. "So, about the will."

"Yes. The will." Jill pulled out a folder and handed it to him. "Your uncle left most of his sizable estate to you. I've made a copy of the will for you to read at your leisure. It's fairly long, with lots of asides and opinions. There are a few donations to charities."

Riley didn't bother opening the folder. "I'm surprised," he said. "I didn't think the old man had it in him."

"I know the two of you were estranged, but your uncle did a lot for the town. He will be missed by many."

Riley's dark eyes filled with loathing. "At the risk of sounding like a complete bastard, I don't give a shit. As far as I'm concerned, my uncle was a miserly old prick who lived to torture those less well-off. He let his own sister die of cancer. By the time I learned she was sick, it was too late. After her death I found a letter she'd written to him asking for money for the operation that could have saved her life. He sent it back, along with a note telling her to get help from the government."

Jill didn't know what to say. "I'm sorry," she murmured.

"So am I. I was nineteen at the time. Fresh off my divorce. I'd left town to make my way in the world and my mother knew I didn't have any money myself. Of course if she'd told me what was going on, I would have gotten it out of her brother one way or another. But she didn't. The first I knew anything was wrong was when the county hospital called to tell me she was dying." He leaned forward. "So I don't care about my uncle's donations to charity. I want to take whatever he's leaving me and spend it in a way that will make him turn over in his grave. I consider it a personal mission."

She could understand his need for revenge. Riley didn't strike her as the kind of man who would forgive and forget. There was also the fact that his uncle had committed an unforgivable act of neglect. To have turned away his own sister. She shivered.

"I'm surprised you didn't try to get back at him while he was still alive," she said.

Riley relaxed back in his chair. "Who's saying I didn't? As far as I could tell, the only thing he loved in his life was that damn bank. But times have been hard on financial institutions and he'd been forced to take on a partner."

Jill had heard something about that. "You?"

Riley nodded. "Just as soon as I find out who he's left his share to, I plan to buy them out and close the bank."

"Yes, well, there are some complications."

"Of course there are." He crossed his legs, resting his right ankle on his left knee. "Tell me about them."

Jill knew he wasn't going to like what she had to say. "While you are your uncle's sole heir, the inheritance isn't left to you outright. His share of the bank, along with the assets, will be given to you upon meeting his conditions."

He raised one dark eyebrow. "Which are?"

"You have to become respectable. Apparently your uncle was concerned about what he called your wild ways. Therefore to inherit his portion of the bank and his assets, you have to run for mayor of Los Lobos and win. The election is next June. That gives you just over ten months to make this happen."

Riley stood and crossed to the far side of the room. Despite the heat of the moment, Jill couldn't help but notice the butt Tina had admired. It was pretty amazing.

"He was smart," Riley said contemptuously. "I can just walk away, right?"

"Sure. If you want. The assets go to charity and the bank gets sold."

"Great. I can buy it and—"

She shook her head. "You can't. He makes it clear you're not allowed to bid on the bank if you don't meet the conditions of the will." There was one more thing. She wasn't sure if Riley would consider it good or bad.

"Your uncle's assets were considerable. If you don't go through with running for mayor, you're not just walking away from the bank, you're turning your back on a lot of cash."

"How much?" Riley asked.

"After taxes?" She pushed a few buttons on her calculator. "My conservative estimate is ninety-seven million dollars."

CHAPTER SEVENTEEN

MAC ROUNDED the corner by Jill's office only to nearly run into someone coming the other way. He took a step back to apologize, then stared in disbelief at the man standing there.

Tall, dark with perfect features. He even recognized the scar by the right corner of the guy's mouth—Mac had been the one to give it to him.

Mac shoved his hands into his slack pockets—whether to keep from shaking hands or punching, he wasn't sure—and allowed his surprise to show in his voice.

"Riley Whitefield. I never expected to see you back here."

Riley frowned. "Mac? Holy hell." He looked him up and down. "You're the sheriff?"

At least for the next couple of months, Mac thought grimly. Until he'd taken his temper out on Andy Murphy, the last fight Mac had been in had been his senior year of high school, and his opponent had been Riley. Funny how both events had completely changed his life.

"What brings you to town?" Mac asked, ignoring Riley's question. "You're not staying long, are you?"

Riley grinned. "I see you're still determined to be

one of the good guys. Guess that means you're still finishing last."

The comment cut a little too close to home for Mac's liking. "You didn't answer my question."

"Going to run me in if I don't?" Riley glanced around at the shops on either side of the street, at the overgrown trees and the kids playing in the park on the corner. "It looks the same. I can't decide if that's good or bad."

Mac shrugged.

"I'm here because my uncle passed away. I had to stop by and see the lawyer handling the case."

Jill, Mac thought, and wondered what she'd thought of his old friend.

"Get your check?" Mac asked.

"It's a little more complicated than that. But I'll be taking everything that old bastard had."

Mac remembered how Donovan Whitefield had made his nephew's life hell. He'd heard that the cheap son of a bitch had let his own sister die of cancer rather than pay for her medical bills. While he might not want Riley around making trouble, he couldn't blame the man for hating his uncle.

"Got a time frame?" Mac asked.

"You that eager to get rid of me?"

"Pretty much."

"Sorry, Mac. I'm going to have to become a temporary resident. But don't worry. It's just until I satisfy the terms of my uncle's will. I don't want to be here any more than you want me here. See ya."

With that, Riley walked to the curb and climbed into

his car. A rental, Mac thought, taking in the stickers on the back of the rearview mirror. So what had become of the man who had once been his best friend? Where did he live and what did he do?

Mac would put money on Riley being successful, regardless of his occupation.

He glanced toward Jill's office, then turned and headed back the other way. He didn't want to talk to her right now. Not while he had questions about Riley and the will and he knew she wouldn't give him answers.

Funny how he thought taking the job of sheriff in Los Lobos would mean long, slow, boring days. Right now he could use a little dull in his life, but it didn't look as if he was going to get it.

JILL CAME HOME to an empty house and an uncomfortable silence. She didn't need to check around to realize that her aunt was still out of town with Rudy, although she did push the flashing message light button.

"Hi, Jill, it's Bev. Rudy and I are still in San Francisco. It's so beautiful here, I can see why you love it. We're going to stay a few more days. I've made arrangements for Emily to stay with my friend Chris during the day. Chris has that fabulous craft store by the supermarket. She teaches classes and Emily will simply love it. Anyway, I'm fine." Her aunt sighed, then laughed. "Better than fine. Rudy's amazing." She lowered her voice. "I'll fill you in on the details when I get home. Love you."

There was a click, then the message ended.

Jill stared at the machine. "How much of this impromptu visit is about young love and how much of it is you avoiding me, Rudy?"

She still didn't know what to think about all that had happened. What other secrets had he been keeping from her?

She hated to have been played for a fool, but there was no other way around it. Rudy had acted all normal and righteous around her, but in truth he was a criminal.

"It shouldn't be a surprise," she told herself. "You knew he was a snake when you let him in."

True, but she'd thought he was a good snake.

In her bedroom she found a Post-it note on her mirror and a letter tucked into the frame. The Post-it reminded her of a pier committee meeting in a couple of days. The time for the celebration neared and there was plenty of work to be done.

"I get to stuff goodie bags," Jill muttered. "What a fabulous use of my talent."

The letter was an offer from the firm in San Diego. She fingered the expensive paper, but didn't pull it out and read it again.

The job offer was fabulous. Great salary and benefits. A clear plan for promotion. A chance to learn about different industries while continuing to advance in her specialties. As she'd been careful to never mention her relationship with Rudy and the potential three million in billing, they wouldn't miss the money. It was perfect. So why hadn't she called?

Jill didn't have an answer, although she knew she should. Was she waiting to hear back from the partners at her old firm in San Francisco? Did she think that they would suddenly discover Lyle was a rat fink lying weasel dog and beg her to return?

"Pathetic but true," she said as she began to change her clothes.

Her gaze dropped to the phone on the nightstand. Should she call Gracie and tell her that Riley was back in town? Would her friend want to know? Jill had warned him there would be a lot of interest in his return and he'd given her permission to say he was going to be around dealing with the contents of his uncle's will and that was it.

Gracie would have a lot of questions that Jill wasn't prepared to answer. Nor did she think her friend wanted to hear that her one-time crush still looked like a walking, breathing poster for a female sexual fantasy.

She pulled a T-shirt over her head and walked to her window. From there she could see Mac's house. The truck was in the driveway. It was too early for lights to be on, but she could hear noises from next door. He was home.

She ached for him and not just for the afternoon of lovemaking that had been derailed. She missed talking to him—both for what he had to say and for the sound of his voice. She missed laughing with him and seeing him smile. She missed Emily.

But after what had happened, she wasn't sure if they were still speaking. She could tell herself that none of it was her fault, but she still felt some measure of guilt. Rudy had come to Los Lobos because of her. She hadn't listened when Mac had warned her the man was trouble. Then Mac had lost his temper and taken it out on

Andy Murphy. Not that the wife-beater didn't deserve it, but there were consequences for Mac. Huge ones.

Still, there was no point in wishing for the moon, she told herself as she turned away from the window and walked toward the stairs. If Mac wanted to get in touch with her, he knew exactly where to find her. She wasn't going to be the one to go crawling to him.

SOMETIME AFTER TEN, Mac told himself he had to go up to bed. The way his days were going, he needed his sleep to stay sharp, or at least not to be stupid again.

He and Emily had spent a quiet evening together, playing games, then watching a video. He treasured the closeness as she snuggled against him, giving him the honor of holding Elvis. He liked the way she smiled at him during the funny parts of the movie and how she'd flung herself at him when Ariel had gotten herself into some trouble and had whispered she knew Mac could save her.

He liked being both her father and her hero. So what the hell was going to happen to the love in her eyes when he was officially charged and lost custody of his daughter?

He didn't want to think about it. He didn't want to deal with it, but there it was—waiting for him. Lurking and giving him a knot in his stomach. He'd been a fool and now he had to pay the price.

"Anything but Emily," he said aloud. He would cut off his arm rather than lose her.

A knock on the door caused him to sit up and glance at his watch. Who would come calling now?

He knew who he wanted it to be, but Jill wasn't likely to show up at his door. Not after all that had happened between them. Still, he hadn't heard a car pull up.

Expectation propelled him to his feet. He crossed to the door and pulled it open. Pleasure poured through him.

"It's not what you think," Jill said as she pushed past him and walked into the living room. "I am absolutely not crawling here. I'm walking with strength and dignity. As your friend and as an attorney, I feel it's important to discuss certain things with you. As with all free advice, you can ignore it, but in this case, you'd be a complete ass to do so. Am I making myself clear?"

She stood there, spine stiff, shoulders back. Determination radiated from her and, even in her shorts and T-shirt, she looked damned impressive. He would have wanted her under any circumstances, but it was her long curly hair that did him in.

He grabbed her and pulled her against him. "I've missed you," he said right before he kissed her.

Her mouth instantly yielded. Her arms wrapped around his neck and she molded her body to his. Her scent and her heat surrounded him, offering comfort and promise. Or maybe that's what he wanted to read into it all.

She was the one who drew back a few seconds later. "We have to talk."

Four words every man in the universe, except maybe Dr. Phil, would rather eat glass than hear. "Can't we just go upstairs and make love instead?"

She hesitated. "I'm tempted."

"Good."

He took her hand with the intent to lead the way, but instead he found himself curling his fingers around hers and tugging her toward the sofa. He could never admit this to another living soul, especially not another guy, but maybe they did need to talk.

"How are you?" she asked when she had settled next to him on the sofa, her body angled toward his, their knees touching.

"Fine."

She shook her head. "I don't think so."

"Okay, I feel like shit. What was I thinking?" He straightened and slid to the front of the sofa where he rested his elbows on his knees and dropped his head to his hands. "I risked everything by punching out that bastard. He's a human cockroach and he's going to cost me Emily."

"You don't know that."

He turned his head to look at her. "I'm going to be formally charged. Hollis has already called to set up an appointment. I'll put him off as long as I can, but you and I both know it's just a matter of time."

Jill rubbed her hand across his back. "You need a lawyer, Mac. Someone brilliant. I want to ask around and find the right person."

"Not you?"

"No. First of all, we have a personal relationship and that's a serious no-no. Second, I don't handle criminal cases."

"A lawyer isn't going to be able to change what I did. I lost my temper and now I have to pay the price."

"But Andy deserved it."

"Are you sure?" Mac straightened. "Does anyone deserve to be beaten by someone in authority?"

"He does it to his wife. He's breaking bones."

"An eye for an eye?" he asked.

She glared at him. "If you're going to take the moral high ground, I'm not having this conversation with you."

"Okay. Then just have sex with me." He grabbed her hand and pulled it toward him. Knowing she was watching, he pressed an openmouthed kiss to her palm and had the satisfaction of feeling her shiver.

"You're not playing fair," she whispered.

"I'm a guy, sweetheart, and I want you naked. There is no fair."

She cupped his jaw. "I have to tell you something first."

He didn't like the sound of that. "I'm reasonably confident it's not that you were once a man."

The corners of her lips quivered, but she didn't smile. "No, it's not that. Riley Whitefield is back in town and he might be staying for a while."

Mac already knew that firsthand, but he appreciated Jill wanting to tell him.

"I know. We ran into each other earlier today."

Her eyes widened. "You're kidding. How was it?"

"Weird." He flopped back on the sofa. "It's been a long time and yet it felt like yesterday. Funny how

Riley was the last guy I had a fight with and he shows up now. Maybe it's a sign."

"Of what?"

"I haven't a clue."

She shifted close and rested her hand on his chest. "Did you guys talk?"

"We spoke, but it wasn't friendly."

"You used to be best friends. What happened?"

"A lot of things."

He put his hand on top of hers and laced their fingers together. He and Riley had been best friends forever. They'd been on the fringe of bad, getting into trouble, staying out late, drinking and, as they got older, racing their cars. But at the beginning of their senior year, something had happened to fundamentally change their relationship. Mac had stolen Judge Strathern's Caddy and had taken it for a joyride. And he'd been caught.

"When your dad came to talk to me after I stole his car, I thought I was totally screwed," Mac admitted, remembering the fear of that long-ago morning. A long night in the local jail had given him plenty of time to imagine the worst.

"He can be pretty intimidating," she admitted. "If you haven't seen him dancing around the house in his underwear."

Mac chuckled. "I'll admit I never have."

"I did way too many times. When I was a kid I thought it was funny, but as I got older, it began to scar my psyche."

"Well, that morning he terrified the hell out of me. You know he took me up to Lompoc. A few hours in a prison cell put me right on to the straight and narrow."

She sighed. "Riley didn't like losing his partner in crime."

"You got it."

"So you fought?"

"At first he was just mad and kept expecting me to change. One day we had it out and I told him I wasn't interested in getting in trouble. I wanted to graduate from high school and join the Marines. He laughed and I punched him."

"About that anger-management book Hollis gave you…"

"Yeah, yeah. So I have a temper. I'm doing better. Or I was until Andy Murphy pissed me off." Mac didn't want to think about that. "Riley and I both walked away bloodied and bruised. That was the end of our friendship. We graduated. I left town and he married Pam."

"Which lasted all of five months," Jill said. "It turned out she wasn't as pregnant as she'd claimed. Then Riley took off to parts unknown."

"So what happened to him?" he asked.

"I haven't a clue. I didn't ask and he didn't say."

"How long is he back for?"

She rested her head on his shoulder. "I'm thinking until next spring, but I'm not sure."

He knew there was more she wasn't telling him. Information about the will, but he wasn't going to ask. He didn't want Jill violating her ethical code for him.

Not that she would if he asked. She had principles. He liked that.

"I was wrong," she said in a low voice.

"Can I have that in writing?"

She nudged him with her knee. "I'm serious, Mac. I feel horrible about what happened with Rudy. You were right about everything and I didn't listen. I thought I knew him. I thought because of all the legitimate business dealings we'd had that he wasn't a criminal. But he is and now he's brought gambling to Los Lobos. I never wanted that."

"I know." He turned and kissed her forehead.

"Aren't you mad at me?"

"I can be if you'd like."

She looked at him. "I'm serious."

"So am I. I'm not mad. You made a mistake. It's nice to know I don't have a corner on that market."

"He's gone. Bev's with him. I think they're in San Francisco."

"I knew that. Bev called to let me know she wouldn't be around to look after Em."

She squeezed her eyes shut. "I thought coming back here would be so simple. I thought I'd hate everything and leave at the first chance I got. But it's not like that. I got another job offer. This one is in San Diego and it's really great."

A sharp pain cut through his chest. No way in hell did he want to try to figure out what that meant.

"You should take it," he said.

"Should I? I'm not sure. Something doesn't feel right

and I don't know what. Everything is confusing. I hate this town. Really, really hate it."

He tucked her hair behind her ear and tried not to notice how great she smelled.

"Who are you trying to convince?" he asked.

"Don't ask me that," she said.

"Okay. What would you like me to do?"

"Make love with me."

"My pleasure."

MAC DIDN'T WASTE any time, Jill thought happily, as he instantly stood and pulled her to her feet. Before she could think about where or how or even what, he had her in his arms.

His hands were everywhere. Her back, her hips, her arms, her hair. He roamed her body like a blind man paying tribute. At the same time, he pressed his mouth to hers and claimed her with an intimate kiss.

She parted for him instantly, wanting to taste and feel him. When their tongues touched, she felt the heat pour through her. It was like standing under a waterfall of desire. Every inch of her skin tightened in anticipation. Between her legs, her body softened, dampened and swelled in anticipation. Her breasts began to ache, while her muscles clenched.

He explored her mouth, then broke the kiss to nibble his way along her jaw. Her head dropped back and she felt her breathing quicken. She held on to him, her fingers curling into his shoulders.

"Bed," he murmured against her neck, his breath

teasing the places he'd already dampened with his kiss.

"What?"

She couldn't think, not when he made her feel so delicious. Tiny shivers rippled through her with each brush of lips, teeth and tongue.

"Upstairs. My bedroom."

"Oh."

Of course. They couldn't make love here, not with Emily in the house. They had to go behind closed doors and be quiet and make sure Jill was gone well before dawn. And they would. In a second. As soon as he stopped licking the side of her neck and...

"Go," he said, straightening and pushing her toward the stairs.

Laughter filled his voice while passion darkened his eyes. The irresistible combination had her scampering toward the second floor. She headed for his bedroom and waited until he'd shut and locked the door behind him before carefully peeling off her T-shirt and dropping it on the ground.

"I like a woman who takes charge," he said as he removed his own shirt.

"Do you?"

She hadn't bothered with shoes when she'd come over, so she only had to unfasten her shorts and let them fall to the floor. Then she stood before him in only her bra and panties.

He followed her actions, dropping his jeans. He, too, had been barefoot. Now he stood before her in briefs that did little to disguise his erection.

"All that for me?" she asked as she pressed her hand against his belly before moving lower to stroke him.

"There's more," he said, nudging her toward the bed. "Come on. I'll show you."

He waited until she stopped next to the mattress before reaching behind her to unfasten her bra. After pushing away her hand while muttering "Later, I promise," he drew her onto the bed and knelt beside her.

"So beautiful," he said in a voice that was thick with need.

His words made her shiver, the intensity of his stare made her want. She shimmied out of her panties and tossed them onto the floor.

"My kind of girl," he said with a smile before lowering his head toward her breast.

The first brush of his lips on her tight nipple had her arching toward him. When his tongue teased the sensitive flesh, she actually whimpered.

"It feels so good," she whispered.

"I'm glad."

He cupped her other breast and matched the movement of fingers to his tongue. Heat exploded low in her belly and radiated to the very tips of her fingers and toes. Her legs moved restlessly as she tossed her head from side to side.

He moved slowly, then faster. He nipped, he licked, he sucked, and he whispered how much he wanted her. The contact, the words, and when she opened her eyes, the visual of what he was doing sent her perilously close to the edge. So much so that when he left her breasts and began to kiss his way down her belly, she wasn't sure she was going to hold off long enough to actually let him get there.

But somehow she managed to keep control so that

when he parted her legs and knelt between her knees, she could draw in a deep breath in anticipation of his soul-stirring kiss.

His fingers gently parted her slick flesh, then he unerringly found that one central point of pleasure and swirled his tongue around it.

Jill covered her mouth with her hand to hold in the scream of pure pleasure. It was better than she'd imagined, better than she'd ever felt. The heat, the speed, the movement, the *something*. Her toes curled, the soles of her feet burned, her back arched, her body shook.

He kissed and licked and teased and soothed until she couldn't stand it another second. She was already too close and when he took her to the edge, she hung on as long as she could before giving in to her explosive release. The orgasm ripped through her like a tidal wave of pleasure, tossing her back and forth, filling her with ecstasy before slowly seeping away and leaving her boneless.

"Earth to Jill," Mac said as he settled in beside her.

She blinked, not exactly sure when she'd closed her eyes in the whole thing. Not that it mattered. She stretched and turned toward him.

"You're really good at that."

He grinned. "Thanks."

"No, seriously. You could teach a class or something." She had a vision of an entire classroom of men eager to learn technique. "Hmm, you'd need some volunteers for them to practice on. I bet I could find a few."

He tunneled his fingers in her hair. "Not a good idea."

"The class or the volunteers?"

"Both."

He leaned in and kissed her. She moved against him and felt his erection pulse.

"I think I like this," she murmured as she slid her leg between his. "A lot. But one of us is still seriously overdressed."

"I can take care of that."

He rolled away and tugged off his briefs. She took advantage of the moment and collected a condom from the nightstand. Seconds later she was on her back, he was between her thighs and they were both starting to breathe fast.

"Ready?" he asked after he'd pulled on the protection.

As he spoke he slipped a finger deep inside of her. Instantly she clamped her muscles around him and felt the first thrill ripple through her.

"More than ready."

He eased himself inside of her.

Jill reached for his hips and pulled him in deeper. "Don't hold back."

His blue eyes dilated. "Are you sure? I don't want to hurt you."

"I'm too wet and swollen for that. Just do it hard."

He groaned with the pleasure of a man just given a free pass. Then he braced his hands on the mattress and thrust in all the way. The sharp, erotic movement made her insides quiver with delight. She wrapped her legs around his hips and gave herself up to the feelings.

"Just like that," she breathed when he did it again and again.

Harder. Faster. Slick. Hot. It was the perfect mating between a man and a woman. When she felt herself once again falling into paradise, she opened her eyes and found him staring at her. They climaxed together, watching each other. Bodies stiffened, muscles tightened and, at that moment, she understood exactly what all the fuss was about.

CHAPTER EIGHTEEN

LATER, WHEN SANITY RETURNED and Jill found she could breathe normally, she curled up next to Mac and pulled the covers over them.

"I can't fall asleep," she said quietly.

"I know, but I don't want you to go yet."

His words warmed her from the inside out. "I don't want to go, either."

She wanted to stay right here, to be with him, around him, making love, touching, talking. Being.

He rubbed her bare back, then played with her hair. She sensed he was with her, but also miles, or maybe years, away.

"What are you thinking?" she asked.

"Just looking over my life."

"That's a pretty serious topic. Listing highlights?"

"No."

"Because of Emily?"

"Yeah. I don't want to lose her."

She wished she could tell him he wouldn't, but she wasn't sure. She didn't know the details of his arrangement with the court, nor did she know what had happened in his past.

She pushed herself up on one elbow. "Tell me what happened, Mac. Why did Carly leave you?"

He stared at the ceiling. "It's a long story."

"I don't have a whole lot of plans for the rest of the night."

He was silent for a long time. Not sure if she should prompt him or let it go, she said nothing. Eventually Mac began to speak.

"I met her while I was still in the Marines. We had a couple of long weekends together. Good times, but nothing special. Then she turned up pregnant and I wanted to do the right thing, so I left the service and became a cop. I thought it would be more stable, and the pay was a hell of a lot better."

Jill did her best not to react, while inside small explosions of fireworks shot up in celebration. He hadn't loved Carly. She didn't want to think *why* the information was important, but it was and she accepted that.

"So you moved to Los Angeles," she said.

"Right. I'd been an MP, so it was an easy transition. I liked my job, the people I worked with. Carly and I had to adjust, but then Em came along and I knew, whatever else happened, she'd made everything worth it."

He exhaled slowly. "I loved her from the second I held her. She's my best girl and the best I'll ever be."

Jill's heart sighed at the words. "I think she's pretty terrific, too."

"Thanks. So there we were. One happy family. Carly and I had our problems, but we were good friends and that helped. Then I went to work in South Central L.A., in the gang division." He turned and looked at her. "I was excited because I thought I could make a difference. I was wrong. Those kids live a life the rest of us can't begin to imagine. Violence is what they know and understand. I got weighed down and I started to drink to escape."

Jill hadn't expected that and she didn't know what to say. Mac didn't wait for her to comment.

"I got more distant at home and Carly didn't like that. We started fighting. I knew I had a temper, but I was determined not to show it to her, so I buried it and drank more." He returned his attention to the ceiling. "One day my partner and I were on routine patrol. We saw some kids jump an old lady and take her purse. We headed out after them, rounded a corner to an alley and ran headfirst into an ambush."

Jill tensed even as she began running her hands up and down his torso. "Are you okay? Were you shot?"

He glanced at her. "Twice." He patted his chest. "Right here. I had on a vest. So did Mark. The difference is, they shot him in the head."

She gasped. "Oh my God."

"They said he was dead before he hit the ground. I couldn't think, couldn't breathe, couldn't do anything but react. I was past rage, to whatever the hell place that is. I came out shooting and got every one of them. There were four of them." He closed his eyes. "Not one of them was older than sixteen."

She shifted so she could stare into his face, and shook him until he looked at her. "They tried to kill you, Mac, and they murdered your partner. What were you supposed to do? Let them go?"

"That's what everybody said. Even the department psychologist. But here's the thing. There's a difference between killing someone because you're trying to save your own skin and putting a bullet in them because you're so furious you can't see straight. I acted out of anger, not fear. I wanted them dead. And I killed them."

Did he really blame himself? "All strong emotions are closely linked. Passion, rage, fear. They slide into each other. Would it have been better to let them get away?"

"They were children."

"They were murderers."

"You didn't have to watch them die."

She nodded slowly. "You're right. I didn't. So what happened? Did you get in trouble?"

"No. The kids all had serious records, all involving murder."

"So you didn't accidentally shoot someone innocent."

"I'm not saying they were decent, I'm saying I didn't want to have been the one to pull the trigger, and sure as hell not because I was angry." He rubbed his temples. "I started drinking more. Eventually I quit the force and locked myself in the bedroom. Carly left and took Emily. God, I missed my little girl so much, but I couldn't get myself to do anything. I knew if I stopped drinking, I'd have to remember, and there was no way I could survive that."

She settled back down on the mattress and rested her head on his shoulder. "So you let her go because it was too painful to focus enough to find her."

"Something like that. Nearly as unforgivable a sin."

"Is that it?" she asked. "You can't forgive yourself for what you did?"

"I'm supposed to be one of the good guys."

"I think you are."

"You're biased."

"In some ways, but not about this. If you hadn't shot those kids, who's to say they wouldn't have turned around and put a bullet in your head?"

He gave her a weary smile. "People with a lot more training than you have tried to convince me I did the right thing."

"Let me guess. It's not working."

"No."

Men could be so stubborn. She understood he had a lot to work through, but if he didn't stop punishing himself, those kids might as well have killed him.

"So how did you get here?"

He smiled. "One day someone pounded on my front door and no matter how I yelled he wouldn't go away."

Jill wrinkled her nose. "My father?"

"Uh-huh. I don't know how he found out what had happened. He said something about keeping track of me. I was too drunk to remember much. He stuck me in a cold shower until I sobered up, then he ripped me a new one. Told me I didn't have the right to waste a life he'd helped save. Then he offered me the job here and a chance to get Emily back."

His mouth twisted. "Sleeping with his only daughter is a hell of a way to pay him back."

She leaned close so she could whisper in his ear. "I've been married. I don't think my dad believes I'm still a virgin."

"I sure as hell hope not."

She grinned. "Trust me. You're fine. Besides, he's clear on the other side of the country. He won't find out."

"Want to bet?"

She thought about all the people her father kept in touch with. "No. Not really."

He wrapped his arms around her and held her tight. "I'm going to lose her."

Emily. She squeezed him. "No, you're not. I won't let it happen. I'm going to find you the best lawyer I can."

"Why bother? I earned this."

She pushed into a sitting position and stared at him. "Dammit, Mac, you're not going to take this lying down. Do you hear me? Didn't you just do fifteen minutes on how much you love your daughter? How dare you not fight for her?"

He narrowed his gaze. "Jill, I broke the rules. I lost my temper and punched someone."

"So? There are extenuating circumstances. You made a mistake, but you can't just give up. You have to fight. She's worth it, isn't she?"

"She's everything."

There was something in the way he said the words. Something in his eyes, as if he'd been haunted by a specific reality all his life. And then she got it—Mac's universal truth. In his mind the person who wasn't worth it was him.

"No," she breathed as she collapsed against him and held him. "Can't you see how amazing you are? Everyone has flaws, but not everyone is capable of being honorable and owning up to them."

"You don't know what you're talking about."

"Don't I? If you won't do it for yourself, then do it for her. Don't let Emily lose her father a second time."

He didn't speak for several seconds, then he nodded slowly. "You're right. I promised her I wouldn't go away again and I have to make sure I keep that promise. Even if it means crawling to that prick Hollis."

"The crawling is an entertaining visual, but personally I'd go the lawyer route."

"I'll leave that to you. You're the resident expert."

She kissed him and smiled. "You got that right."

"I CAN'T BELIEVE he's here," Jill said, sounding both surprised and furious as they entered the room for the last pier committee meeting before the celebration the following week. "I want his head on a stick."

Mac looked where she pointed and saw Rudy talking to the mayor.

"Hey, I'm the one with the temper," he reminded her. "You're supposed to be the cool, collected lawyer."

"Not today. I'm still pretty steamed over him playing me for a fool all those years." She shrugged. "Okay, I suppose technically I knew what he was, but I never really believed it. Sort of like making friends with a guard dog and then being surprised to find out it has teeth."

"Big teeth and deep pockets," Mac said, watching the mayor laugh at something Rudy said.

Jill clutched his hand. "Are you okay?"

As there were a number of things on his plate right now—the charges, an upcoming meeting with Hollis, a potential run-in with Rudy and the mayor, he wasn't sure what she meant. Not that it mattered. He'd managed to confess his deepest, darkest secret and she hadn't turned away from him. Instead, she'd offered support and had believed in him. He couldn't remember the last time that had happened...if ever.

"I'm fine."

"No punching," she said, her expression earnest.

He grinned. "Not even Hollis."

"He's earned it, but you really shouldn't."

"I promise, I won't." Hollis. He started to laugh.

"What?" she demanded.

"Hollis and his ideas that all cops make lousy fathers. Ironic that he's wrong about everyone else, but right about me. I do have an anger-management issue and I haven't always been there for Em. I've been so busy hating him, I never bothered to listen to what he had to say." His humor faded. "Too bad I won't be able to tell him. I have a feeling that today's meeting isn't going to be fun."

"I'm more than willing to come with you."

He loved her for offering. "Thanks, but I don't think showing up with a lawyer is going to help my case."

He could offer explanations, but the truth was, he

couldn't talk away what he'd done. He was going to have to find a way to pay the price without losing Emily.

Franklin Yardley moved to the front of the room and called the meeting to order. Mac and Jill found seats in the back.

"I have wonderful news," the mayor said excitedly. "We have received a large donation that will completely cover the refurbishment of the pier."

Everyone else in the room applauded. Beside him, Jill groaned. "Didn't Rudy already write a big fat check? What is he buying this time? The right to bring in prostitution? I swear I want that man's head on a stick. A really big one."

Mac took her hand in his and squeezed. "Deep cleansing breaths."

"Do they help?"

"Not with the temper, but eventually you start to hyperventilate and then you have something else to think about."

She grinned.

The mayor waited until the room had quieted to continue. "I propose that in addition to celebrating the pier centennial next week, we make Rudy Casaccio an honorary citizen of Los Lobos and give him the key to the city."

Several people yelled out their agreement. Jill sank down in her seat. "Great. Now we're going to be the *Sopranos—West.*"

THE MEETING SEEMED to go on for days, but it was only about thirty minutes until it ended. While Mac headed out for his meeting with Hollis, Jill worked her way through the crowd until she stood next to Rudy. She took hold of his arm and dragged him toward a side door.

"Hey, Jill," he said cheerfully. "Where are you taking me? Not that I'm not flattered, but Bev and I..."

She turned to glare at him. "Don't you dare make jokes with me." She saw Mr. Smith trailing after them. "You stay out here."

"No can do," he said, and she realized they were the first words she'd heard him speak.

She eyed the bulge under his jacket and knew it had nothing to do with him being happy to see her and everything to do with an illegal gun.

"Fine, then keep back because I want some room when I yell at your boss."

She hated that Mr. Smith glanced at Rudy for confirmation before easing back a few feet when they entered the dimly lit utility corridor behind the meeting rooms.

Rudy, well dressed as ever in chic resort wear, gave her a big smile. "So what's the problem, Jill? How can I help? Is it Lyle?"

She stared at him. "Help? You think I need a favor? You couldn't be more wrong." She really wanted to punch him or something, but several things held her back. First, the thought that Rudy might hit back and that could hurt. Second, it wasn't her style. Third, and most important, Mr. Smith and his ever-present weapon.

"You lied to me," she said, sure she was practically

spouting steam. "You said you were here on vacation. You said you *liked* the town."

He looked genuinely baffled. "I do. Very much."

"You set up gambling," she yelled. "You brought organized crime to my town, and nobody does that and gets away with it."

He smiled. "Jill, honey. Calm down. You don't even like being here."

"So? This may not be my idea of paradise, but you don't have the right to screw with people's lives. How could you do this?"

He frowned. "A couple of card games don't hurt anyone."

"They're against the law."

"What does that have to do with anything?"

She couldn't believe it. "I...you..." Okay, so speaking had just become impossible.

Rudy put his arm around her. "You're taking this way too hard, Jill. I was having a little fun with your boyfriend. I knew the gambling would piss him off. That's all. I didn't mean anything by it."

Her boyfriend?

"You leave Mac out of it."

"Sure. Whatever you say. We're practically family. I don't want you to be upset. Hey, if you don't want to have gambling here, then it's gone."

Her mind swirled with too much information. There was only one way they could be "practically family" and she didn't want to think about that.

"I don't just want the gambling gone, I want you gone."

His friendly expression hardened. "That's not a choice you get to make. I like it here and I'm not leaving."

Damn him, she thought. She had no way to make him.

"Then just stay away from my aunt."

"Bev's more than capable to make her own decisions." He stepped toward her. "What's going on, Jill? We've always been friends."

Had they? Had she really allowed herself to be friends with someone like him?

"We're not friends and I don't work for you. In fact, I don't want to have anything to do with you ever again. So leave your business where it is. I'm sure you and Lyle will be very happy together—you're both exactly the same."

She pushed through the metal doors back into the now-empty meeting room and walked out. Why had it taken her so long to see the truth about Rudy? Worse, he was already in the town and in her aunt's life. However was she going to get him out?

"I'M SORRY TO BE RIGHT, but there we are," Hollis said as he laced his fingers together and rested his hands on his desk.

Mac had to gather every single ounce of self-control to stay calmly seated in his chair.

"I'm not sure what the sequence is," Hollis continued. "Do violent men with short tempers get drawn to law enforcement, or does the profession change them once they're ensconced?" He paused expectantly.

"I'm the last guy to have an opinion," Mac said dryly.

"Yes, of course. You served in the military first, didn't you?"

"Let me guess. You think they breed violence and abuse, as well."

"Military institutions don't help."

Mac looked Hollis over. He took in the slight build, the glasses, the air of prissy nerdishness that practically screamed "come bully me."

"You had a hell of a time when you were a kid, didn't you?" Mac asked. "I'll bet you couldn't go twenty-four hours without someone beating the crap out of you."

Hollis stiffened. "You couldn't be more wrong. I had a very supportive and loving childhood."

"Probably at home, but school was another story. You're the guy I spent my high school years beating up and that's what really pisses you off."

Hollis pushed up his glasses. "I find it interesting that your history of violence started so young."

"I'm sure you do." Mac leaned forward and put his hands flat on the other man's desk. "Here's the thing, Hollis. I don't care what you think of me. I do care about my daughter and I will fight you to the ends of the earth to keep her."

"You should have thought of that before you assaulted Mr. Murphy."

"You're right," Mac said. "I should have. And while we're assigning blame, where the hell were you?"

Hollis blinked at him. "What do you mean?"

"Just what I said. Where were you? Where was the

social services department while Andy Murphy used his wife as a punching bag? Why aren't you out there lecturing to him on the pitfalls of violence? How dare you sit in your office while that man breaks bones in his pregnant wife?"

"We can't—"

"You can't what?" Mac asked, interrupting. "Get involved? Care? When does it become your job? Because we both know what's going to happen. Andy shows a clear pattern of escalation, which means this is going to get worse until someone gets killed. What are the odds of it being him? I'm going with less than ten percent. I think it's going to be his wife or his kid in the morgue. You're going to sit here with your rules and regulations and do nothing. How does that make you right?"

Hollis stared at him for several seconds, then pulled out a file. "After your preliminary hearing, I'll be sending a letter to the judge in the custody case. Should you be charged, you will, of course, lose custody of Emily."

Mac stood. "As always, your understanding is what keeps me going."

He turned and left the room.

Anger bubbled inside of him. There had to be a solution. There had to be a way out. Dammit all to hell. Yet even as he searched for an answer, he knew he'd brought this on himself and he only had one person to blame. There had to be—

Mac stepped out of the building only to find Rudy Casaccio standing next to the patrol car.

"Afternoon, Mac," he said. "How did your meeting go?"

"You don't want to talk to me right now."

"That's where you're wrong," Rudy said easily. "I do want to talk to you and I think you want to listen."

Mac started to unlock his car door, but Rudy stepped in the way.

"Hear me out. You have something I want and I have something you want."

For one horrifying second, Mac thought Rudy had taken Em. All the blood rushed from his head. Fury turned the world red.

"You're making life difficult for me," Rudy said, as if he were unaware of Mac's reaction. "I'd like you to get off my back. In return, I can make Hollis Bass disappear." He chuckled. "Not literally, of course."

Rational thought returned. This wasn't about his daughter—at least not directly. He realized he'd automatically grabbed for his gun. Now he relaxed his hand and let it fall back to his side.

Mac tossed his keys into the air, then caught them. "Let me get this straight. You want the freedom to bring organized crime to Los Lobos and in return you'll make sure the social worker gets off my back."

"We're talking about a little gambling, some number running, nothing big. No drugs. I don't approve of drugs."

Mac supposed that everyone needed standards.

"You're in trouble, Mac," Rudy said. "Hollis doesn't approve of you."

Mac didn't ask how he knew. Rudy's business was all about having the right information at the right time.

"No deal," he said as he unlocked his patrol car.

"You're in a tough place. You have to know that."

Mac knew exactly where he was. He could lose Emily forever.

"Aren't you even a little tempted?" Rudy asked.

More than a little, Mac thought honestly. He would do just about anything to prevent that from happening, but he wouldn't sell his soul.

"I'm not interested in anything you have to offer," Mac said, and closed the door.

"SO HOW ARE THINGS?"

Jill clutched the phone tighter and wasn't sure if she should laugh or cry. "To be honest, Dad, I don't have a clue as to how to answer the question."

"Just start at the beginning and go slow. I'm getting old and I'm not as sharp as I used to be."

That made her laugh. "Yeah, right. That's why you're running everyone's life from three thousand miles away."

"Whose life am I running?"

"Mine. Mac's." She was sure there were more but she didn't know their names.

"Okay, so I've offered a little input now and then."

Jill thought about how her dad had twice saved Mac. "You're a good man and I love you."

"I love you, too, sweetie. Now what's going on?"

She drew in a deep breath. "My secretary, Tina, used to hate me but now she's taken down all the fish so that's cool, but some of my cases are hideous. I mean dog sperm? What's up with that? And I have Lyle's car and I'm trying to get someone to dent it, but nothing is happening to it. I swear it's been protected by Gypsies or something. Then there's Bev, who is dating a guy. I really like that because the gift thing was never real, except the guy is a former client of mine and while I always knew he was sort of in organized crime, I never dealt with any of that and somehow I convinced myself he was one of the good guys only he's not. And now I have to tell her and I don't want to. Plus Mac's in trouble. He pounded this guy who totally deserved it—Andy beats his wife and she's pregnant and it's horrible—but now Mac's going to be charged and as soon as that happens he'll lose Emily. And I've been going on job interviews and I have a great offer from a firm in San Diego and I should take it because that's what I want to do with my life, but I can't seem to pick up the phone and say yes and what's up with that. Oh, and the pier centennial is next week."

"Sounds like a good time for a visit," her father said calmly.

"You want to come here now?"

"I wouldn't miss it for the world."

CHAPTER NINETEEN

Jill was surprised to see the front door open when she pulled up at Bev's house. As she climbed the stairs, her aunt appeared in the doorway and pushed open the screen.

"Hi. I'm back. We had the most amazing time. San Francisco is beautiful. I can certainly see why you've enjoyed living there."

As Bev spoke, she stepped back to let Jill into the house. Jill followed, not sure how she was going to keep her mouth from falling open. Bev wore tailored white slacks and a trim lightweight sleeveless turquoise sweater. Delicate gold earrings hung from her ears. Gone were the gaudy dangling beads, gone was the ever-present floral-print dress, the multiple bangles and ankle bracelet. Most shocking of all, her long wild red hair had been cut short and styled in such a way as to emphasize her pretty features.

"You look great," Jill said, not quite able to believe the transformation.

"Not so bohemian?"

"Not even close. What happened?"

Bev smiled. "I decided it was time to grow up."

Jill's delight evaporated like water in the Sahara.

"This is all because of Rudy," she said flatly. "You're in love with him."

Bev beamed. "I know it's very fast and you probably think I'm too old, but I have fallen for him completely. He's funny and charming and he makes me feel so incredibly special and feminine. We had the most wonderful time."

Jill felt as if she were about to kick a very cheerful puppy. She couldn't remember the last time she'd seen her aunt this happy. To think she'd finally found the right guy, only he wasn't right. He was a criminal, possibly a murderer, and there was no way Jill could let this happen.

"We have to talk," she said, taking her aunt by the hand and leading her to the sofa in the living room.

When they were seated next to each other, Jill drew in a deep breath. "You know that I love you. I barely remember my mother. You were always there for me, including a few weeks ago when I had nowhere to go."

Bev smiled. "Jill, honey, this isn't necessary. Of course I know how you feel. You mean the world to me."

"Then please believe me when I tell you I'm so sorry to have to be the one to tell you this. Rudy really is in the Mafia. It's not a game or an affectation. He's bringing organized crime to town and he has to be stopped."

Bev stared at her. "What are you talking about?"

Jill explained about the gambling.

Bev dismissed the information with the flick of hand. "He told me about that. It wasn't him at all. There are some other people responsible."

Jill sprang to her feet. "You can't believe that. He's the one. He claims to like the town, but he's only interested in making trouble. I've told him I won't have anything to do with him anymore."

Bev stood as well. "Then we have a serious problem, because I intend to marry him. If you can't accept the man I love, then you're not the person I thought you were."

This couldn't be happening. "You have to see—"

Her aunt cut her off. "I see a lot of things, including a young woman who is too stubborn for her own good. I'm sorry your marriage didn't work out, but that's no reason to be bitter about my happiness. I thought you were a better person than that."

Jill winced at the accusation. "I'm not bitter. I want you to be happy, just not with Rudy."

Bev walked out of the room. In the hallway, she glanced over her shoulder. "I've been waiting for Rudy all my life. No one is going to stand in the way of that, not even you."

"OKAY, WHAT'S UP?" Mac asked three evenings later. They sat on his back porch in the quiet of the night.

Jill leaned against him and squeezed her eyes shut. "I'm fine," she whispered.

"You're a lousy liar."

"I know."

He put his arm around her and pressed a kiss to the top of her head. Emily and her friend Ashley were in the living room watching a movie together. The evening was cool and still with a thousand stars overhead. With Jill next to him and the promise of her in his bed later that night, he could almost forget all the hell in his life.

"So tell me," he said.

"When I came back, the only problem I had was getting a new job and taking revenge on Lyle. Now those things seem so unimportant. My aunt isn't speaking to me, you're facing a preliminary hearing in less than a week, my father arrives tomorrow and I don't know how much of all of this I should tell him."

Mac smiled. "Your father has an information network that would make the CIA weep with envy. I'm guessing he pretty much knows everything."

"That doesn't mean he won't ask questions. I told him some stuff, but not all of it. You know how he is. All that gentle understanding wrapped around some serious probing. I doubt we'll be out of the airport parking lot before I start spilling my guts to him."

"Is that so bad?"

She lifted her head and smiled at him. "Not really. I guess I'm more upset about Bev than him."

He'd heard about their fight. "Have you tried to make things right with her?"

"She doesn't want to talk to me. As soon as my dad heads back to Florida, I'm going to move out. That will make things easier for everyone."

He rubbed her back and wished he could offer to let her move in with him. Only two things stood in his way. Make that three. If he lost Emily, he wasn't going to be fit company for anyone. If he didn't lose Emily, he couldn't issue the invitation. Last, but equally important, Jill wasn't going to be around that much longer.

"Won't you be moving to San Diego soon?"

"I thought we weren't talking about that," she said.

"We have to. It's a great job. You should take it."

"Trying to get rid of me so quickly?"

"No. Trying to say the right thing. It's everything you want. Isn't that what you told me?"

"I guess."

"There's enthusiasm," he said teasingly.

"I'm having a hard time getting any extra energy together right now," she admitted. "What about you? Will you be staying here if things don't go well?"

"I haven't thought that far ahead." Nor did he want to. Life without Em? The only thing that could make the situation worse was life without Jill.

The unexpected realization made him stiffen and swear silently. Life without Jill? They'd talked about her taking a job somewhere else, but he'd never considered the consequences. That she would leave. That she wouldn't be next door, or his friend, or as of late, his lover.

He turned to her and cupped her face in his hands, then kissed her. She responded with an eager sweetness that made him ache.

"You're really good at that," she said when he pulled back.

He forced himself to smile. "So are you."

Don't go.

He wanted to speak the words, bargain with her, explain why it was important for her to stay. He wanted to talk about building a life, of families and love and forever.

Sometime, when he hadn't been paying attention, he'd fallen for her.

"What on earth are you thinking?" she asked. "You have the most peculiar expression on your face."

He shook his head. What was there to say? What could he offer? Jill hated it here. She wanted the big city and corporate law. He wanted…aside from her and his daughter, he wanted to find a place to belong. He had thought that was here. With Rudy muscling in, he wasn't so sure. The mayor had—

"I have to fight them," he said.

"What? Who?"

"Rudy and the mayor. I'm not going to let them take over Los Lobos. Somehow I'm going to have to convince the town that they have to fight with me against Rudy and the mayor."

"It will be an uphill battle."

"Maybe, but after the hearing, I may have a lot of time on my hands." Time, because Emily would be gone.

"I want to help," she said, taking his hands in hers. "We'd make a good team."

"You won't be here."

She looked at him, then dropped her chin to her chest. "Let's not talk about that."

They could avoid it, he thought, but that didn't change the truth.

"NICE WHEELS," William Strathern said as he slid into the passenger seat of the 545. "New?"

"Lyle's," Jill said. "I was going to keep the car, but I don't love it and he does."

Her father clicked his seat belt in place. "Since when do you care about what Lyle thinks? I thought he was a lying weasel rat fink dog, or some variation on that."

"He was. Actually, he still is. But I don't want the car, and I'll get no satisfaction from driving it. I guess I could sell it, but that seems childish."

"What happened to the plan for revenge?"

She shrugged. "I don't care anymore. I have no energy where Lyle is concerned. Marrying him was a huge mistake and now I'm fixing the problem. That makes me feel good. As for Lyle, I can't tell you how much I'm not interested in him or his life. He's buying me out of the condo, I'm getting a cash settlement for the car and fifty percent of everything else."

"That sounds mature."

She pulled onto the main highway that led to Los Lobos. "It is. Which is very exciting. But the big news is that I know I'm going to be fine and I have a feeling Lyle never will be. Not because of me, but because he's a complete idiot. Screwing around at work? What's up with that? It's only a matter of time until he gets caught and then what? He's not my problem anymore and I couldn't be happier."

Her father patted her shoulder. "That's my girl. So what's new since we last spoke?"

"About four billion things."

"That's going to be a long list."

She smiled. "Okay, maybe only a couple of dozen. I have that job offer from a great law firm in San Diego."

"Sounds like exactly what you're looking for," he said.

"So you'd think. They're starting to get impatient."

"Of course they are. You're a catch."

The constant, unconditional support was one of the things she loved most about her father.

"I want to wait until after Mac's hearing to make a decision. They weren't happy, but they've agreed to wait."

"When is the hearing?"

"Two days after the pier celebration. You're just in time for all kinds of fun stuff." She tightened her fingers on the steering wheel. "Just so you know, Bev and I aren't exactly seeing eye-to-eye these days."

"Because of Rudy."

"Yeah. She thinks I'm wrong, I think she's an idiot." Jill sighed. "Okay, that's harsh, but it sums up the situation. Plus Rudy keeps leaving messages for me and there's no way I want to talk to him. He's either going to try to convince me that I overreacted about him or it's going to be something about Mac. I don't want to hear either."

"Speaking of Mac, has he found a lawyer yet?"

Jill glanced at him. She'd hoped they would get around to that. Her father might be into his sixties, but he was still an impressive man and he knew the law better than anyone she knew.

"Not one he's happy with. I sort of thought you might want to take that on."

Her father raised his eyebrows. "I'm not sure he'd be interested."

"Of course he would. I think you'd enjoy the challenge. It would be a change from dating age-inappropriate women."

He chuckled. "I have no idea what you're talking about."

"Of course not. That's why your current girlfriend is only five years older than me."

"How did you find that out?"

"I have my ways."

"Kelly's a lot of fun."

"I can only imagine and no, I don't want details."

"Good. You don't talk about my love life and I won't talk about yours. Although I will say it took you long enough."

Jill was so stunned that she nearly drove off the road. "What?"

"You and Mac. You've been crazy about him for ages, although I'm very grateful you kept your feelings to yourself instead of acting like a complete nutcase like your friend Gracie."

"She *was* enthusiastic about loving Riley."

"That's one way of putting it. I was afraid I was going to have to issue a restraining order so that poor boy could finish high school in peace."

Jill wondered what Riley would think to know that someone in town had actually thought of him as "that poor boy." She doubted he would be amused.

Not wanting to pursue that topic, or the issue of how long she might have been interested in Mac, she returned to the question of his legal defense.

"Are you going to take Mac on?" she asked.

Her father glanced out the side window. "I'll have to give it some serious thought."

THE MORNING of the pier celebration dawned bright and hot. Local motels had been booked for weeks in advance. Mac figured the beach parking lots would be full by ten. At least he had the off-site parking and bus service ready to go. Now if they could just get through the day without anything out of the ordinary happening, he would be relieved. Once this was done, he could concentrate on spending as much time with Em as possible before the preliminary hearing.

But until then, he had to deal with too many tourists, underage drinking, patrolling the beach, keeping the crowd on the pier to a manageable number so the old supports didn't give way. There was parking enforcement, the usual fights, arguments and minor medical emergencies.

"Hell of a way to make a living," he said as he stood, grabbed his clipboard and started to step out of his office.

D.J. stopped him with a quick, "Boss, can we talk?"

Mac winced. "This isn't a good time to tell me that we're underfunded and undergunned to fight terrorists," he said with barely concealed impatience. "Let's take it up next week."

D.J. swallowed. "It's not that."

Mac was about to push past him, but there was something in the kid's eyes. Something that made him step back into the office and jerk his head toward one of the chairs in front of his desk.

"What seems to be the problem?" he asked.

D.J. hunched over, his hands twisting together. He scuffed his feet, then raised his head and announced, "I've met somebody."

Mac swore silently. Just his luck. His junior deputy had knocked up some summer bimbo. Did he want Mac's advice on getting married or keeping the kid? Mac figured he wasn't exactly the right person to ask.

"Maybe you should talk to one of the women," he said knowing this didn't bode well for the day. "They're better at this sort of thing."

D.J. nodded but didn't move. "The thing is we get along great. Not just, you know, in bed, but we can talk and laugh. We like the same things." He smiled shyly. "It's really great."

Young love, Mac thought, feeling about ninety years old. "That's great, D.J. I'm really happy for you. You'll have to bring her around sometime."

"I can't."

"What?" He couldn't bring her around? Because why? Mac got a bad feeling as he considered the possibility that D.J. was trying to carry on a relationship with a ghost, an extraterrestrial or God knows what.

"I can't..." D.J. cleared his throat, glanced at the floor and then at Mac. "He's not a she. I mean...I'm gay."

Mac knew his first thought should be one of compassion or some such shit but all he could think was why the hell was this happening today?

"I know you're disgusted," D.J. said in a small voice. He wasn't looking at Mac now. "I am. If my dad knew, he'd kill me. I mean, I played football. I'm a jock. I'm in law enforcement."

Mac carefully put down his clipboard and settled on the corner of his desk. Whatever crisis was happening with the pier celebration was going to have to wait.

"I'm not disgusted," Mac said. "I'm the last person to make judgments on anyone's choices. If this makes you happy, then I'm okay with it."

Jeez, was he really saying this touchy-feely stuff? Not that he cared about who or what D.J. did in bed, but it was like channeling Oprah.

The kid looked at him. Hope glimmered in his eyes. "Yeah?"

"Sure."

"Do I have to quit?"

"What?"

"You know. The department. I didn't know, because there's a don't-ask, don't-tell policy in the military and I told and…"

Mac put his hand on D.J.'s shoulder. "You're not in the Marines, kid. As long as your significant other is over eighteen and not wanted for a felony, have at it. But not today. Today I need you out on the beaches."

"Okay." D.J. stood and grinned. He looked as happy as a puppy with a new chew toy. "I'm glad I told you. I wanted to before, but I wasn't sure and I've really felt guilty and bad. But this is great."

D.J. stepped forward as if he was going to hug Mac. Mac quickly held out his hand to shake.

"All right, Deputy. Stay safe."

Mac winced when D.J. actually saluted before heading out of his office.

Mac waited until the kid was gone, then he raised his eyes heavenward. "Could this be as bad as it gets? I'd be really grateful if you'd take care of things." Then he grabbed his clipboard and his car keys and followed D.J. out of the building.

JILL SWUNG BY her office on her way to the pier celebration. She'd promised Tina to help carry out the last of the fish.

Now that the little critters were down and the paneling stood there in all its old, stained glory, she couldn't help thinking how great the office would look with a nice coat of paint and maybe some wainscoting. New furniture, some varnish on the floor and...

"Stop right there," she told herself as she walked toward the front door. "This is not your rock to carry and not your office to redecorate."

"Morning," she said to Tina as she walked into the reception area. "How are you?"

"Good." Tina pointed at the boxes lined up against the far wall. "Mrs. Dixon wants to know if we would mind donating the rest of these to charity."

"What? She doesn't want them as a testament to the memory of her loving husband?"

"Apparently not."

Jill laughed. "Why am I even surprised? Okay, we're

not going to take them anywhere today. We'll just leave them and drag them to a charity place in the morning. Or maybe we should leave them tonight."

Tina grinned. "Right. Under the cover of darkness so they can't refuse them."

"Exactly."

The two women looked at each other. Jill felt an odd sense of having missed something with Tina. If they'd gotten off to a better start or come to an understanding sooner, maybe they could have been friends.

"You've been a real help this summer," Jill said.

Tina shook her head. "Not even for a second. I'm sorry I was so difficult about coming in and stuff. I had a chip on my shoulder about a lot of things. You're just so perfect and smart and everything. I was determined to hate you."

Jill couldn't believe it. "I'm many things, but perfect isn't one of them."

"Yeah, right. That's why you always look like a model and I'm the example of the cautionary tale."

"You have a family and a life. All I have is my career."

Tina shrugged. "You could have more if you wanted."

"You make it sound so simple."

"Isn't it?"

Jill started to tell her that it wasn't. Life was far more complicated than that. But was it really? Or had she been making it complicated all on her own?

The phone rang before she could decide. Tina

frowned. "Everyone knows it's the pier centennial. Why would someone be calling?"

Jill grinned. "Because it's not yet a national holiday. There is life outside of Los Lobos."

"Oh, yeah. I forgot." Tina reached for the phone.

Jill ducked into her office, where she glanced around at the fish-free decor. A lot had changed in a short period of time. If someone had told her when she'd first arrived that she would feel kind of bad to be leaving Los Lobos, she probably would have driven Lyle's car over them.

Tina walked into her office. "It's for you. A Roger Manson."

Jill put down her briefcase. "That's not possible. Did you say Roger Manson?"

"Uh-huh. He said you'd know who he was."

Of course she did. He was the senior partner at her previous law firm. He was the man who had refused to take her calls after she'd been fired and had given Lyle her office with a window. So he finally wanted to get in touch with her. Well, good. She could give him a piece of her mind.

She marched to the desk and grabbed the phone. "This is Jill Strathern," she said crisply.

"Ah, Jill, I'm glad to have found you. Roger Manson here. How are you?"

She picked up the FedEx envelope holding her offer from the San Diego firm. "Never better, Rog, and yourself?"

"I have to admit, I'm feeling pretty foolish right now."

She'd expected a lot of things, but not that. Did senior partners *ever* admit to feeling foolish?

"I'm calling to let you know that Lyle has been let go."

That perked her right up. She might be over her revenge thing, but that didn't mean she wished Lyle *well*. "Really? Why?"

"It's a long list and I can't discuss all of it, but what I can tell you is that he put false reports in your permanent file and falsified client billings."

Jill sank into her chair. "He lied about me?" she said.

"Yes. He's the reason you were fired, Jill, and I want you to know we feel awful about it. When you were let go, several of us couldn't understand what had happened. You'd done excellent work and the clients all adored you. In fact they miss you terribly. So we started an internal investigation."

He kept talking about what all had happened, but she wasn't listening. Not really. Instead she felt a bubble of happiness float its way up through her body until she thought she might levitate to the ceiling.

It hadn't been her. She hadn't done anything wrong. Vindication felt damn good.

"We want you back," Roger said.

That brought her down to earth with a thud.

"What?"

"We want you back," he repeated, "and we want to show you how sorry we are with a very impressive raise. Of course you'll be promoted and given a nice office. Bigger than Lyle had. Please, Jill, won't you consider coming back?"

She fingered the FedEx envelope. "I'm actually speaking with some other firms."

"I was afraid of that. Is there anything I can say or do to convince you that you belong here?"

"Let me get back to you on that," she said.

Later, when she'd hung up, she walked to the window and stared out at the side street. Lyle was a washed-up has-been. If he'd screwed with client billing, then he was at risk of being disbarred. Funny how without her doing anything at all, he'd gotten what he deserved. So much for him buying her out of the condo. She had a feeling they would be putting the place on the market.

Now what, she wondered. Which offer did she accept? And why did the thought of leaving Los Lobos suddenly make her sad?

JILL DROVE BACK to Bev's house to pick up her aunt and Emily.

"You're late," Emily said as she danced around the living room. "Your dad already left and he said we should hurry. There aren't going to be any good places left."

"I'll hurry," Jill promised as she raced upstairs to get changed. "Besides, I'm on the committee," she yelled from her room. "We get special parking."

It would almost make those hours spent stuffing goodie bags worthwhile.

She tugged off her clothes and pulled on a bathing

suit. After fastening her hair back in a ponytail, she slathered sunscreen all over, then slipped a loose sundress over her head and grabbed her already-packed beach bag.

As she darted out of her room, she nearly ran into Bev, who had paused at the top of the stairs. They looked at each other.

Jill didn't know what to say to make things right between them. She knew that her aunt cared about Rudy. Jill didn't mind that so much as Bev's refusal to see the truth about the way he made his living. Jill's argument that Bev should understand what she was getting into had fallen on deaf ears.

"Ready?" Bev asked.

Jill nodded. "Are we ever going to be friends again?" she asked softly.

Bev's mouth tightened. "We're friends. I'm not angry."

"You're acting like you're angry."

"No. I thought you'd be happy for me."

"I am. It's just…"

"Will you guys *hurry*?" Emily yelled from the bottom of the stairs.

Bev smiled. "We're being paged."

Jill didn't want to let the conversation drop, but with Emily staring up from the bottom of the stairs and the lack of privacy once they arrived at the pier celebration, she didn't see a choice.

"We're coming," she told Emily as she started down the stairs.

VIP parking turned out to be a very good thing, Jill

realized as she locked the 545 and looked around at the mass of people heading toward the beach by the pier. She thought Los Lobos had pulled in a crowd for the Fourth of July, but that was nothing when compared with this. Lines stretched ten deep at the various concession stands. Dozens of body surfers vied for the perfect ride onto the beach.

"Over there," Emily said, pointing. "See. There's Ashley's mom."

Tina had offered to save them a spot, which made Jill grateful that she and her soon-to-be-former assistant were friends.

Jill raised the cooler as a toddler raced by, his mother in hot pursuit. Music poured from dozens of boom boxes. Shrieks and laughter and loud greetings added to the cacophony. The sand was warm, the sky blue and the smell of barbecue mingled with the scent of salt and suntan lotion.

"This is great," Jill said as they approached the spot Tina had marked out with towels.

"I didn't think there would be this many people," Tina said. "I need to make another trip back to the car, but I wanted to wait until you got here. I practically had to fight off people wanting to move in on our territory. I heard someone say that the pier is already filling up, that they'll start limiting how many people can be on it at one time." Tina smiled at Emily. "Ashley is off with her dad. She should be back any second."

Jill turned toward the pier and shielded her eyes. She could see people moving along the walkway and standing at the railing. Two officers in uniform walked toward the stairs leading to the beach. She recognized Mac and started to smile.

At that second, her heart gave a very distinctive *ping*, while her stomach flipped over and the rest of her insides got all warm and squishy.

She stood there, unable to move, unable to breathe as the truth crashed in on her. She loved Mac.

Loved him? No. Wait. It wasn't possible. Sure, she'd had a crush for years and the reality was far better than anything she'd imagined, but that wasn't love. It wasn't anything but means and motive, right? It was great sex and fun conversation. It was him making her laugh and them sharing secrets and…

Oh…my…God.

It was love. She loved him. Maybe she always had, which was crazy. Maybe it was new.

Did it matter?

Several things occurred to her all at once. If he was charged with beating Andy Murphy and lost Emily, he would never forgive himself. Part of that self-punishment could very easily be refusing to be happy with her. Second, what if he didn't love her back? What if this had just been some good times with a little slap and tickle thrown in? Last but certainly not least, what was she supposed to do about her career now? If she—

"Jill?" Emily tugged on her dress. "Can you see my dad?"

"What? Sure. He's right over there." She pointed toward the pier.

"He's gonna come have dinner with us later."

"Good." Not good. How could she face Mac knowing that she loved him and that he might not love her back? What was she supposed to say to him? How and when would she tell him the truth and what if he rejected her? She'd gotten over Lyle pretty easily because she'd never really cared. But Mac was a whole different kind of man.

Think about that later, she told herself, not sure if she was happy or panicked when Emily started jumping up and down and waving her towel to get her dad's attention. It only took a couple of seconds for Mac to spot them and wave. When he started down the stairs, Jill had a bad feeling he was heading this way.

Act natural, she told herself. Pretend nothing has changed. This wasn't the time or place to deal with how anyone was feeling.

"I'm heading to the car," Tina said.

"Do you need help?" Jill asked, eager to disappear for a while.

"No. You stay here and guard our stuff. I'm telling you, people are ruthless."

With that, she walked off.

Jill busied herself spreading out towels while Bev marked the corners of their plot with the coolers.

"It's like a fort," Emily said with a laugh. "We have to take turns standing guard."

Jill sat down and started to tug off her sandals. Just then Rudy walked up. Aware that Mac was quickly approaching and not wanting the two men to get into anything, she stood quickly, prepared to tell him to get lost, but something in his expression stopped her.

"We have a problem," he said by way of greeting.

Mr. Smith hovered closer than ever and Jill noticed he had one hand tucked under his coat as if he were going to grab his gun at any second.

Bev walked over and took Rudy's hand. "What is it?"

"An associate of mine is in town and he's angry about the recent death of his brother."

Fear gripped Jill. Another Mafia guy here looking for payback? In this crowd?

Her first thought was for Emily and she moved close to the girl. Where to go? Where could Emily hide and be safe?

"Rudy, I don't understand," Bev said, sounding frightened. "What are you talking about?"

Jill wanted to scream out the truth, but she was aware of Emily listening. She scanned the crowd, looking for an angry stranger, for Mac, for Tina's husband.

Rudy pulled Bev to him. "You know those conversations you've been having with Jill?"

Bev nodded.

"She's not wrong."

Bev sagged against him. "No."

"I'm sorry. I should have told you myself. I was afraid if I did you wouldn't love me anymore."

"I'm getting Emily out of here," Jill said, taking the girl by the hand.

"What's wrong?" she asked. "Why is Bev crying?"

Jill turned and ran smack into Mac.

"What's going on?" he asked, but before anyone could answer, a woman screamed.

CHAPTER TWENTY

MAC TURNED toward the scream and saw Andy Murphy holding a knife to his wife's throat.

"Get back," Andy yelled. "Everyone get back."

Mac swore and motioned for everyone to move away. Kim, pregnant and pale, her eyes wide with fear, didn't say anything. Her husband locked his left arm around her just above her belly, pinning her arms at her side. The tip of a hunting blade brushed against her skin and a bead of red appeared. She whimpered and someone in the crowd screamed.

Mac could feel the weight of his own gun against his side. If he pulled it out, Andy would cut his wife's throat. If he didn't...

"This is your fault," Andy said, his voice thick with rage. "You set that dumb-ass social worker on me."

"What?" Mac demanded. "What the hell are you talking about?"

Just then he saw Hollis inching forward. Dammit all to hell, what had the idiot done?

"Get back," Mac yelled at Hollis.

Hollis, still prissy in Bermuda shorts and a button-down short-sleeved shirt, walked purposely forward. "I'm a professional and I know what I'm doing."

"You take another step toward me and I'll slice her head off," Andy growled.

Hollis came to a dead stop.

Mac ignored the social worker and focused on Andy. Information poured into his brain—who was nearby, the sharpness of the knife, Andy's rapidly deteriorating mental state. He wondered if the guy was drunk or just pushed to the edge. Had that bully nature of his finally snapped, forcing him to believe he was trapped and this was the only way out? Mac had to convince him otherwise. If he couldn't do that, he needed time to get off a clean shot.

"You shouldn't kill her," Mac said quietly. "If you let her push you that far, you know she wins."

Andy stared at him. "What?"

"Don't *you* have to win? Don't you have to be the one to walk away while she begs you to forgive her?"

Andy frowned. He glanced down at Kim and started to nod. Just then Hollis moved in.

"What are you talking about?" he asked. "Andy, put that knife down right now so no one gets hurt."

Mac physically shoved the social worker out of the way, but it was too late. Andy's anger returned.

"I'm going to slit her throat," he yelled. "I'm going to ruin everybody's party. How's that for fun, huh?"

Where was the rest of his team, Mac wondered, and what would they do when they arrived? He had to defuse Andy, but with Hollis around, not to mention the damn crowd, that wasn't going to happen.

"Andy," he said, hoping Hollis wouldn't interrupt him. "You know she's not worth it."

Andy dug the knife in a little more and Kim gave a strangled cry. Blood trickled down her throat. Mac judged the distance. If he went for his gun, would the other man have time to seriously injure Kim? A knife wasn't a gun, but it could still be lethal.

Mac could hear the worried conversations around him. He could feel Andy's control slipping. He had to move or—

A dark-haired man in a light-colored suit came up behind Andy. Before Mac could figure out who he was or what he was doing here, the man put a gun to Andy's temple.

"Let the woman go," he said in a low voice.

JILL TOLD HERSELF not to scream. Freaking out wouldn't help anyone, but she couldn't believe this was happening.

Andy jerked slightly, then clutched the knife tighter. "If you shoot me, she's dead for sure."

"I don't think so," the stranger said calmly. "Now put the knife down."

Andy lowered his arm, but kept hold of Kim. Jill wanted to grab the pregnant woman and pull her to safety, but the guy in the suit looked too dangerous to mess with.

Mac glanced at him as he pulled out his own gun. "Let me guess. You're here for Rudy."

"Yeah."

The man looked past Mac. Jill instinctively turned and nearly fainted when she saw another stranger holding a gun on Rudy. Mr. Smith lay unconscious on the ground.

"Looks like we're going to have a gunfight," the first man said conversationally.

"I don't want any innocent people hurt," Mac said.

"Sometimes they get in the way."

This wasn't real, she thought frantically. It couldn't be. They were at the beach. All around them people were laughing and surfing and eating hot dogs. This sort of thing didn't happen where there were hot dogs.

"I don't care what happens to Rudy," Mac said evenly. "But I'm not going to let you take care of business in my town."

"Mr. Casaccio hasn't given me and my associates much choice."

Mac glanced around and Jill had a feeling he was wondering where his deputies were. The man with the gun obviously had the same thought.

"Two of your men are tied up in their cars. Uninjured," he added. "The others are too far away to get here in time. I'm sorry to interrupt your party, Sheriff. I don't usually like public displays like this, but I don't have another option."

Jill turned toward Emily. She had to get the girl out of here. Relief poured through her when she saw Bev already had the girl and was inching back from the unbelievable tableau. Suddenly she heard the faint sound of sirens.

"Looks like my guys are on the way," Mac said, sounding relieved. He pointed his gun at the man close to Andy. "Put your weapon down now and we'll get this straightened out."

"I don't think so, Sheriff. Your men will get here too late."

"Goddammit, this is about me and my bitch of a wife," Andy yelled. "I'm going to kill her right now."

"You're annoying," the slick guy in the suit said, and kicked the back of Andy's knee.

Andy started to go down. Kim might be slight, but she was pregnant and awkward. She stumbled as her husband slipped. Andy pushed her away, regained his footing and ran toward the guy who had kicked him.

"Hollis, protect my daughter," Mac yelled as he charged Andy and the other guy.

Jill heard a grunt. When she turned, she saw Rudy punching the man who'd held a gun on him. Hollis ran toward Emily, who broke free of Bev and started to run toward Jill. Jill grabbed her, pulled her against her body, then bent over, trying to cover as much of her as possible.

Mac plowed into Andy and his assaulter and the three of them went down. His only intent was to keep anyone from getting shot. He guessed the knife had gone flying. It would be a problem in a minute or two but right now he had to get the other gun.

A kick to the gut pushed all the air out of him. He fought the instinct to stop and breathe and continued to punch any flesh that wasn't his own. A glint of metal had him grabbing, then the muzzle turned toward him. He ducked. There was a flash and he waited for the hot impact.

His heart beat once, twice. Nothing. Not sure what had happened, he cracked his gun against the wrist holding the other weapon. There was a grunt of pain and the gun in question fell to the sand. Mac grabbed it and scrambled to his feet.

"Don't even think about moving," he told the stranger.

The man rolled over onto his back and Mac saw the gushing bullet wound in Andy's chest. Instinctively he glanced up toward Kim. The young woman saw her husband, screamed, clutched her belly and dropped to the sand. A couple of people in the crowd caught her.

Just then D.J. ran toward him. "I heard gunshots," he yelled, looking more excited than scared. "What happened?"

Instead of answering, Mac turned to check on Emily and Jill. He saw them huddled together and drew his first steady breath since the trouble had started.

"You okay?" he asked.

Jill nodded.

He looked past her to where Rudy and a slightly wobbly Mr. Smith held the second stranger at gunpoint.

"Start with them," he told D.J. "Arrest them all."

JILL WATCHED the hospital elevators, tensing every time they opened. Wilma had promised Mac would arrive as soon as he took Emily home and finished up his preliminary paperwork. Three hours after leaving the beach in the ambulance with Kim, she was starting to go crazy.

Just as she was about to call the sheriff's office again, the elevator doors opened and Mac stepped out. Even as she took in the bruise on his jaw and careful way he held his arm, she rushed toward him and threw herself at him.

"Are you all right?" she breathed, holding on as tightly as she could. "Is Emily?"

"We're both fine." He kissed the top of her head. "How are you?"

"Shaky, but otherwise okay. What happened? Is Andy still down in emergency or did they take him to surgery? Did you really arrest Rudy?"

He led her to a bench along the hallway wall and pulled her down next to him.

She touched the bruise on his face. "Does it hurt?"

"I'll survive," he said. "I find it ironic that I've been in more fights in the past couple of weeks than in the past ten years. It's a pattern I'd like to break."

He tucked her hair behind her ears, then brushed his thumb across her mouth. "How's Kim?" he asked.

"In labor. She's about three weeks early, but the doctor said the baby looks fine. I talked to Kim's mother. She's driving up from Los Angeles and should be here within the hour. The poor woman had no idea what was going on with her daughter. She feels horrible and wants to take Kim home with her." She took one of Mac's hands in hers and squeezed. "Kim keeps asking about Andy and I can't get any information from the staff. How is he?"

The bleakness in Mac's blue eyes told her the truth

before he spoke the words. "He didn't make it. They pronounced him dead on arrival at the hospital."

She shuddered. "He was a horrible man, but to die like that."

She didn't want to think about it.

"I know." Mac pulled her close. "Rudy's friends have been arrested for murder and attempted murder. We'll be tacking on a few other charges."

"What about Rudy?"

"As much as I'd love to put him away, in this case, he didn't do anything wrong."

"You don't sound happy about that."

"I'm not."

There was too much to think about. Too much to consider.

"What about Emily?" she asked. "She has to be in shock."

"She's with Tina and her family right now. I spent about an hour with her first. Fortunately she didn't see that much, but the whole situation still scared the hell out of her. Hollis keeps paging me." He grimaced. "I'm sure he thinks this is all my fault."

"No, it's not. He can't blame you."

"Want to bet?" He shrugged. "That's the least of it. I've got a call in to Carly. This whole thing is bound to piss her off big time."

Jill had a feeling he was right. "Does she know about the preliminary hearing?"

"She will after we talk."

If Carly reacted badly—a circumstance Jill could see happening—then she could go directly to the judge in charge of the custody case and insist Mac give up Emily.

"We'll fight," she said, staring at him. "No matter what, you're not going to be in this alone."

He smiled sadly. "Your father stopped by the police station to tell me he wanted to represent me. Is that your doing?"

"He was interested already. I just told him there was an opportunity."

"Thanks."

He drew her close and kissed her. Jill let herself sink into his embrace and the feeling of his mouth on hers. This is what she wanted, she told herself. To be with Mac always. But when to tell him? Certainly not now. If the hearing went badly, would he even care about her feelings?

"I need to get back to the station," he said. "Wilma volunteered to tell Kim about her husband, but we want to wait until after the baby's born."

"Good idea. Her mom will be here then. That will help. Although she's going to be destroyed. In her own way, she really loved him."

"I'm not sure what she felt was love." He stood and pulled her to her feet. "You take care of yourself."

"I will.

A LITTLE AFTER TEN the next morning, Mac lay stretched out on his sofa with his feet up on the coffee table. Emily was curled up next to him, still sleeping. She'd begged him not to put her to bed the previous night and he hadn't had the heart to refuse her. So they'd watched Disney movies until after midnight, then she'd fallen asleep in his arms.

He wanted to believe everything would work out and that his life would return to normal, but he had his doubts. Andy might be dead, but that didn't take away what Mac had done. Andy being so close to going over the edge offered something of a defense, but was it enough?

He didn't want to think about what might happen and he couldn't seem to think about anything else. Carly had already called twice to yell at him. She couldn't get away until the following morning, but she would be in town in time for the hearing. Hollis had left nearly fifteen messages—thank God for caller ID—and Mac had been fielding calls from the local press. He'd taken the morning off to stay with Em, but at this rate, they weren't getting much time together.

He glanced down at her and stroked her beautiful blond hair. Funny how when she'd been little he'd assumed that the worst he would have to deal with was her rolling her eyes at him when she turned thirteen and beating the boys off with a stick. He'd never thought he'd screw up so badly that he might actually lose her.

He told himself not to anticipate the worst, but the instruction didn't stop the pain from ripping through his heart. He'd already let her down too many times and it was about to happen again. If he lost custody of her, she wouldn't understand anything more than the fact that her father had once more disappeared. He doubted he would get a second chance to set things right.

He heard footsteps on the porch, then someone knocked. He thought about ignoring it, but when he heard Jill's voice, he straightened and shifted Emily from his lap to the sofa.

"What is it, Daddy?" she asked.

"It's Jill. You go back to sleep."

She rubbed her eyes and yawned. "Okay."

He stood and walked to the front of the house. When he pulled it open, he saw Jill was not alone and nearly slammed the door in her face.

"Wait," she said. "You want to hear this."

He looked past her to where Rudy stood. "You have nothing I want to hear."

"I understand you're upset," the other man said. "I came to apologize and tell you I'm leaving."

Mac stared at him for a long time before stepping back. As Jill walked in, he nodded toward the living room.

"Em's in there. Would you please take her upstairs? She's still upset about what happened yesterday and I don't want her to see Rudy."

"No problem."

Jill hurried into the other room. He heard murmured voices, then saw the two of them going up the stairs. Only then did he nod at Rudy.

"You have five minutes," he said.

"Fair enough." Rudy stepped into the house and glanced around. "Nice place."

Mac folded his arms over his chest and waited.

Rudy shrugged. "You're not happy with me. That makes sense. In your place, I'd be plenty pissed off, too." He shoved his hands into his slacks' pockets. "I first came to town to see if Jill was okay. You know, after what Lyle did. After a couple of days I realized I liked the area. I'd thought about leaving Vegas and this little place seemed perfect. Then I met Bev."

One corner of his mouth turned up. "She's an amazing woman. I thought it was a sign—the town, meeting her, wanting to ease toward retirement. You were difficult, but I had the mayor in my pocket and I knew there was an election coming up and I could make sure you didn't win."

Mac did his best not to react to the information. None of it was news.

"The gambling was a mistake," Rudy said with a grimace. "I don't know why I did it. Knee-jerk reaction, I guess. I wanted to piss you off."

"It worked."

"The thing is I felt kinda bad afterward. Then Bev and I went away and I realized I'd been looking for her all my life. She's a really decent woman. Special. She didn't know what I did, and I knew if she found out, she'd be furious. Especially about the gambling. But I didn't want to leave. It was a serious dilemma."

"Then your friends showed up yesterday."

Rudy nodded. "That was bad. People could have gotten hurt. People like your daughter, or Jill or Bev. So I did some thinking and I've realized I'm not right for Los Lobos. I need to be back in Vegas where I understand how things work and there aren't any surprises like yesterday."

He drew one hand out of his pocket and handed Mac

a card. "I'm leaving in a couple of hours. If you need to get in touch with me for anything, here's how to reach me."

Mac took the card but didn't look at it. "The gambling?"

"All shut down. I feel kind of bad about the mayor—the money I gave him. I'd like to give you the same amount for your campaign."

"No, thanks."

"Yeah, I figured you'd say that." Rudy looked him over. "You're a good man. I don't meet very many in my line of work. If you ever need anything, just call."

"I'll keep that in mind."

Rudy nodded, then walked out of the house.

"What did you think?" Jill asked from the stairs.

"I'm not sure. Is he really leaving?"

"Uh-huh. He's all packed up."

He glanced toward the ceiling. "Emily?"

"She fell right to sleep." Jill walked down the stairs and over to him. "Bev's going with Rudy. We talked most of the night. While she now understands who and what he is, she still loves him and wants to be with him. She's moving to Las Vegas. At first I felt kind of strange about it, but the longer I thought about it, the more right it seems. How crazy is that?"

"Pretty wild." Looking at Jill made him ache inside. "She's selling the house?"

"I guess. We didn't talk about it."

Why would they? Jill wouldn't want it; her life was somewhere else that wasn't here.

He dropped Rudy's card on the entry tabletop, then

cupped Jill's face in his hands. As he stared into her eyes, he told himself it was for the best. He had nothing to offer her—certainly nothing of value.

"You'll be happy," he told her.

"What?"

"In your new life. Away from here. In time this will all seem like a bad dream. I don't know what's going to happen tomorrow at the hearing. I know that whatever is decided, I'm going to keep fighting for Emily. We both deserve that."

Jill smiled at him. "I'm glad."

"But I'm not going to fight for you."

"What?"

He rubbed his thumbs against her cheeks. "You're an incredible woman, Jill Strathern. I wish only the best for you."

Her gaze narrowed. "That sounds amazingly like goodbye."

"It is."

"That's it? Thanks for the good times and goodbye?"

"What else do you want me to say?"

"I don't know. Something. I appreciate that you're willing to fight for Emily, but why *aren't* you willing to fight for me? Don't I matter?"

"Of course. I love you."

"What?"

He brushed his mouth against hers. "I love you."

She pulled back and glared at him. "Let me see if I have this right. You're telling me you love me and not to let the door hit me in the ass on the way out?"

"No."

"But you fully expect me to leave?"

"Yes. It's what you want." This wasn't going well, but he wasn't sure why.

"You think you know everything, don't you?" she told him. Anger hardened her words until they felt like bits of glass. "For someone who thinks he knows so much, you're incredibly stupid."

"I don't understand."

"Obviously."

She walked past him and out the front door. At the top of the steps she turned back. "I'll see you in court."

CHAPTER TWENTY-ONE

JILL GRUMBLED the entire way to the courthouse.

"You seem to be in a temper," her father said calmly from the passenger seat.

"I am. Mac is really stupid. I want to slap him."

"He has a lot on his mind."

She stopped at the light and glared at her father. "Don't even *think* about taking his side against me."

"I have to defend him."

"For hitting Andy, not for what he did to me."

"This would go better if you told me what he'd done."

She raised her eyebrows. "Do you really want to have an intimate conversation about my personal life?"

Her father held up both hands. "Excellent point. You're right. Whatever he did, Mac was a jerk and I hope the two of you work it out."

She sniffed without answering. Men. Were they all idiots? How on earth could Mac say he loved her and then turn around and let her go? What was up with that? Had he thought it through? Did he think the words were enough? Didn't he know that she was willing to compromise and find a solution that worked for them both? But no. He made the grand gesture and the decision without once consulting her. It was just so typical and when she stopped being so mad that she wanted to spit, she was going to tell him.

She pulled into the courthouse parking lot and found a spot for the 545. Before she opened her door, she looked at her father.

"You have a plan, right?"

He smiled. "Are you doubting me?"

"Sort of. Normally I wouldn't care, but this is Mac. I might want to beat the crap out of him right now, but that doesn't mean I want to do it with him in prison."

"Interesting point. I'll keep it in mind."

She opened the car door and stepped out into the morning. It was beautiful and clear, much as it had been a couple of days ago at the pier celebration. Not that she wanted that experience repeated again. If there—

A sharp sound like a gunshot made her jump. Before her heart could leap out of her chest, she realized it was just another car door nearby.

"I'm going to need therapy to get back to normal," she muttered right before someone grabbed her arm.

"There you are!"

She shrieked and spun away only to find herself staring into the pale gray eyes of her ex-husband.

"Lyle? What are you doing here?"

"What do you think?" he asked, his face flushed and his veins throbbing. "You ruined me."

She shook her head. "I think you have me confused with, oh, say, yourself. I've been here in Los Lobos for the past several weeks, trying to put my life together. You've been in San Francisco. How exactly could I have ruined you?"

He looked young and upset, as if he were about to cry. "Everything is gone. My job, my career. There's talk of disbarring me."

"I know. I'm sorry."

Surprisingly, she found she meant the words.

"I want my car," he said, sounding as petulant as a child.

"Of course you do." She handed him the keys. "Here you go."

He stared at her. "Just like that? Why are you being nice?"

Because he didn't matter. Because he had nothing and even if Mac was an idiot, she still had a chance for perfect happiness.

"I agreed to give you the car," she said. "Take it."

He brushed back his thinning hair and grabbed the keys, then turned to the BMW and ran his hands along the smooth roof.

"Are there any dents?"

"Not a one. Not even a scratch."

She thought about telling him her theory that the car was somehow protected by a higher force, but what was the point?

"Enjoy," she said, and started walking toward the courthouse.

Her father fell into step with her. "I never knew what you saw in him."

She glanced back as Lyle got into the car and started the engine. "Me, either. I sold myself way short with him, and I can tell you that's not going to happen again."

"Good." He put his arm around her. "You know there's a very good chance Lyle's going to be living out of that car."

"I heard."

They'd reached the steps of the courthouse and started to climb them. From the street came the squeal of brakes followed by a huge *crash*. Jill turned to see that Lyle had driven the gleaming black 545 into the side of a delivery truck. He got out and started screaming. She stood there for a second, trying to care, then realized she didn't and walked inside.

MAC HAD THOUGHT a few folks from town would come to the hearing. Events like this were always of interest, but even he hadn't expected there to be standing room only.

"You seem to be a popular figure around here," William Strathern said as he opened his briefcase and pulled out some papers.

"I doubt they're offering support," Mac said.

He turned away from the crowd when he spotted Hollis waving at him. He'd been avoiding the social worker for two days. No way did he want to hear the prissy pip-squeak gloating now.

"You might be surprised at what the people want," Strathern told him. "Have you talked to Jill lately?"

"Not since yesterday."

Not since he'd told her he loved her and she'd stalked out of his house as if he'd insulted her.

"She's in a temper," her father said. "I wonder why."

Mac swallowed but didn't speak.

"You know about her job offer in San Diego."

"She told me."

"Her old law firm wants her back, too."

Mac hadn't known that. "Great. She must be happy."

"Oddly, she's not. Oh, I'm sure there's a nice sense of vindication, but apparently Jill wants to make other arrangements for her future."

Mac felt sure there was a message in the other man's words, but he wasn't sure what it was.

"I don't..."

Jill's father stared at him. "Did it ever occur to you there was a reason you and Jill both returned to Los Lobos at exactly the same time?"

Before Mac could absorb the question, let alone answer it, Carly came up. He hadn't seen her in nearly a month and she didn't look very happy.

"Where's Emily?" she asked by way of greeting.

"With her baby-sitter. I didn't want her to see this."

"At least you got that right." She glared at him. "Dammit, Mac, how could you do this? How can you act like this and expect me to trust you with our child? What if you're charged? What if you go to prison? What will she think about that?"

"Mrs. Kendrick?"

Mac nearly growled when he saw Hollis approaching. "Get out of here," Mac said.

Hollis ignored him. "Mrs. Kendrick, I'm the social worker in charge of your case. If I could have a moment of your time, please?"

Mac wanted to grab the other man by the shirtfront and shake him. "Stay out of this, Hollis."

Hollis pushed up his glasses. "I'm afraid I can't do that, Mac. There are some things that Emily's mother needs to know about you."

Mac sank down in his chair and knew he was completely and totally screwed.

"Not a fan?" Strathern asked.

"More like someone who would like to see me do hard time."

The bailiff appeared, along with the judge, and court was called to session. Mac stared straight ahead, not wanting to see what was going on behind him or look at the district attorney.

The charges were read. William Strathern rose and introduced himself to the judge.

"Good to see you, Bill," the man at the bench said. "I thought you'd moved to Florida."

"I have. This is a special case." Strathern slipped on his glasses. "I'm sure the district attorney told you that Andrew Murphy is dead."

"I heard that, yes. The court sends condolences to the family, but his death doesn't change what happened."

Much as Mac had thought.

"Are you also aware that my client has temporary custody of his minor-aged daughter and that there are certain limitations to that custody?" Strathern asked.

"Yes. Mr. Bass from our Social Services department has given me all of the particulars. If Mr. Kendrick is charged, I'll be informing the court in Los Angeles."

"Ah, Your Honor?"

Mac turned and saw Hollis had risen.

"Yes?"

"I'm Hollis Bass. About that report to the other court. It's not really necessary."

The judge frowned. "What are you talking about?"

"Just that whatever happens here, whatever Mr. Kendrick did, he still loves his daughter very much."

"There are rules, Mr. Bass."

"Yes. Of course." Hollis adjusted his glasses and cleared his throat. "In the past few days I've come to see that Mac, ah, Mr. Kendrick is an extraordinary father. What he did to the deceased was wrong, but he did it for the best of reasons. He was trying to protect a young woman's life. A pregnant young woman. He stepped in when my department did nothing. For all we know, he saved Mrs. Murphy's life."

Mac felt as if he'd stepped into an alternative universe. Hollis defending him? Was it possible?

Several people started whispering. The judge banged his gavel and called for order.

"Mr. Bass, are you arguing for Mr. Kendrick to keep his daughter or for the district attorney to drop the charges?"

"Oh." Hollis looked surprised. "Both, actually."

"And this would be by what authority?"

"Well, ah, none, but I've gotten to know Mr. Kendrick and when I saw how he handled the situation on the beach, it was amazing. So many people could have been killed. There were ample opportunities for—"

"Thank you, Mr. Bass. I'm sure if either side wishes you to testify, they'll call on you. Please be seated."

Hollis nodded vigorously and sank back in his chair.

Mac shook his head. Was that why Hollis kept calling? Had he wanted to reassure Mac that he was now on his side?

"Your Honor?"

The judge looked up. "Yes? You are?"

"Carly Kendrick. Mac's ex-wife and the mother of his daughter."

Oh shit, Mac thought.

"Whose side are you on?" the judge asked, sounding weary.

"Mac's. I was furious when I found out what had happened, but since arriving in town, I've heard nothing but praise for how he handled a very difficult situation. Plus, if you consider that Andy Murphy tried to murder his wife, I would say he had a beating coming. Not that I want to speak ill of the dead."

Mac turned around and stared at her.

"Of course not," the judge said. "Anything else?"

"Just that Mac and Emily, our daughter, have a wonderful relationship and I would hate to see that taken away from either of them. She's only eight and she needs her father."

The judge narrowed his gaze. "Can we all be clear here? Mr. Kendrick's custody arrangement isn't in question. We are here to discuss whether or not he's going to be charged with assault."

"He didn't do it," a man in the back yelled. "He couldn't have done it. He was with me at the time."

"And who are you?" the judge asked.

"Marly Cobson. I run a couple of tour boats. Mac and me were having a beer at the time someone else beat the crap out of Murphy. He had it coming. Murphy, not Mac."

"I was with them, too," another man said.

Nothing made sense, Mac thought, even as the unexpected support warmed him.

"Did you arrange this?" he asked Strathern.

Jill's father shook his head. "I prepared a brilliant legal argument. Makes me think I wasted my time."

"Fred and me here, we were with them, too," another man said.

"I baked cookies for the whole lot of them," Tina said as she stood. "There was a real crowd."

The judge banged his gavel on the desk and glared at the spectators. "I'll remind you again to be quiet. If you all listen, then I won't bother with a lecture on the dangers of perjury."

John Goodwin, the D.A., stood. "Your Honor. In light of this new evidence, I'm going to have to ask that the charges be dropped while my office does a more thorough investigation."

A cheer went up in the crowd. Mac looked at his lawyer and shook his head. "We both know it can't happen like that."

"You're right," Strathern said, and rose. "Your Honor, my client would like to speak."

"It seems to me this is a good time to stay silent," the judge grumbled. "Go ahead."

Mac stood. "Your Honor, I don't want anyone to get in trouble for what they said here today. They're being kind and I appreciate that, but the truth of the matter is I lost my temper and I hit Andy Murphy. It was wrong. He beat his wife and in the end, he tried to kill her, but that doesn't give me the right to punch him. We have laws and as the sheriff of this town, it's my responsibility to set an example by following them. I don't want to go to prison and I don't want to lose my daughter, but I'm not going to do the wrong thing for the right reason again."

The judge glanced at him, then the D.A. "Any other surprises?"

"No, Your Honor."

The judge returned his attention to Mac. "You planning to take the law into your own hands again?"

"No, but that doesn't change what I did."

The judge leaned forward. "Bill, you want to instruct your client to answer the question asked and nothing else."

Mac felt Jill's father nudge him in the ribs.

"I won't be taking the law into my own hands again," Mac said.

"Good. I don't want to see you again in this courthouse. At least not on the wrong side of the law." The judge banged his gavel. "Case dismissed. Everyone, get the hell out of my courtroom."

JILL WATCHED everyone surround Mac. It seemed the entire town of Los Lobos wanted to congratulate him and take part in the victory celebration. Somehow she didn't feel comfortable in that crowd.

So she walked out of the courthouse only to realize she'd given her ride home to Lyle. The BMW was gone, as was the delivery truck. It was about an eight-mile walk back to Bev's place, which meant she was going to have to call and ask to be picked up.

She punched the number on the cell phone. When Bev answered, she explained what had happened.

"We have cookies in the oven," Bev said when she'd finished. "Give us fifteen minutes and we'll be there. Tell Mac we're delighted for him."

Jill had no plans to talk to Mac so Bev was going to have to deliver that message in person before she packed up and left for Vegas.

Jill planted herself on a top step off to the side of the courthouse. It didn't take long for the people to make their way out and leave. She supposed she could have gotten a ride from nearly anyone, but she wasn't in the mood to talk. Not when everything hurt.

Now what? If she didn't stay mad at Mac for being an idiot, she was going to have to feel horrible because he wasn't willing to fight for her. How could she love a man so very willing to let her go?

Her eyes burned. She blinked hard, because there was no way she was going to cry over him. He wasn't worth it. Except he was, and she loved him and why couldn't he see that?

She felt someone approach and turned her head so whoever it was wouldn't notice the tears. Then, before she realized what had happened, Mac had slipped a pair of handcuffs around her wrists. She stared from them to him.

"What do you think you're doing?" she asked in outrage.

"Getting your attention."

"Are you arresting me?"

"Do you want me to?"

She held out her hands. "This isn't funny."

"I know." He sat next to her and stared out at the horizon. "I love it here, Jill. Los Lobos has always been my home. I want to run for election next November and I want to serve here for the next thirty years."

"Nice to know you have your future mapped out. Now unlock these."

"I don't think so. See, I've been trying to figure out why you got so mad at me yesterday and I think I know what happened."

"Gee, I'll have to put a star by this day on the calendar."

He leaned over and kissed her. She sat there as stiffly as she could, refusing to kiss him back, even when he nibbled on her lower lip.

"You love me," he murmured.

"I don't."

"Yeah, you do. You love me a lot and you don't want to go anywhere, but you didn't want to come out and say that. You wanted me to ask." He kissed her again. "You wanted me to prove you were more than a convenience and that I thought you were worth fighting for."

Her eyes started burning again and she knew she was seconds from crying but for very different reasons than before.

"Maybe," she admitted.

"So if I hadn't asked, were you just going to go away?"

"No," she said, her voice low. "I already turned down

both jobs. I was going to stay in Los Lobos and make you see sense."

"Really?"

She nodded. "But I have to tell you, I gave the BMW back to Lyle."

"That's okay. I prefer to buy American. Maybe we can get a minivan. You know, for all the kids we're going to have."

She stared at him. "What?"

He smiled. "I love you, Jill. Please stay in Los Lobos and marry me. Although if it's really important, we can go somewhere else so you can practice your big-city law."

The first tears slipped down her cheek. She raised her handcuffed hands over his head and pulled him close.

"I would rather stay right here," she said with a sniff. "With you. We can buy Bev's house and have babies, but I'm not sure I'm ready for a minivan."

"I thought you hated Los Lobos."

She thought about the town and how everything had changed. "Actually, I think it's grown on me. Besides, you love it and I can live anywhere with you."

He kissed her, and somewhere in the distance she heard the sound of applause.

"We have an audience," she whispered against his mouth.

"I know."

"You should probably stop kissing me and let me out of the handcuffs."

"Yeah. I will." He pressed his mouth to hers. "In a second."

She pulled back slightly and grinned. "I think we should keep the handcuffs, though. For later."

He laughed. "Jill, I have to tell you. I've always admired your style."

* * * * *

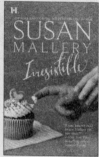
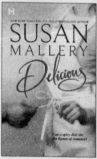

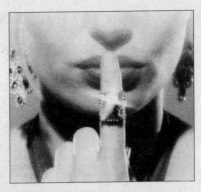

NEW YORK TIMES AND *USA TODAY*
BESTSELLING AUTHOR

JOAN JOHNSTON

Bella Benedict's dying wish is to give her grown children what she once had: a marriage of passion.

Wealthy playboy Max Benedict has no interest in long-term commitment. Working as a sometime spy for the CIA, he's asked to investigate a threat against the president. Then he hears who he'll be working with.

FBI special agent Kristin Lassiter is losing everything, so when Bella Benedict offers to pay her debts, she's tempted. The catch: Bella wants Kristin to win the heart of her son Max, the very man who destroyed Kristin years ago. But can she win Max's heart without falling back in love with him?

INVINCIBLE

Available wherever books are sold.

REQUEST YOUR
FREE BOOKS!

2 FREE NOVELS
FROM THE ROMANCE COLLECTION
PLUS 2 FREE GIFTS!

YES! Please send me 2 FREE novels from the Romance Collection and my 2 FREE gifts (gifts are worth about $10). After receiving them, if I don't wish to receive any more books, I can return the shipping statement marked "cancel." If I don't cancel, I will receive 4 brand-new novels every month and be billed just $5.74 per book in the U.S. or $6.24 per book in Canada. That's a saving of at least 28% off the cover price. It's quite a bargain! Shipping and handling is just 50¢ per book.* I understand that accepting the 2 free books and gifts places me under no obligation to buy anything. I can always return a shipment and cancel at any time. Even if I never buy another book, the two free books and gifts are mine to keep forever.

194/394 MDN E7NZ

Name   (PLEASE PRINT)

Address   Apt. #

City   State/Prov.   Zip/Postal Code

Signature (if under 18, a parent or guardian must sign)

Mail to The Reader Service:
IN U.S.A.: P.O. Box 1867, Buffalo, NY 14240-1867
IN CANADA: P.O. Box 609, Fort Erie, Ontario L2A 5X3

Not valid for current subscribers to the Romance Collection
or the Romance/Suspense Collection.

Want to try two free books from another line?
Call 1-800-873-8635 or visit www.morefreebooks.com.

* Terms and prices subject to change without notice. Prices do not include applicable taxes. N.Y. residents add applicable sales tax. Canadian residents will be charged applicable provincial taxes and GST. Offer not valid in Quebec. This offer is limited to one order per household. All orders subject to approval. Credit or debit balances in a customer's account(s) may be offset by any other outstanding balance owed by or to the customer. Please allow 4 to 6 weeks for delivery. Offer available while quantities last.

Your Privacy: Harlequin Books is committed to protecting your privacy. Our Privacy Policy is available online at www.eHarlequin.com or upon request from the Reader Service. From time to time we make our lists of customers available to reputable third parties who may have a product or service of interest to you. If you would prefer we not share your name and address, please check here. ☐

Help us get it right—We strive for accurate, respectful and relevant communications. To clarify or modify your communication preferences, visit us at www.ReaderService.com/consumerschoice.

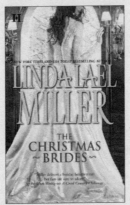

SUSAN MALLERY

(limited quantities available)

TOTAL AMOUNT $ _____
POSTAGE & HANDLING $ _____
($1.00 FOR 1 BOOK, 50¢ for each additional)
APPLICABLE TAXES* $ _____
TOTAL PAYABLE $ _____

(check or money order—please do not send cash)

To order, complete this form and send it, along with a check or money order for the total above, payable to HQN Books, to: **In the U.S.:** 3010 Walden Avenue, P.O. Box 9077, Buffalo, NY 14269-9077; **In Canada:** P.O. Box 636, Fort Erie, Ontario, L2A 5X3.

Name: _____
Address: _____ City: _____
State/Prov.: _____ Zip/Postal Code: _____
Account Number (if applicable): _____
075 CSAS

*New York residents remit applicable sales taxes.
*Canadian residents remit applicable GST and provincial taxes.

HQN™

We *are* romance™

www.HQNBooks.com

PHSM1110BL